"What is this idea of yours?"

"We court each other."

"We, what?" Isobel stared at him in confusion. Surely she'd misheard him.

But no, Alec repeated nearly the same words. "We're seen around town courting each other."

"How does that help the problem, Alec?"

He took a step closer to her. His eyes were lit with the same enthusiasm she'd seen whenever he talked about his profession or the ranch in North Dakota. Tipping his head, he indicated the other church members who were still eyeing them with open curiosity. "They're all wondering if we're courting or not, so we give them what they want."

"You really think that would silence the gossip?"

Alec gave a confident nod. "It'll take the mystery and speculation out of what we're doing or not doing. Without that, it'll eventually become old news."

"What then?"

"I figure if we let a few people know we didn't suit, the news will get around. Then we're free to court whomever we like."

A courtship between them would have to be believable to be effective. Could she be that vulnerable again with a beau, especially in public, after having her heart broken twice in the past?

Stacy Henrie has always had a love for history, fiction and chocolate. She earned her BA in public relations before turning her attention to raising a family and writing inspirational historical romances. The wife of an entrepreneur husband and a mother of three, Stacy loves to live out history through her fictional characters. In addition to being an author, she is also a reader, a road-trip enthusiast and a novice interior decorator.

Visit the Author Profile page at Harlequin.com.

STACY HENRIE

Their Wyoming Courtship Agreement

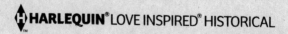

LOVE INSPIRED BOOKS

ISBN-13: 978-1-335-00522-9

Their Wyoming Courtship Agreement

www.Harlequin.com

Printed in U.S.A.

The Lord is my strength and my shield;
my heart trusted in him, and I am helped:
therefore my heart greatly rejoiceth;
and with my song will I praise him.
—*Psalms* 28:7

To my husband and kids.
I love being me with you
and you being you with me.

Chapter One

Sheridan, Wyoming, April 1902

"I have two pieces of news!"

Isobel Glasen glanced up from the sewing draped over her lap as her assistant seamstress breezed into the back room of the dress shop. "What sort of news?" she asked, bending over the gown again. The commissioned dress of red print silk would be picked up this afternoon, and Isobel needed to finish hand-stitching the black braiding along the bodice.

"First, I've fallen in love." Stella Ivy sighed dreamily as she plopped into the vacant seat in front of the nearby sewing machine.

Unsure whether to groan or smile, Isobel settled for raising her eyebrows in a mild show of interest. This was not the first time Stella had declared herself in love—and Isobel suspected it would not be the last. The girl traded hearts like seasonal gowns.

Isobel didn't fault her too much. After all, at twenty-two years old, Stella was still young with her whole life ahead of her. A life that would likely include a husband and children.

"Who is the fortunate beau this time?" Isobel asked.

The girl removed her hat from her strawberry blonde coif and smiled, her green eyes sparkling. "He's a newly hired wrangler for the Running W ranch and his name is Franklin."

Isobel finished one line of braiding and used the tiny scissors pinned to her shirtwaist to cut the excess thread. "When did you meet Franklin?" She couldn't recall Stella mentioning a young man with that name last week.

"Just now." Stella jumped up to hang her hat and coat on the hat tree.

The girl had met this boy minutes ago and was already convinced it was love? Isobel suppressed a skeptical chuckle. Not that romance couldn't happen in such a way. It just hadn't happened in that way for Isobel. In the past, she'd taken her time to get to know a man before choosing to risk her heart. Even then, that hadn't lessened the reality of getting hurt.

With her thoughts focused elsewhere, she accidentally poked herself with the needle. She put her thumb to her lips to alleviate the smarting. How she wished old pains could be as easily soothed and forgotten. At least she had no fear of being hurt in the future. Her courting days were long past. She was content with her dress shop, her cozy apartment on the second floor above and the company of her beloved aunt and uncle who lived not too far from town.

"I encountered a huge puddle of mud on the walk to the shop this morning," Stella said, her hands gesturing, animating her story. "As I was trying to figure out how to cross without getting my shoes dirty, this handsome wrangler happened by. He introduced himself and insisted he help me cross the street."

Isobel couldn't help a genuine smile this time, even if it was a small one. What girl could resist a gallant hero? "When will he be in town again?"

"This Saturday. He wants to take me for a buggy ride."

Holding the next line of braiding in position, Isobel began sewing it into place. "What will Gerald think?" Stella's last beau was the son of the bank manager.

"It hardly matters. I don't care what he thinks anymore," the girl replied with a sniff. "He was standing right outside the bank, waiting to talk to me, and didn't even bother to come over to help."

Poor Gerald. He would now join the handful of suitors who found themselves on the receiving end of Stella's cooling infatuation. Or perhaps the real people Isobel ought to feel sorry for were Mr. and Mrs. Ivy. The couple had expressed their frustration and fears that Stella would never settle down. It was part of the reason they'd been so eager to have their daughter come work for Isobel three years ago. Not necessarily for the monetary benefits but for what they called the blessing of being around Isobel's "mature and ladylike character."

At the age of twenty-eight, Isobel knew that was the Ivys' diplomatic way of saying Stella might profit from being around a spinster.

Whether their motive was to show their daughter what might befall her if she remained fickle in love or a hope that Stella would gain greater restraint and wisdom working at the dress shop, Isobel couldn't say. Perhaps it was a bit of both.

"Which dress do you want me to work on this morning?" Stella asked, pulling Isobel's attention to the present.

She pointed with her needle at the half-finished, black-and-white striped afternoon dress lying on top of the cutting table. "I told Mrs. Kitt that we would have it ready for her to pick up tomorrow."

The wives and daughters of Sheridan's elite didn't change their gowns nearly as often as their wealthy counterparts back East did—something Isobel hadn't minded giving up when she moved to Wyoming seven years ago. However, her customers did like to feel that they looked every bit as stylish as the rest of the country, even way out here in the shadow of the Big Horn Mountains. And her dress shop had thrived as she'd provided those fashionable gowns.

Bringing Stella on as an assistant had been a blessing for Isobel, too. Together they were able to produce nearly twice as many dresses as Isobel had by herself. So much so that a year ago she'd begun to seriously consider the idea of expanding her shop. When the building next door came up for sale, it had seemed more than fortuitous.

Isobel had been saving for months now in order to buy the building. She'd even hoped Stella's interest in Gerald might help sway the bank manager to champion her plans, though that was less likely to happen now that the young man was no longer a suitor.

"If I hurry and finish Mrs. Kitt's gown, can I keep working on my May Day dress?" Stella picked up the striped gown and returned to the sewing machine.

Isobel nodded. The girl had a natural knack for sewing, and her gown would surely be the envy of many at the town gathering. And since Mr. Ivy was the city council member in charge of this year's May Day festival, Stella had talked of little else the past few weeks.

"Are you going to make yourself a new dress for the celebration?" The girl looked over her shoulder at Isobel. "A yellow one would look so lovely with your amber eyes."

It wasn't the first time Stella had made such an observation, nor was she the first to do so. Whitman Russell had often complimented Isobel when she'd worn yellow, even before they'd become engaged. A few years older, Whit had been handsome and successful, so she'd been inclined to believe his opinion. However, when he'd ended their engagement, Isobel vowed never to wear yellow again—and she'd held fast to that commitment.

"If I decide to attend and make a new dress, it won't be yellow. Maybe something red, like this one."

Stella gave her a contemplative look. "Red would be nice, too." She returned her focus to the garment on the sewing machine. "Whatever color you pick, I think you ought to wear your hair down, Issy. If mine was half as thick and pretty as yours, I'd never wear my hair up."

Another style choice that was out of the question. Beau Doyle, Isobel's second fiancé, had preferred it when she wore her hair down. He'd grown up out West and didn't put much stock in anything stylish—be it hair or clothes. Isobel had fallen for him nevertheless, only to have her half-patched heart shattered all over again when Beau asked for his ring back. That had been six years ago and she hadn't worn her hair down in public since.

After snipping the last bit of thread from the braiding, Isobel held up the dress. It was simple yet elegant. She smiled and rose to her feet as something else Stella had said earlier repeated through her mind.

"What was your other piece of news?" Isobel placed the finished gown on the table.

"Hmm?"

"You said you had two pieces of news."

Stella spun in her chair. "You're right! In all the excitement of telling you about Franklin, I almost forgot." She paused, likely for dramatic effect, then announced in an incredulous tone, "Gerald was waiting to tell me that the building next door has been sold."

"What?" Isobel's joy over the completion of another beautiful gown snapped. Sharp disappointment rushed in to take its place. "It's already been sold?"

"I'm afraid so." Stella climbed to her feet and came to put her arm around Isobel's shoulders. "I'm sorry, Issy. I know you wanted to buy it."

Isobel glanced down through tear-brimmed eyes at the red dress. "I was sure that, once we completed the spring and summer orders, I'd have enough money." She ran her hand over the silk material, her dreams of a larger dress shop tearing apart like tattered pieces of fabric. "Has the new owner moved in?"

"That's what Gerald said."

Willing back her tears, Isobel lifted her chin. "Then I ought to go next door and welcome him or her." It was the proper, ladylike thing to do, no matter how much it hurt to give up on her original plan. And a lady was what her late mother had raised Isobel to be.

You must embody those refined qualities, my dear Isobel. For that is the only way you'll survive and thrive in a world that measures a woman's worth far differently than God does.

The memory elicited another ripple of pain, both from the accuracy of her mother's words and the grief Isobel still felt at times since Lydia Glasen's passing eight years earlier. Now was not the time to dwell on the past, though. Tucking the grief away, Isobel placed her hat on top of her dark brown hair and slipped on her coat. It might be spring, but it was still chilly outside.

"I'll be back," she said as she moved to the door.

"You're a better woman than me, Isobel." Stella folded her arms and leaned back against the cutting table. "I'd likely march into Gerald's father's office and demand he rethink the sale."

Isobel allowed a soft laugh. If she'd had any siblings, she would have enjoyed having a younger sister like Stella. "I can't say the thought hasn't crossed my mind, but it would accomplish little. I didn't have the money in time. This new owner did. There's nothing more to it than that."

"I still wish it had worked out for you."

"Thanks, Stella." Her young friend's support meant a great deal.

She walked into the dress shop's main room and paused to angle the dressed mannequin in the picture window before stepping outside. A brisk breeze swished her light blue skirt around her shoes. A stab of frustration pricked Isobel anew as she surveyed the building next door. But, as she'd told Stella, there was nothing more to do but accept things and be neighborly.

Squaring her shoulders, she covered the short distance of sidewalk between her shop and the next. The door had been propped open. Isobel spied a man in wrinkled work clothes crouched before the counter, a paintbrush in his hand. He wore no jacket and his sleeves had been rolled back. Was this the new owner or a hired worker?

"Good morning." She rapped a knuckle against the doorjamb and curved her lips into a friendly smile. "I own the shop next door and was hoping to meet the owner of this establish—"

Her greeting ended on a startled gasp when the man spun around and stood. Isobel blinked, hoping and praying she was dreaming. That in another moment she'd realize she was wrong about the new shop owner's direct connection to her painful past.

There was no mistaking those blue-gray eyes and dark blond hair, though, even if she hadn't seen them in ages. Which meant the man staring wide-eyed at her was none other than Whit's younger brother, Alec Russell.

* * *

"Isobel Glasen?"

Alexander "Alec" Russell lowered the paintbrush in his hand and took a step toward her, unsure who was more shocked—Isobel or himself. While she looked older than the last time he'd seen her, he would recognize Isobel anywhere. Those beautiful amber eyes were unequivocally hers, as were the lovely face and dark brown hair. But he certainly hadn't expected her to be among the first people to walk into his newly acquired building.

"Wh-what are you doing here?"

"I was thinking the same about you," he said, giving her a playful smile. "I knew you'd come West to live near your aunt, but I didn't know you'd come to Sheridan."

Isobel inclined her head in a stiff nod. "I've been here for the last seven years."

So this was where she'd come after her broken engagement with Whit. Alec had wondered, especially since his older brother had claimed not to know where Isobel had ended up.

Letting Isobel go had been the only big mistake Alec could ever recall his brother making. In every other area of life—business, family—Whit had achieved great success with innate skill and seemingly little effort. On the other hand, Alec hadn't initially gone into owning a business as his father and brother had. He'd completed schooling in veterinary medicine and had worked more than a decade at a dude ranch in North Dakota. Even so, Alec still felt obscured by his brother's shadow.

His father's edict last month had handed Alec his first real opportunity to prove himself. In order to receive the rest of his inheritance when he turned thirty in August, Alec had to put his veterinary skills to real use by establishing a successful clinic. He'd been given half his bequest to start his business and he'd been allowed to pick the location. Given that his best friend, West McCall, who also came from a wealthy family in Pittsburgh and had worked at the dude ranch, too, had married the year before and was now living near Sheridan, Alec had chosen to set his clinic up here.

Getting his veterinary practice running wasn't the only challenge he faced, though. He'd also been instructed to find, court and marry a good woman by his birthday. His father wanted Alec to finally settle down, something Alec wanted, as well. However, anytime he'd liked a girl in the past, he would inevitably discover that she had feelings for someone else—usually his brother or a friend.

That had been the case with Isobel, too. Alec had secretly harbored feelings for her, but before he'd braved sharing them with her, she and Whit had announced their engagement. Alec had even considered going after her when that engagement was over, but in the end, he'd decided against it. He wanted to find a girl who wasn't interested in him just because she'd been thrown over by his brother or someone else Alec knew.

Despite what had happened in the past, Alec was still glad to see Isobel standing in front of him. It wouldn't hurt to have another friend here in Sheridan. She didn't look as pleased to see him in return, though. Her demeanor radiated the same ladylike poise and beauty he remembered, but her expression bordered on panic.

"Are you relocating to Sheridan permanently?" she asked in a strained tone that broke the charged silence that had settled between them.

Alec nodded. "I just bought this place." He gestured to the walls with his paintbrush. "I'm setting up a veterinary clinic—once I have everything ready."

"A veterinary clinic?"

A flicker of disappointment shot through him at her confusion. Didn't she remember he'd become a veterinarian? He remembered nearly everything about her— at least, the things she'd liked and disliked seven years ago. Maybe he was being foolish to think they could resume being friends or that she'd see him as anything other than the younger brother of her former fiancé. "I graduated from veterinary school…"

"I remember," Isobel said quietly. "You were home for a month in the spring the last time I saw you."

Pleasure wound through him at her recollection. "My father's been hinting in his letters for over a year now that I need to set up a practice. I figured with West McCall living nearby, this was as good a place as any to do it."

"Were you in town for West's wedding last year?"

Alec smiled at the memory of his friend's happy day. "I was."

If only Alec had known then that Isobel was living here, he could have stuck around to see her. "How did you hear about the wedding?" The Russells and the McCalls had been longtime family friends, but Alec didn't think Isobel knew West's family well and she hadn't been at the wedding. He would have definitely remembered if she had.

"I made the bride's dress." She glanced around the room. "So you bought this building?"

He followed her gaze. "Yes, I'm hoping folks around here will let me take care of their sick and injured animals."

"Animals?" There was no mistaking the horror on her face this time.

Alec chuckled. "That's what a veterinarian does, Isobel. Cares for—"

"I know that, but you can't do that here." She retreated a step, her fingers kneading together at her waist. "I-I own the dress shop next door."

He'd always suspected she would make something of herself and her extraordinary talent for dressmaking. "Congratu—"

"Which is why you can't have animals in this building," she said, cutting him off again. "What would my customers have to say about that?"

Fighting a frown, Alec folded his arms. "Your customers won't need to step foot in here, unless, of course, they have an animal that needs tending to."

"You don't understand." She matched his stance by crossing her arms, as well, her eyes throwing off yellowish-brown sparks. "What about the noise or... or...the smell? My customers expect cleanliness, quiet and style."

Annoyance heated his neck. Though he secretly feared he wouldn't turn out to be a born businessman like his father or Whit, he wasn't completely inept, either. "I plan to run a neat, respectable establishment, too. But you'll have to forgive me on the *style* factor. That isn't so much of a requirement when working with God's four-legged creatures."

Isobel looked as if she wanted to spit nails at him, but she wouldn't. One thing Alec knew, even after all these years, was that Isobel Glasen never acted in a way that wasn't in keeping with being a proper lady.

"It's a pleasure to see you again, *Doctor Russell*," she ground out. "Welcome to Sheridan." Head held high, she stepped over the door's threshold. "Seeing as I have no pets or animals of my own, I doubt we'll need to interact more than is customary for two neighboring business owners."

Alec's irritation deflated in the wake of her cool formality. "I hope we'll get to see each other more—"

"Good day."

Throwing him a tight smile, which looked anything but genuine, she spun on her heel and marched away.

"Good day," he repeated to himself.

Alec turned to face the room and ran his hand through his likely paint-flecked hair. His excitement at seeing Isobel again had exited the building right along with her. If he couldn't win over an old acquaintance with his plan for a veterinary practice, would he ever be successful in convincing the rest of Sheridan that they needed his services? With a sigh, he returned to painting the counter.

While he didn't know what had caused the rift between Isobel and his brother, Alec had experienced enough heartbreak of his own to recognize the glimmer of hurt he'd seen in Isobel's gaze and demeanor just now. He hated the idea that his older brother might be the cause and that Isobel might harbor lingering resentment toward Alec because of his connection with Whit.

You knew where she was, God, he prayed as he painted, *when I felt good about coming here. So help me understand why.*

Maybe another reason for his being in Sheridan was to help Isobel heal from the past. Or maybe it was simply to convince Isobel, and thereby the other townsfolk, that a veterinary practice was more than a smelly, noisy establishment. Either way, he wanted to do right by her if he could.

The one thing he wouldn't allow himself to consider, though, was that he'd been given a second chance with Isobel. Her ringless finger attested to her unmarried status, but she might still have a beau. Regardless, Alec wasn't going to let history repeat itself.

He needed to find a girl to court and marry, but he wouldn't knowingly pursue someone who years ago hadn't been able to see past Whit to the eligible man standing behind him. This time, Alec was determined to find a girl whose feelings matched his own, a girl who liked him first and foremost for being himself.

Chapter Two

Isobel shut the outer door of the dress shop more forcefully than she'd intended. No, that wasn't true. She'd slammed it—on purpose. Leaning back against the door, she shut her eyes. She could forgive herself the unladylike show of emotion after her encounter with Alec.

She wasn't sure which upset her more, the fact that Whit's brother was now residing next door or that he planned to run an animal clinic alongside her dress shop. It wasn't that she didn't like Alec Russell. She'd always thought he was kind and funny. His casual, fun-loving demeanor had been a welcome and interesting contrast to Whit's confident, driven personality.

However, the thought of Alec knowing the cause of her broken engagement to Whit brought a renewed feeling of panic to Isobel. She'd naively believed she would never have to face another member of the Russell family or their unwavering emphasis on marriage and children, and now one of them was back in her life.

"Is something wrong, Issy?"

Isobel opened her eyes to find Stella watching her

from the doorway of the back room. She hurried to put on a smile. "I'm fine."

"Did you meet the new owner?"

She swept across the room and slipped past Stella. "I did." She didn't want to say more, but it might be best if her assistant heard about her history with Alec from Isobel rather than someone else. "I know him, actually. From back when I still lived in Pittsburgh."

"Oh?" Stella trailed her. "Is he handsome? Is he a bachelor?"

Alec hadn't spoken about a wife. "I think he is a bachelor." Isobel deliberately ignored the other question. Not that she didn't find Alec handsome, but it didn't matter what she thought of his good looks. "I thought you were in love with Franklin."

"I am," the girl said with an offended sniff. "I was thinking of *you* and how you haven't had a suitor since I've known you."

Despite the frustration over her thwarted plans and seeing Alec again, Isobel couldn't help laughing. Stella's desire to matchmake was sweet in its intent but entirely pointless. Especially when it came to the Russell brothers.

"What sort of business is he setting up?"

Isobel wrinkled her nose as she took off her hat and coat. "A veterinary practice."

"A…what?"

"He's an animal doctor."

Stella brightened. "A bachelor doctor. Sounds even more promising." She waggled her eyebrows at Isobel.

"Maybe you can get him to take you to the May Day festival."

"I don't think so."

"Why not? You're friends, aren't you? You wouldn't have to go as a couple. Just as friends."

Were she and Alec friends? Isobel had once considered him a friend, and yet, interacting with him now had been more painful than cordial. "We may be friends, but I don't think we'll see much of him. Our customers are women in need of high-quality dresses, while his are likely men, looking for advice on caring for livestock and animals."

"I suppose you're right," Stella conceded. "What will you do now about expanding the shop?"

Isobel mulled over the question as her gaze swept the tidy back room. She didn't want to give up on her dream just yet. Expanding her shop would not only mean her business was successful but that she was successful, too—in spite of not being married.

"I'm going to continue to save," she answered as she stepped up to the cutting table. "Perhaps I can turn my apartment into useable dress space and find another place to live." Or if Alec's business didn't prove to be the right fit for Sheridan, then she could revert to her original plan.

Stella nodded approval. "You're sure about the festival? It would be fun to go all together. You, me, Franklin and your friend…"

"You'll have more fun without us," Isobel said, giving her an understanding smile. "Besides, if I choose to go, I'm perfectly content to go by myself."

With a shrug, the girl resumed sewing. Isobel heated an iron on the still-warm stove and began to press the wrinkles from the new dress. She enjoyed the simple task, though it didn't keep her mind as busy as her hands.

Despite how much she wished to, she wasn't going to be able to avoid seeing Alec altogether or the reminders of the past that he brought with him. However, she hoped such interaction would be brief and infrequent. Nothing in her carefully constructed life and business had to change simply because Alec Russell was setting up shop next door.

Using his thumb, Alec tested the paint on the sign he'd created. It was dry. *Veterinary Clinic, Doctor Alec Russell.* Though he'd commissioned an official sign to be made, it wouldn't be ready until next week. And he didn't want to wait that long to help passersby identify his business. Not when he planned to open his clinic as soon as possible.

It had been four days since he'd taken ownership of the building, and the main room was beginning to look more like a clinic. The new paint on the counter and walls gave the place a clean, fresh look. This morning the iron bars that would separate the waiting area from his apothecary station had been put into place. Wooden benches for seating now stood along the walls, though Alec had also ordered a set of nice, comfortable chairs from the mercantile for any elderly or female customers.

Picking up his sign, he walked to the large display window and set the placard in the corner. Then he stepped outside to ensure the sign was straight and readable. A thrill of satisfaction as well as trepidation shot through Alec at seeing his name and business clearly identified.

Would his practice be as successful as he needed it to be to get out from under Whit's shadow and impress their father? Over the past few days, more than one pedestrian had ducked inside, asking what sort of business Alec would be running. Every one of them had looked surprised when he'd explained Sheridan would now have its own veterinarian.

At least they hadn't looked as appalled as Isobel had. Alec had seen very little of her since that first day. Just a glimpse here and there when they both headed up to their apartments at night or came down in the morning. They'd exchanged a series of nods, but that was all. Alec wasn't sure if he felt more disappointed about that or relieved.

He shot a glance at her shop. What would Isobel think of his clinic now that it was nearly ready? He caught sight of her dark brown coil of hair in the picture window of her store as she moved a headless mannequin around. The mannequin's dress seemed as stylish as those worn by women back East. Though that didn't surprise Alec. He'd never seen Isobel wear anything that wasn't fashionable.

Before he could retreat inside his own building, the door to the dress shop opened and Isobel stepped onto the sidewalk. "Afternoon," he said in an effort to be polite.

Her amber eyes widened in surprise when she saw him. "Afternoon."

"Did you design that dress?" He pointed to the lacy, frilled confection.

Isobel frowned. "I made it, but no, it isn't my own design. I patterned it from a picture in a magazine."

"Didn't you used to design your dresses?" Alec thought he remembered her saying she'd designed the yellow gown he'd complimented her on.

"I haven't designed a gown in years." At his questioning look, she faced the window again. "Women want to know their dresses are in keeping with the styles of Paris and back East. They don't want to spend money for gowns created by an unknown designer."

Alec eyed the showcased dress again. "I'd think there are people here who'd like to look unique. Besides, I always thought your dresses were pretty."

Look at that, he thought, smiling smugly to himself. He'd not only been polite and conversational, but complimentary, too.

"While I appreciate the tribute," she said, her lips curving attractively upward, "I'm afraid you know very little about fashion."

Alec chuckled. "Can't say that isn't true."

A trio of women approached Isobel and she greeted them by name. "I'll be with you momentarily," she told them. "Feel free to look through the new magazines on the table inside." They entered the shop, leaving him and Isobel alone once more.

Falling back a step, he motioned to the dress shop. "Maybe if I knew something about style, I could have the kind of enthusiastic customers you seem to have on a regular basis."

Isobel looked in the direction of the clinic window.

"You're welcome to borrow one of my gowns. You know, if you wish to dress up a stuffed cat or dog."

It had been years since he'd last seen that sparkle in Isobel's gaze or been the recipient of her witty teasing. But the feeling Alec had experienced back then was no different than the emotion he felt now. It was a feeling of pleasure, of being given a gift.

Not for the first time, he wondered how Whit could have let Isobel slip away.

Alec feigned a thoughtful look, then shook his head. "Given that I'm not runnin' a taxidermy business, I think a cat or dog in fancy clothes might send the wrong message. I want people to know I'm here to help their animals—not turn them into a tableau."

She lifted her shoulders in a shrug, though Alec could tell she was fighting a full smile. "If you change your mind, you know where to find a fashionable gown. I'd even throw in some style advice, free of charge."

"Are you saying *I* could use some style help and not just my clinic?" he joked, sending a smile her way.

Isobel waved her hand at his work clothes. "Well, you are a doctor, but you dress like a cowboy."

His smile faded. "That's because, as you may recall, prior to coming here, I was a cowboy on a ranch in North Dakota."

"Still, you're not a cowboy now." He thought he saw her chin lift a notch. "But how are people to know that if you insist on wearing the attire that you do?"

Alec cocked his head. "So you're adding my clothes to the list of things that bother you about having a veterinarian as a neighbor?"

"All I'm saying is if you want more customers, you might try dressing the part of a doctor. Such as wearing a suit perhaps."

His pleasure at talking with her was dissipating faster than a bout of good weather in late October. She'd accused him the other day of running a smelly, noisy establishment, and now, she deemed his current attire unworthy. "I'll keep the unsolicited feedback in mind."

"I'm only trying to help." Her mouth had become a tight line.

He started for the clinic door but stopped short of it to turn back. "If we're swapping unwelcome advice, then here's mine. Why don't you stop worrying about what other people will think and offer them your own designs instead of hiding behind someone else's?"

Isobel gaped at him, then her expression hardened. "If you'll excuse me, *doctor*, I have customers to attend to." With that she turned away.

Alec marched into his clinic, irritation tensing his jaw, and tossed the door shut with a loud *bang*. His handmade sign toppled to the floor. A jab of regret stabbed him as he picked it up. He stared down at the lettering, wishing he hadn't been so bothered by Isobel's advice. But he was already dealing with enough uncertainty. Her reminders, especially from someone who'd proven successful in business, had only served to fuel his misgivings.

After returning the sign to the window, Alec surveyed the room. He knew he had the medical knowledge and skills to properly care for livestock, fowl, even the occasional lapdog. What he didn't feel as self-assured about was his ability to establish a prosperous clinic.

You know what opening this place means to me, Lord, he petitioned silently as he lowered his chin and stared at a hard knot in the floorboards. *Please help me in my endeavors and guide me to know what to do as I move forward.*

He'd keep working as well as praying. Otherwise, he might have to resort to staging that fancy animal tableau Isobel had suggested. And following such misguided counsel wasn't going to help him achieve what he wanted. Of that, Alec felt confident.

Isobel couldn't get Alec's parting remark out of her head as she half-listened to her three customers exclaim over the spring magazines. His words about fearing what others thought and hiding behind someone else's designs had stung, but only because he'd spoken the truth.

He was likely the only person in Sheridan, save for her aunt, who knew Isobel had once designed her own dresses. If she were honest with herself, she still had a strong yearning to create distinctive gowns from her own imagination. Gowns that showcased each woman's unique shape and features—not ones she simply refashioned using someone else's ideas. But when she'd shared her vision with Whit and later with Beau, both men had discouraged her, saying a successful business was built on giving the customers what they thought they wanted. And what they wanted wasn't a dress designed by Isobel Glasen. They wanted dresses like those on the pages of *Harper's Bazaar* or *Vogue*.

How had Alec, someone she hadn't seen in years, so astutely identified her fears? It was as unsettling as his compliment had been earlier. Instead of accepting his flattery graciously, though, she'd handed him unsolicited advice.

Isobel's cheeks warmed with embarrassment at the unbecoming things she'd told him. What was it about Alec's honest face and dancing blue-gray eyes that got under her skin and made her say the first thing that came into her head?

It was nothing about him, she chided herself. It was his sloppy attire and his plan to create an animal clinic next to her fashionable shop that bothered her. He hadn't dressed in such a casual fashion the last time she'd seen him. He'd been looking quite handsome in a tailored suit, though she wasn't sure why she could suddenly recall that detail.

"Miss Glasen?" The oldest of the three women, a Mrs. Maverly, eyed Isobel curiously. "Are you unwell? You look a bit flushed."

Attempting a smile, Isobel shook her head. "I'm quite all right, thank you. Have you found something you like, ladies?"

Mrs. Maverly and her youngest daughter, Rose, spoke over each other in their eagerness to share their preferences. In contrast, the woman's eldest daughter continued to wordlessly scrutinize the magazine on her lap.

"What about you, Miss Annabelle?" Isobel asked.

Annabelle's brow furrowed. "I don't know. I'm not sure I like these new elongated bodices."

Isobel studied the young woman. The girl's figure

would be better enhanced by a gown with a shorter bodice and higher waistline. But did Isobel dare suggest creating something so different? Alec thought her too scared
to say something, and yet, she could be brave. After all,
she'd weathered two broken engagements and had established a respectable dress shop as a female entrepreneur.

In spite of the hard, rapid thumping of her heart, she
scooted forward on her chair and pointed to one of the
two dresses on the open page of the magazine. "What if
I sewed you a lovely blue one like this, but I shortened
the length of the bodice and brought up the waistline?"

"But that isn't how it is in the picture," Mrs. Maverly
protested, her eyes narrowing with confusion.

Isobel wet her dry lips. "No, it isn't. However, I think
a slight change in the style would better suit—"

"She wouldn't have the *S* curve silhouette that's all
the rage." Rose gave Isobel a dubious look.

Annabelle frowned and glanced between her sister
and Isobel. "True, but I like a shorter bodice…"

"I could round the sides of the collar, too," Isobel
said with growing excitement. "That would soften the
blunt lines of that collar."

Mrs. Maverly straightened in her chair. "We want
the mauve-colored dress for me, the tan one for Rose
and the blue one for Annabelle—all exactly as they appear in the magazines." She tapped the page with her
gloved finger for emphasis.

Isobel's enthusiasm wilted like a neglected house-
plant. She wasn't the only one, either. Annabelle appeared displeased with the arrangements, too. But what
could either she or Isobel do? Mrs. Maverly wasn't pay-

ing for unique designs; she wanted a dress similar to what everyone else would be wearing this spring.

"Of course," Isobel managed to say with some semblance of cheer. "My assistant and I will get started on those right away. Would it be convenient for you to pick them up next Saturday?"

Once the arrangements had been made and Isobel had seen the women to the door, she sank onto her vacated chair, too weary to even tidy up the discarded magazines. Her throat felt tight and there was unwanted moisture brimming in her eyes.

Why had she said something? Isobel knew the answer at once. She'd wanted to challenge Alec's opinion, wanted to prove to him that she wasn't lacking in bravery. All she'd proven, though, was that Alec was wrong. The women of Sheridan did not want individually styled dresses.

Climbing to her feet, Isobel gathered up the magazines and thumped them in place on the low table. The whir of the sewing machine in the back room, where Stella was hard at work, was as soothing to Isobel's ears as a lullaby.

She would not let herself be influenced by Alec or his opinion again. Her dream of designing dresses was a thing of the past. Her new dream was expanding her shop one day soon. Giving her customers not what they needed but what they thought they wanted.

That was something Isobel felt certain *Doctor Alec Russell* hadn't yet figured out about running a successful business.

Chapter Three

"I don't think I can eat another bite," Alec declared, pushing his plate forward to indicate he was finished.

He'd willingly accepted two helpings of Vienna McCall's stew and four of her biscuits. It was little wonder the HC Bar, the dude ranch she and West owned, was proving to be a success—on the merit of the meals alone. The food was better than anything Alec had tasted in a long time and certainly trumped the simple Sunday supper he would've made for himself on the stove in his home above the clinic. Even more than the delicious fare, it was the people seated around the table that had made the meal so enjoyable.

"I've got a question, Mr. Alec," Vienna's daughter Harriet said, smiling at him from where she sat perched on West's knee. The blonde little girl might not be West's flesh and blood, but Alec didn't think any father and daughter could be closer than these two.

He bent forward, leaning his elbows on the table. "What's your question, Hattie?"

She glanced up at West, who nodded encouragement. "Daddy says you can do tricks."

"I do know a few," he said, exchanging a smile with West.

After the challenge of the last few days, both with preparing the clinic for opening and his last heated exchange with Isobel, Alec had been more than happy to accept a dinner invitation from the McCalls. It had also given him a chance to drive the horse and buggy he'd purchased for making house calls and would store at the livery stable.

"Would you like to see a trick?" He'd often entertained his nephews with tricks, before and after family dinners whenever he was visiting home.

Hattie gave a vigorous nod, her green eyes bright.

"Mind if I borrow three of these leftover biscuits?" he asked Vienna.

She shook her head. "I was going to insist you take them with you anyway."

"Perfect." He withdrew three biscuits from the basket in the middle of the table. "All right, Miss Hattie. Watch closely."

Alec tossed the first biscuit in the air, followed quickly by the second, then he was juggling all three. He kept them moving around and around for a few seconds before he caught them in his hands. "Ta-dah."

"That's really good, Mr. Alec." Hattie applauded him, her expression full of admiration and enjoyment. "You're a great juggler."

Pleased, he gave her a slight bow and set the biscuits on the table. If only he could as easily win over the townsfolk with his veterinary practice. Maybe he should have gone into juggling, instead.

"Will you come back and juggle for us after my baby brother's born?"

Alec looked from her to Vienna, who was now blushing. "I'd love to. And congratulations to all of you."

"Thank you," Vienna said quietly. "We still have six months to go before the baby arrives." When she glanced at West, the shyness dropped from her face. The two of them shared a smile, a gesture that held nothing but tenderness and joy.

A splinter of jealousy cut through Alec. He wanted to find a woman who would look at him like that. A woman who wanted a family as much as Alec did. He couldn't wait to entertain his own children with dinner tricks.

"You feel like it's a boy?" He directed the question to Vienna.

Still blushing, she laughed and gave a shrug. "Who knows?"

"You might be right about having a brother, Hattie girl," West said, grinning at her. "And what are we going to name the baby if it's a boy?"

She pressed her forehead to his. "Lawrence."

Alec nodded with understanding. "Your father's name." Lawrence McCall had passed away last year, but not before he and West had reconciled with each other. Unlike Alec's family, West's hadn't condoned his decision to leave his wealthy life back East and embrace the life of a cowboy. It had pained Alec to see his best friend, a man as hardworking and skilled with horses as anyone, unrecognized by his own family for his talents.

Or was some of that pain an echo of his own? His father and mother had certainly championed his decision to go to veterinary school and work far from home, but Alec still hadn't felt that those things measured up to his brother's success.

"I think Lawrence is a fine name," Alec said, returning to the conversation.

West reached out to take Vienna's hand in his own. "If it's a girl, though, we want to name her Maggy, since she's largely the reason Vienna and I were reunited."

"Also a great name." He smiled at the couple.

At the wedding last year, Alec had met the McCalls' friends and former employers Maggy Kent and her husband Edward. He'd liked them both immediately. Edward was one of the area's most successful horse ranchers, and Maggy, in addition to helping with the ranch and being a mother, ran a small detective agency.

"Hattie, why don't you help me with the dishes," Vienna said as she stood, "so Daddy and Mr. Alec can visit before he has to head back to town?"

The little girl wrinkled her nose, which had Alec chuckling, but she obediently climbed to her feet. "All right, Mommy."

"Thank you for the exceptional meal, Vienna." He pushed back his chair to stand.

She gave him a genuine smile. "You're welcome, Alec. Anytime you tire of cooking for yourself, you can come by."

"I appreciate that."

West led the way from the kitchen to the parlor. "How goes everything with starting your clinic?" he asked as he knelt before the hearth to start a fire.

"It's had its challenges," Alec admitted as he took a seat in one of the armchairs in front of the fireplace.

His best friend shot him a look over his shoulder. "Not going so well?"

"I'm close to opening the doors, but that's not the part I'm concerned about."

"What are you concerned about, then?"

Alec frowned as he sat back in the chair. "People's perceptions, mostly. I know what a good majority of folks think about horse doctors. We're either seen as dishonest and of low reputation or no smarter than the average farmer. Man has been tending to his animals for hundreds of years, so why call in a veterinarian?"

"I get that's what they may think, but it's only because they don't know how much they need your help." West finished making the fire and sat in the other chair. "There were times as foreman, working on Edward's ranch, I'd wished you were around to help identify some of the more complicated horse ailments. We usually tried our own remedies or called in a regular doctor, but they couldn't always figure out what was best for the animal."

The compliment cheered Alec but only for a moment. "Apparently it's not just my practice people might not find favorable, either. I guess I wear the wrong clothes for a doctor, too." He glanced down at his worn shirt as Isobel's words repeated through his mind.

West laughed until he seemed to realize Alec wasn't joining in. "Who thinks that about your clothes?"

"Do you remember me telling you that Whit was once engaged to someone else before he and Jocelyn married?"

His best friend drummed the chair arm with his fingers, his expression thoughtful. "I believe so. But how does that apply to you dressing like a doctor or not?"

"Whit was engaged to Isobel Glasen for a while before he broke it off."

Resting his foot on his other knee, West watched the fire. "Glasen? Is she related to the shipping Glasens?"

"Yes, Robert Glasen was her father. He passed away when Isobel was about fifteen. Fortunately, he left enough money for her and her mother to survive on." Alec tried to recall other details about Isobel. "Her mother died the year before Isobel met Whit. After their failed engagement, she left Pittsburgh and headed here to live near her aunt and uncle. She owns the dress shop next door to my clinic."

West threw him a surprised look. "Wait. Isobel Glasen lives in Sheridan?"

"Of course, she made my wedding dress," Vienna said, coming into the room with her daughter. "She's an exceptional seamstress. Miss Glasen makes all of Maggy's dresses."

Hattie circled the chairs to give West a hug and kiss. "Night, Daddy. I love you."

"I love you, too, Hattie girl." He kissed her blond head. "Sleep well."

The little girl turned to face Alec and presented her hand like a grownup. "Nice to see you, Mr. Alec. Thank you for the trick."

"My pleasure, Hattie." Smiling, he shook her out-stretched hand. "By the way, I'm hoping you get a little brother, too," he whispered loudly.

Hattie giggled as her mother led her from the room. The moment the pair disappeared down the hall, West resumed their conversation. "So let's see if I have this right. Isobel Glasen, who was once engaged to Whit, has a dress shop in Sheridan, which happens to be next door to your clinic."

"That's correct," Alec said with a grim nod.

"Is she the one who mentioned your clothes?"

Alec wagged his finger at him. "Also correct."

"It makes sense." West smirked when Alec threw him a disparaging look. "Well, she is a maker of dresses, so fashion and clothes is likely something she notices."

Leaning forward, Alec studied the rug. "That isn't all she commented on. She's also worried about me run-ning a smelly, noisy, unstylish establishment."

West's laughter filled the warming air. "Again, it—"

"If you say it makes sense one more time," Alec countered, "I'm going to find Vienna right now and tell her every embarrassing moment of yours that I either heard about or witnessed. And you know there's some really good ones."

The smile didn't fully ease from his best friend's face, but West did hold his hands up in surrender. "Sorry. You and I both know you're not going to run a smelly, noisy practice, Alec. So why should Isobel's opinions matter to you?"

It was a fair question, though Alec needed a long mo-ment to mull over the answer. Were his past feelings for

Isobel making him give her views greater weight than he needed to? He figured that might be partially true. But that wasn't the main reason her ill opinion of his business and clothes bothered him.

"Her opinions matter because she has the same knack for business as Whit does." Alec ran his hands through his hair, the old feelings of inferiority creeping back in as he voiced his thoughts. "She set up her own shop by herself and it appears she's been quite successful at it. You should see the steady stream of customers she has. What if I'm not like them, West? What if this venture fails? Not only will I lose the other half of my inheritance, but I'll lose my parents' respect and my one chance to prove I'm as good as Whit."

West didn't reply right away, for which Alec was grateful. It meant his best friend was considering his words and wasn't going to throw out some platitude about Alec being good enough or not having any reason for concern.

"I get the fear of trying something you've never done before, even when you want it badly." West glanced around the room. "Starting this dude ranch didn't come without difficulty. There was even a time Vienna and I weren't sure we'd even have guests. But you can't compare the start to the end result, Alec. It wasn't so long ago that Whit and Isobel were starting off, too, with no guarantee of success. Just a desire to try and a hope that things would eventually prove profitable."

Alec stared at the flickering flames as he contemplated West's reminder. "You're right. Whit and Isobel, and even you and Vienna had to start somewhere, even without promises of success. But is there more I should be doing?" He rested his elbows on his knees and studied his hands. "I have the skills to doctor animals, but I'm not sure if that's enough to really get my practice going. Or to push back on people's misconceptions about veterinary medicine."

"Asking questions is helpful," West said, twisting in his seat to face Alec. "I certainly had a lot of them before starting this dude ranch. That's only half of the benefit of asking, though. The other half is being open to the advice you're given."

He didn't need West to explain what he meant. After straightening, Alec leaned his head against the chairback. "You're suggesting I listen to what Isobel said."

"And from the pained look on your face I can tell how thrilled you are about that."

The remark drew a partial smile from Alec. Talking things out with his best friend had been the right thing to do. Right now he felt less apprehensive about the future than he had the past few days.

"All I'm really saying," West continued, "is that if you respect Isobel's business prowess, then I think it's worth your time to consider her suggestions. Even if they seem unimportant to you."

Alec slowly nodded. "I can do that."

Isobel's suggestions about his clothes or having a "stylish" clinic did seem unimportant and irrelevant to him. However, he respected what she'd accomplished with her business. So maybe there was something to her advice, as unsolicited as it had been, and Alec intended to find out.

* * *

A knock at the shop's main door drew Isobel's attention from her task of tidying up in preparation for heading up to her apartment by way of the outside staircase at the back of her building. Another day of sewing and consulting with customers was behind her. Instead of feeling tired yet satisfied, though, she felt on edge.

Her frustrating conversation with Alec two days earlier, followed by her disastrous attempt to provide the Maverlys with her own designs, wouldn't leave Isobel's thoughts and had sapped her of her usual energy for dressmaking. Even attending Sunday services the day before hadn't rejuvenated her as she'd hoped. Though that likely had more to do with seeing Alec among the church members in attendance.

Today, Stella had expressed concern that Isobel didn't seem herself. But she didn't want to recount Alec's words to her assistant or her failure to convince someone to use her own designs. Instead, Isobel cited the need for a more restful night's sleep, which was true. Ever since Alec had shown up in town, she hadn't slept well.

The person at the door knocked again. Was it a customer ignoring the Closed sign? Isobel peeked out the door's small window and found Joanna Clawson, her aunt, standing there.

She quickly turned the lock and opened the door. "Aunt Jo! Come in, come in."

"Did you close early or did I linger too long over coffee?" Joanna asked as she slipped inside. Her dark coiled hair showed touches of gray here and there, but it was the only outward sign of aging. Joanna's striking facial features and figure did much to mask her true age.

Isobel shut the door. "It must have been the latter. I only just closed up."

"How are you, Issy?"

Moving to the counter, Isobel picked up the two gowns lying there. "I'm a bit tired this evening. What about you?"

"I'm well. And since I was already in town, I couldn't leave without stopping by." Joanna pulled down the dress draped over the changing screen and followed Isobel into the back room.

Isobel hung up the three dresses. "I'm glad you did." She'd wanted to visit Aunt Jo and share everything about Alec, but renting a horse and buggy and driving to their ranch was something she only had time for every other weekend.

"Is something wrong, Issy?" her aunt pressed gently. "You look more than tired. You seem sad."

The weightiness of all Isobel had experienced the past few days pushed up her throat. The words filled her mouth, begging for release. "I lost my chance at acquiring the building next door."

"Oh, my dear." Joanna led Isobel by the hand to the twin armchairs. "I know you were so excited about expanding the shop."

Isobel nodded stiffly as she took a seat. "I only needed another month, maybe two. But now…" She fiddled with the scissors at her waist, disappointment rising fresh inside her.

"I'm so sorry. When did you find out?"

"A few days ago. That isn't the worst part, though." She pulled in a full breath, eager to unburden herself, but before she could speak again, the pounding of a hammer shook the dress shop's wall.

Isobel frowned. What was Alec doing hammering away at this hour instead of fixing supper in his apartment?

"Has the new owner already taken possession of the building?" Joanna spoke loudly to be heard over the noise next door.

Nodding, Isobel looked from the wall back to her aunt. "He moved in the day I found out I wouldn't be expanding," she replied at an equally loud volume.

"So there was no…" The hammering stopped, and the room was suddenly filled with silence. Joanna gave her rueful smile and lowered her voice to normal tones. "There was no warning, then?"

"None. But I decided to go next door and introduce myself. To be neighborly."

Her aunt tipped her head in a nod of approval. "How were you received?"

"I—"

Bang, bang, bang. Isobel gritted her teeth.

"You what?" Joanna prompted more loudly.

The quiet resumed. Isobel waited for another interruption. When it didn't come, she continued. "I was well received at first. But you see, the gentleman who's set up his business next—"

The noise started up again. Exasperated, her head throbbing in time with the blows of the hammer, Isobel stood. "I'm going to see what he's doing." She nearly had to shout. "And if he can possibly wait until we've finished our conversation."

"Do you want me to go with you?" her aunt hollered back, her dark eyes twinkling with more amusement than annoyance.

Isobel shook her head. She hadn't yet told Aunt Jo that the man next door was the younger brother of her former fiancé. "I'll be right back."

"I can look through your new dress magazines while I wait."

Grateful for her aunt's patience, she hurried through the shop and outside, not bothering to grab her coat. She wouldn't be long. At the door to the clinic, she rapped her knuckles against the wood. But Alec began hammering again at that same moment, and Isobel doubted he could hear her above the noise.

She hated to barge in, but surely this was a case for desperate times calling for desperate measures. Making a decision, Isobel tried the handle. The door was, thankfully, unlocked. She pushed it open and stepped into the room. Alec stood in front of the wall that abutted her dress shop, hammering a nail into it. A whole series of nails now dotted the wall.

When Alec paused to eye his handiwork, Isobel took the opportunity to cough—noisily. Alec turned to face her, but instead of wariness or annoyance, his blue-gray eyes shone with delighted surprise.

"Isobel." The smile he gave her stirred a fluttery sensation in her stomach. "What brings you into my clinic this evening?"

For a moment she couldn't remember. All she could

think about was the pleasure his smile inspired and how she much preferred the anticipation in his expression tonight to the irritation she'd last seen there. Then her gaze dropped to the hammer gripped in his strong-looking hand.

"I...uh...wondered if you'd be so good as to keep the noise down." She waved a hand in the air. "My aunt and I are trying to have a conversation, but the hammering is making it rather difficult."

Alec's smile turned sheepish as he, too, glanced down at his hammer. "Oh, sorry about that. I guess these walls are thinner than I thought. I'm actually done, though." He set his tool on a nearby wooden bench. An array of picture frames sat there, as well.

"What exactly are you doing?" She'd meant to leave, and yet her curiosity over the frames and nails drew her forward a step.

He lifted a framed picture in the air. "I'm giving the clinic some style."

"Some..." Isobel pressed her lips together in embarrassment as the memory of what she'd accused him of came rushing back. "There's something I need to say, Alec. To apologize for, actually. I shouldn't have said what I did the other day."

Hanging the picture on one of the nails, Alec stepped back. "No, you were right. The place does need some style, some sprucing up." He moved to the bench again and selected another frame. "Which is what I hope these photographs will accomplish."

Isobel stared at him in surprise as he hung another frame on the wall. When was the last time a man had taken her ideas or suggestions seriously? Whit and Beau certainly hadn't. Her father had genuinely listened to her and considered her words, but that had been so long ago. The fact that Alec Russell was willing to heed her words, especially after their less than cordial exchange the other day, left her feeling as cautious as she did pleased.

"What sort of photographs do you have?" she asked, closing the distance between them.

Alec showed her the one in his hands. "This one was taken last year." Isobel recognized his family, though the young woman and two small boys were unknown to her.

"Is that Whitman's wife?" She prided herself on sounding cheerful and unaffected. It wasn't that she didn't wish Whit happiness, but it still smarted a bit to see evidence that he'd been blessed with what he'd always wanted—marriage *and* children.

"Yes, that's Jocelyn. And these two rascals are Harry and Ernest." He pointed at the boys in turn. "They're also the best nephews in the world, and this month they'll be joined by another brother or a sister."

The pride in his tone was unmistakable and couldn't help but draw a small smile from Isobel, in spite of the ache she felt at seeing Whit's family. "What are your other pictures of?"

"That's one of my favorite horses from my time in North Dakota." Alec indicated the first photograph he'd hung up, where he stood smiling as he held the bridle of a black horse. "This other is of President Teddy Roosevelt. Of course, he was the vice president when this was taken."

Isobel looked closer at the picture. It was easy to pick out which of the group was the former vice president. "Very impressive."

"Other than the one of my family," he said, hanging the frame alongside the others, "all of them are from the dude ranch in North Dakota."

Picking up one of the frames off the bench, Isobel studied the picture. A group of men, some young, some older, sat on horseback. She thought she recognized the man on the far left as Alec. "Is this you?" She pointed at the figure.

Alec looked down and nodded.

"Do you miss working there?" She'd noticed his voice held a bit of nostalgia each time he mentioned the ranch.

He took the picture from her and added it to the wall. "I miss it a lot more than I thought I would."

"How come you left, then?"

Turning, he folded his arms and regarded her, his eyes full of teasing. "Wishing I'd stayed there?"

"No," she blurted out. He raised his eyebrows in obvious suspicion of her quick answer. "What I mean…" She straightened her shoulders, remembering her mother's admonition that a lady was honest and humble, especially when owning a wrong. "I felt that way, at first, but I've had time to think it over and I believe things will be fine…between us." Isobel motioned to the pictures that now graced the wall. "It doesn't hurt that you listened to my advice about giving the place style."

Alec laughed, and Isobel found she liked being the

inspiration behind the deep, elated sound. "Glad you approve. Because there's one other piece of your advice I'm going to need some help implementing."

"What is that?"

He plucked at the collar of his wrinkled work shirt. "I'd like to get some new clothes. Maybe even a suit. Something that looks more fitting of a doctor, and I'd be most appreciative if you could help me."

Chapter Four

Isobel couldn't help staring at Alec. He'd not only listened to her but he wanted her help with new clothes, too. This interaction was so different from their last that she was struggling to keep up with the changes in their rapport.

Before she could give him an answer about the suit, a voice at the door had them both looking in that direction. "Hello," Joanna said as she stepped inside. "I came to see if you were all right, Isobel."

"I'm sorry, Aunt Jo. I didn't mean to linger overly long."

Her aunt shook her head. "Not to worry." She stepped toward Alec, her hand extended. "I'm Joanna Clawson, Isobel's aunt."

"Alec Russell." He smiled as he shook her hand.

Joanna inclined her head in a friendly nod. "A pleasure to meet you, Mr. Russell. What sort of business are you planning to operate next door to my niece's shop?"

"A veterinary clinic."

Genuine interest lit her aunt's face. "How fascinating. So it's Doctor Russell, then." Joanna glanced about the room. "Will you treat your patients here?"

"Not typically, no," Alec said, shaking his head. "I'll likely do more house calls than any real treatment here. Though I do have a place to make the medications the animals might need." He pointed over his shoulder to indicate a section of the clinic separated from the rest of the room by a set of iron bars.

He wouldn't be treating most of the animals here? How had Isobel not known that? Then again, she hadn't given Alec much of a chance to explain the intricacies of his business that first day. Instead, she'd run rough-shod over him with her preconceived opinions.

Fresh mortification scalded Isobel's cheeks. Linking her arm through her aunt's, she smiled at Alec. "Unfortunately, we need to go. The pictures look quite nice, though, and I would be happy to assist you with that other matter, Doctor Russell."

"Really?" He looked as surprised as he did relieved at her agreement. "That would be—"

Isobel steered her aunt toward the door. "Come by tomorrow morning and we can discuss some appropriate options. Good evening."

"Good evening," he echoed.

Outside on the sidewalk, Joanna stopped and eyed her curiously. "Why the rush to leave? I found your neighbor friendly and charming."

"I'll tell you once we're back inside the shop." Isobel cast a glance at the closed door of the clinic. It wasn't likely that Alec would overhear their conversation, but she wasn't taking any chances.

She could tell her delay in an explanation only further piqued her aunt's interest. But the woman patiently followed Isobel into the dress shop and waited until she'd secured the door before asking another question.

"Is he married?"

Isobel shook her head. "No." If she hadn't been sure before, she was now. None of the photographs Alec had featured him with a young lady.

"He's a handsome young bachelor, then." Joanna lifted her eyebrows as she smiled.

Confusion tumbled through Isobel again, over Alec's sudden interest in her suggestions and the way she'd reacted to his smile. "He may be, but he's also the brother of Whitman Russell."

"Oh." Her aunt's eyes widened, her expression full of pained empathy. "I thought his last name sounded familiar."

Sinking into one of the chairs, Isobel rubbed a tired hand across her forehead. "His best friend lives nearby, so Alec chose Sheridan as the place to set up his veterinary practice."

"I imagine it was quite a shock," Joanna said, taking a seat, as well, "to discover he was the new owner of the building next door."

Isobel nodded as she recalled that first conversation with him. However, tonight she'd felt more frustration with herself than with Alec. "Twice I've acted rudely to him, Aunt Jo. Not at all as Mama and Papa raised me to do."

"I dare say you were shocked and upset to run into Whitman's brother with no warning." Joanna's hand covered Isobel's. "Have some gentleness for yourself, Isobel. It's never too late to apologize, either, and choose to be more amiable."

She squeezed her aunt's hand, grateful for the reminder to be compassionate with herself. "I apologized to him earlier, but you're right. That's only half of what I need to do. I must be more amiable."

"My guess is he already finds you amiable."

Isobel stood to hide her blush. "I'm not sure what you mean." She moved to rearrange the fashion magazines, though they didn't need straightening.

"Only that he seemed genuinely at ease with you."

Alec had been more open and jovial than he had during their previous encounters. Did he really feel at ease with her, though? It didn't seem possible, given how flustered she still felt, her stomach fluttering with more than hunger.

"Even if that's true, nothing more can come from a friendship between us." Isobel leaned back against the counter and folded her arms against the tight ache rising inside her.

Her aunt climbed to her feet. "He strikes me as different in temperament and attitude than his brother, at least with what you shared with me about Whitman." And Isobel had shared a great deal, especially during those first few weeks after she'd come West, devastated and heartsore. It was her aunt and uncle's loving kindness and encouragement, along with many nights on her knees, that had helped Isobel weather both broken engagements. She wouldn't willingly enter into a third, especially with another Russell.

"Alec is different," she admitted. "But it doesn't matter. We both know how important family is to the Russells." The ache flared stronger with old memories. "I doubt their views on the subject have changed in the past seven years."

Joanna crossed the room and gave Isobel a hug. "Knowing something doesn't always make the burden of what we're called to endure any easier to bear."

"No, it doesn't." Isobel hugged her fiercely back. Her aunt's compassion stemmed from more than an understanding heart—it flowed from parallel personal experience. "I'll be amiable and friendly to him from now on," she said with determination as she stepped back, "and that is all there will be between us."

Her aunt cupped her face with her hand, her smile almost sad. "Would you like something more between you, Issy?"

Isobel thought of Alec's laughter and the way it had enhanced the handsome features of his face—just as his smile had. She'd enjoyed talking with him tonight, rather than their throwing barbs at each other. But he was still Whit's brother.

"It doesn't matter. I could never have more with Alec, whether I wished to or not."

The truth of her own words hurt, but Isobel kept her chin up as she moved toward the door. "Besides, even if I could provide someone with a family, it isn't likely that I'm going to find a young man who would consider me a catch at my age."

Joanna laughed, coming to stand beside her at the

door. "Evan believed I was a catch and I was only a year younger than you are now when we courted."

"Uncle Evan is exceptional."

Her aunt's gaze softened. "Yes, he is. And I believe there is yet an exceptional man out there for you, too, my dear. At least, that's what I'm praying for."

"Then by all means keep praying," Isobel teased.

"Oh, I intend to." Joanna opened the door of the shop. "Always wonderful to see you, Issy. Good night."

Isobel kissed her cheek. "Good night, Aunt Jo."

She'd always thought Joanna Clawson would have made a wonderful mother to any child. Indeed, since Isobel had come to Sheridan, Aunt Jo had become a second mother to her.

After locking the door behind her aunt, Isobel moved through the shop to the back door. Spending time with her aunt never failed to cheer and bolster her with renewed strength, even if she was soldiering on as a young woman on her own.

Still, as she let herself out the back of the shop, secured the door and started up the stairs to her apartment, she had another thought. She wasn't less tired just because of talking with Aunt Jo. Her friendly exchange with Alec had helped a great deal, too. So much so that Isobel found herself humming as she prepared supper. Even more surprising was the realization that, far from dreading the next morning, she was actually looking forward to it.

Alec straightened the collar of his best shirt and eyed himself in the dresser mirror. It felt strange to put on a suit when it wasn't a Sunday or a visit home, but he wanted Isobel to get a feel for what he liked. She would probably see right off why he needed a new suit—and not just for working at the clinic. This one had been new several years ago and was now looking a bit worn.

After running a comb through his hair, he put on his tie and exited his apartment. He filled his lungs with the cool morning air. Nervousness gnawed at him as he went around Isobel's building to the front door. It wasn't like he was coming to court her or anything, he reminded himself. This was a tailoring visit. Though he still wasn't sure how Isobel felt about helping him.

He'd been more than pleased with her reaction to his hanging photographs inside his clinic. Their conversation yesterday evening had also been enjoyable. And yet something had caused Isobel to scurry away after her aunt showed up. Alec didn't know the reason, but he wasn't going to turn his nose up at her offer to help him.

The door to the dress shop was still locked, so he tapped a knuckle against the frame. A few moments later, Isobel answered. She wore a dark blue dress today and a tentative smile.

"Good morning."

"Morning," Alec echoed, his nerves churning anew as she held the door open for him. "Am I too early?"

Isobel shook her head. The action caused a single lock of her hair to slip from its pins and fall against the back of her neck, making him wonder what her hair looked like down.

"You're right on time."

He cleared his throat. "I appreciate your help, Isobel."

"If that grimace is your way of expressing appreciation," she countered, her amber eyes glowing with mirth, "then I can't wait to see what you're like when you're truly feeling thankful."

The teasing remark put him at ease and sent his nervousness fleeing for the hills. He gave an exaggerated nod. "It's true. You should have seen me when I landed my first job."

Alec pulled a face, a cross between a smile and a smirk. Isobel laughed, as he'd hoped, and he couldn't help grinning at the sound. It had been years since he'd heard her laughter, but it was as pleasant and beguiling as ever.

"Have a seat." She waved at one of the two armchairs before sitting down herself.

Alec did his best to ignore the decidedly feminine print and took a seat. "I thought I'd wear my Sunday suit so you could see what I've been wearing."

"Do you like your suit?" She studied him thoroughly, her lips pursed in thought.

He tried not to squirm beneath her scrutiny. "I guess so."

"I think the color may be wrong. Dark gray is too stark and stiff for you. Black would be, too."

Chuckling, Alec sat back against the chair. "Don't let my father or Whit hear you say that. They've always worn black or dark gray suits."

Instead of encouraging another laugh or a smile, a flash of pain crossed Isobel's face. Was it the mention of her former fiancé that had induced her reaction? Alec had seen a similar flicker of emotion last night when Isobel looked at the picture of his family, complete with

Jocelyn and his nephews. However, the hurt was gone in an instant as she reached for a magazine.

Alec caught a glimpse of the cover before she turned it aside. It was a men's tailoring magazine. Why would Isobel subscribe to such a publication when she ran a dress shop?

"I think maybe a light gray one," she said, flipping to a page with the corner turned down. "Or perhaps a brown pinstripe similar to this." When he remained silent, she glanced up. "Is something wrong? If you don't like either of those, we can find something else."

It was his turn to shake his head. "No. I like them both. I'm just curious why you have a men's tailoring magazine in your women's dress shop."

Color filled her cheeks as she directed her answer toward her lap. "I walked down to the mercantile earlier and asked the owner if I could borrow the magazine."

The realization that Isobel had put thought into his request for help left Alec feeling more satisfied than he had since coming to Sheridan. Perhaps she wasn't as averse to having him next door anymore. At least, that's what he'd begun to hope for, since their pleasant exchange last night.

"Now which one would you like me to make?" This time she peered directly at him, the self-conscious young woman replaced by the efficient, pragmatic dressmaker.

"You're going to make the suit?"

The corners of her mouth turned up. "Yes, doctor. That's what I do. I make clothes."

"Right." His neck heated with embarrassment. "I just thought since you typically make dresses…"

She stood and moved toward the counter on the other side of the room. "I haven't made a suit in a long time, but it's less complicated than some of these dresses." She waved a hand at the various gowns on display. "So, which color would you like?"

"Uh…" He looked down at the magazine. "The brown?"

Picking up what appeared to be a measuring tape and pencil, Isobel gave a light laugh. "What color do you like best?"

He studied the picture again. "I like the light gray."

"Then gray it is." She walked toward him. "If you'll stand up, I'll take your measurements."

Alec did as he was told. "Can't you just use my old suit as a pattern?"

"I could," Isobel said, "but it doesn't fit you quite right. Take off your coat and I'll measure your arms and shoulders."

Removing his coat, he set it on the chair and held his arms out to the side. "It doesn't fit because it was made for Whit."

"You wear his old suits?" She placed the measuring tape along his left arm, then wrote something on a slip of paper. "Can't you afford…" She let the words trail off as she measured his other arm.

He nodded in answer to her unfinished question. "I could afford a suit, but there wasn't a need for a brand new one while I was working on the dude ranch. Whit's suit still had life left in it and it fit." As she crossed around to his back, he gave her a rueful look. "At least, I thought it fit, before today."

"Well, Doctor Russell, when I'm finished, you will be the proud owner of a suit that fits you and only you."

Her words were likely meant to be teasing, but they filled Alec with another measure of satisfaction. He liked the idea of wearing something that was meant for him and him alone.

"Does that mean I'll have an original suit made by designer Isobel Glasen?"

He felt her stiffen behind him. "It will fit you and no one else, but that doesn't mean I'll have done anything more than sew it."

"All right then." Alec lowered his arms and turned to face her. "What would you do differently if you were designing a suit for me?"

She gave a soft sniff of amusement. "There's less creativity that goes into the design for a suit than there is a dress."

"So there's nothing you'd do differently?" He pinned her with a level look. She had talent—and not just with making clothes.

Narrowing her eyes, Isobel folded her arms. "I would change the vest from double-breasted to single and bring the collar up higher so your shirt is protected when you're working." The annoyance in her gaze melted as she kept talking. "I would change the four pockets to two, so the vest feels less cumbersome, but I would give the suit coat a third pocket. Lastly…" She threw him a haughty look. "I would stitch a small IG on the bottom inside corner of the coat."

"Done," he said, grinning at her. "I'll take the gray suit, but only if it comes with all of the alterations you named." Leaning in, he lowered his voice. "Including the initials of the designer."

Isobel raised an eyebrow. "It will cost you more, seeing as it's a custom-made Glasen suit."

"Not a problem."

He managed to match her tone of nonchalance, but inside he was struggling not to be completely charmed by the woman standing in front of him. Who knew having Isobel make his suit and bantering back and forth would prove to be the most fun he'd had since coming to Sheridan?

"Fine." She measured the length of his pants legs and added the number to those on her paper.

"Anything else you need?" he asked.

"No. It's going to take some time to find the fabric and sew the suit." Isobel tapped the slip of paper to her lips, drawing Alec's attention to their lovely rose color. "When do you plan to open your clinic?"

Alec collected his coat off the chair and slipped his arms into the sleeves. "On Thursday, so in two days."

"I'm afraid your suit won't be ready by then. But I can have it for you in another week and a half."

He waved off her apology. "It's all right. I can wear my stiff, dark gray one until then." As he'd hoped, his remark had her smiling again. "Thank you, Isobel."

"You're welcome." She trailed him to the door. "Is there anything else I can help you with?"

The question was more than he would have expected from her the other day. They were definitely making progress toward being friends again. "Nothing comes to mind. What about you? Anything I can do for you?" He opened the door and stepped through it. "Maybe tell all the men who come into my clinic that my stylish suit was designed by the famous Isobel Glasen?"

"No, that's all right," she said, but her expression looked more delighted than upset. "I'll stick with dresses."

He gave a nod, suddenly reluctant for their time to end. "Someday I hope you'll sew your initials at the bottom of those dresses."

"Me, too." The whispered reply was almost lost beneath the shuffle of approaching footsteps, but Alec still heard it. He saw the wishful, vulnerable look on Isobel's face, too, before her expression changed. "Those are my next clients," she said, indicating the pair of women coming down the sidewalk.

It was time for him to go. "Thank you again."

"If you have any other questions about business or your suit, feel free to come next door and ask me." Her tone was nothing but professional, and yet Alec recognized the sincerity behind it.

With a nod to her and the other women, Alec headed back around the building. He'd go upstairs and change his clothes, then head down to the clinic. But as he did so, he felt far more confident in himself than he had in days. He'd humbled himself enough to heed Isobel's suggestions and the reward had been well worth it. Not only were her suggestions likely to help him with his business, but in following them, he'd started to break down the barriers he sensed between himself and Isobel. Perhaps, if he left off all mentions of his family, they could be friends after all.

Chapter Five

Two days later, dressed in his old suit, Alec surveyed the clinic's main room. Morning light filtered through the picture window. Outside, his newly hung sign swayed in the wind. Everything about the clinic, both inside and out, was ready for business. Tension pooled in his gut and tightened his shoulders as he leveled one of the photographs hanging on the wall. This was it—his day of reckoning. He would either fail or succeed from here.

He blew out a long breath and glanced at the clock sitting atop the counter. It was nine o'clock. Time to open. Crossing the room, he twisted the placard he'd made and hung on the door from *Closed* to *Open*.

Not surprisingly, there wasn't a crowd lined up on the sidewalk in front of the clinic, eagerly waiting to rush inside. Still, he couldn't shake the moment of disappointment that no one likely knew it was opening day.

The thought had barely finished passing through his head when he spotted a figure through the plated glass of the door. Could this be his first client? Hope mixed with his uneasiness as the door swung open. Would he remember everything he'd learned in school? Instead of a stranger, though, Isobel stepped inside, a covered plate in her hand. His regret that she wasn't here for his veterinary help disappeared almost at once. Especially when she smiled fully at him.

"Seeing as today is your grand opening..." She waved her free hand at the sign on the door. "I thought I'd bring over something for you and your first customers to eat." Pulling the napkin off the plate, she lifted it for him to see the muffins sitting there.

Alec didn't know which to thank her for first—that she'd remembered he was opening the clinic today or for the muffins that were filling the room with a mouth-watering aroma. "They smell delicious. Thank you."

"My pleasure. It's another business trick I learned." She held out the plate to him so he could take a muffin, then she set the remainder on the counter. "The smell of something homemade usually draws curious customers, regardless of what the business is."

He took a bite, shutting his eyes for a moment as he relished the taste. "These are amazing, Isobel. You sure you don't want to be a baker, too?"

"I'd rather make dresses," she said matter-of-factly. But Alec could tell from her pink cheeks and shining eyes that she appreciated the compliment.

As he finished eating, she slowly circled the clinic, her hands tucked behind her back. "What do you think?" he asked when she reached the front of the room again.

"It all looks clean, tidy, new…" Isobel paused, her lips twitching at the corners. "And though I never thought I'd say this about an animal clinic, it even has an appealing, rustic style to it."

Alec grinned. Her approval meant nearly as much to him as her coming over and bringing him muffins. "I hope others think so, too."

"Given time, they will." She moved to the door. "I'd better get back to the dress shop now."

"Thanks for coming by, Isobel. And for the muffins."

She offered him another smile. "You gave me the perfect excuse to duck out for a few minutes."

"Rough morning already?"

Isobel laughed lightly and shook her head as Alec accompanied her outside. "No, not exactly. My assistant, Stella, went on another buggy ride with her would-be suitor last night and that's all she can talk about."

"Ah. Sounds as if she really likes this fellow."

With a nod, she stopped on the sidewalk in front of her shop. "She does like him, a lot. But last month, it was a different young man who claimed her affections. Three months before that, it was another one altogether."

"So she can't make up her mind." A flash of sympathy shot through him for the girl's castoff suitors. Unfortunately, he could relate, though more often than not Alec hadn't spent more than a few hours or days with a girl before she decided someone else was more to her liking.

Isobel shrugged. "I guess not. She's still quite young, but I'm concerned if she doesn't choose soon, her parents may choose for her. They certainly don't want her to end up like—" She cut off her words as she threw him a flustered look.

"Like?" he prompted.

Ignoring the question, she lifted her chin and smiled. It appeared a bit forced, though. "Enough about Stella's romances. I hope things go well for you today, Alec."

"Me, too. Thank you again."

She waved, then slipped into the dress shop. Still puzzled about the sudden change in her demeanor, he retraced his steps to the clinic.

What had Isobel stopped herself from saying? The way she was acting almost made him think she'd meant to say Stella's parents didn't want their daughter ending up like Isobel. But that made no sense to him. Who wouldn't want their child to be like her? Isobel was clever, witty, beautiful, kind and ran a successful business as a young woman on her own.

The plate of muffins and their tantalizing smell greeted him as he reentered the clinic's waiting room. It would be a shame to let the baked goods grow cold as he waited for his first customer to come by. He decided to eat another.

When thirty minutes had ticked by and the door still remained shut, Alec began pacing the room, his hands tucked into his pockets, his gaze on the floor. He had little but his thoughts for company, so he found himself reviewing the odd turn in his conversation with Isobel. What had she not wanted to admit to him?

A stray notion had him snapping his chin up as he ground to a stop. Stella's parents were probably not worried about their daughter emulating Isobel's fine qualities. But what about her being on her own and unmarried? That might concern them, especially if they saw Stella's indecisiveness over suitors leading her straight down a similar path.

Irritation flooded him as Alec began pacing again. Who were Stella's parents to judge Isobel? She might not be as young as her assistant, but that didn't mean she couldn't still marry. Any man would be fortunate to have Isobel as his wife. Then again, the more Alec thought about it, the more he realized he hadn't seen a man sitting beside her in church or frequenting her shop during the week he'd been here.

So Isobel didn't have a beau or a husband at present. It didn't mean anything, and certainly wasn't cause for worry from Stella's parents. Maybe the lack of a suitor was Isobel's choice. If it wasn't, though, then the bachelors of Sheridan had clearly been struck with some sort of malady when it came to identifying an eligible, amazing woman. And as a doctor, he found that more than a little concerning.

Isobel couldn't believe what she'd nearly confessed aloud to Alec earlier. That Stella's parents feared their daughter would end up a spinster just like her. Her high-heeled shoes tapped out her agitation against the sidewalk, her cheeks burning with a fresh blush that the late morning breeze couldn't fully cool. While she guessed Alec may have already surmised that she didn't have a beau, she didn't need to draw attention to that fact, either.

After her near blunder, she'd found it difficult to

concentrate. She kept seeing the curiosity in Alec's expression when she hadn't finished her thought. Or the enraptured way he'd eaten her muffin. Or the blatant pleasure in his blue-gray eyes when she'd entered his clinic.

It didn't help that the bright spring sunshine had been teasing her from outside the shop window. When one of her scheduled clients failed to show, Isobel had jumped at the chance to stretch her legs. Unfortunately, the stroll down to the mercantile to purchase buttons hadn't proven to be the cure-all Isobel had hoped. Her thoughts were still too focused on Alec for her liking, and it hadn't helped that the buttons she needed were for his new suit.

"Miss Glasen!" a wobbly voice intoned from up ahead.

Isobel lifted her gaze from the sidewalk to find her absent client, Mrs. Mildred Stone, pacing the sidewalk in front of the dress shop. "Mrs. Stone. Have you been waiting long? I didn't think you were still coming."

"Oh, it's horrible. Just horrible." The widow clutched her precious lap dog to her amble bosom and hefted a sigh. "Something's wrong with my dear Frances. That's why I wasn't here on time."

Eyeing the dog warily, Isobel paused in front of the shop door, but she didn't open it. If the dog was truly ill, she would not allow it entrance, no matter how much Mrs. Stone doted on the animal. "What's wrong with her?"

"The poor thing is limping. I fear she's injured or broken her paw." As she lifted the ailing limb, Frances gave a low whine. "See? She's never like this."

It wasn't hard to read the distress in the eyes of both

dog and owner. "I'm so sorry, Mrs. Stone. Would you like to reschedule?"

"Not especially, but I suppose I must. I don't know that I can concentrate on ordering spring gowns until I know what ails my Frances." The woman laid her cheek against the dog's furry head.

Isobel glanced past her to the clinic, an idea forming. A way to help Mrs. Stone, Frances and Sheridan's new veterinarian. She might even be able to help redeem herself from her earlier embarrassment with Alec.

"I know someone who can help."

The woman's face showed a mixture of doubt and hopefulness. "Who?"

"The building next to mine was recently purchased by a veterinarian, and his clinic opened this morning."

Mrs. Stone looked at her askance. "I won't hand Frances over to some disreputable horse doctor. A man like that is no better than an ill-mannered farm hand."

Isobel nearly chuckled until she realized the older woman wasn't jesting. Was Alec aware of what others thought of his profession? Most likely. She'd experienced her own share of skepticism when she'd first opened her shop and had had to work hard to establish herself as a credible maker of dresses.

No wonder Alec seemed so determined to succeed with his clinic. He'd need that same gumption Isobel had to win over the likes of Mrs. Stone. And, as his friend, Isobel would do what she could to help him.

"I hadn't heard that about veterinarians." Isobel straightened her shoulders. "But I can personally vouch for Doctor Russell's character and the quality of his establishment." She couldn't speak regarding his skills, but knowing Alec, they were likely as top-notch as he wanted his clinic to be.

Frances whined again, her brown eyes peering sadly up at her mistress. "Well, I don't suppose it would hurt to have him just look at my dog."

"I don't think so, either." Isobel gave her a reassuring smile. "Why don't I accompany you next door and introduce you and Frances to the doctor?"

The older woman hesitated another moment, then nodded. "If it might help Frances, I'll do it."

Isobel led them the short distance between her building and Alec's. Pushing open the door, she spotted him sitting on one of the wooden benches. His elbows were braced against his knees, his chin lowered. Even without him saying a word, she could tell from his demeanor that he'd had no other visitors all morning.

"Doctor Russell," she called out cheerfully. She discreetly blocked Mrs. Stone from seeing inside.

Alec jumped up. "Isobel? What brings you—"

"I would like you to meet Mrs. Stone." She moved aside so the older woman could enter the clinic. "And her dog, Frances."

With a quick smile, he hurried toward them. "What a beautiful cocker spaniel, Mrs. Stone." He ruffled Frances' ears. The dog wagged its tail a moment, then offered a mournful bark. "Is she hurt?"

"I believe so." Mrs. Stone glanced around the room, seeming to take its measure.

Isobel could tell from Alec's stiffened posture that

he was also holding his breath as they waited to see if the woman approved of him and the clinic.

"I'm hoping you might be able to help her," Mrs. Stone finally said with no trace of her earlier suspicion in her voice.

The relief on Alec's face matched that winding through Isobel. Then he schooled the emotion behind a serious but kind expression. "What seems to be the trouble with Frances?"

Mrs. Stone described the dog's odd behavior as Alec ran a hand over the animal's head and spine. When he reached her left front leg, the dog whimpered.

"Would you mind taking a seat, Mrs. Stone?" He indicated one of the benches before removing his suit coat and rolling up his shirtsleeves. "You can still hold Frances, but I'd like to get a better look at that paw of hers."

Isobel had planned to deliver the woman and her dog into Alec's capable hands and then return to her shop. Stella was surely wondering what had taken her so long. But she couldn't walk away from the scene unfolding before her. Even dressed in his dark gray suit, Alec looked every bit the skilled, caring doctor as he knelt before the seated Mrs. Stone to examine her dog.

"I think I know what the trouble is," he announced after a long moment as he sat back on his heels. "Frances has a thorn caught in her paw."

Mrs. Stone gave the dog's head a consoling pat. "Can you remove it?"

"Quite easily, and free of charge, too." He stood. "I'll even tie a bandage around the paw to help it stay clean."

The older woman beamed at Alec. "Oh how wonderful. That's just wonderful, doctor."

"Let me get a pair of tweezers," he said, stepping toward the counter.

Isobel decided it was a good time to exit. "I'll leave you and Frances in the doctor's care, Mrs. Stone. When you're finished here, come over to the dress shop. You can let me know then if you'd like to reschedule your dress appointment or not."

"Will do, Miss Glasen. Thank you."

She moved to the door, but before letting herself out, she hazarded a final glance at Alec. Her reward was a smile that set her heart thumping in a way she hadn't experienced in a very long time.

Leaving the clinic behind, Isobel walked halfway past the dress shop before she realized her mistake. She was as lost in thought as she'd been before her errand, but now she no longer felt embarrassed. Alec's smile had held more than gratitude. Without words, he'd seemed to convey that he didn't judge or pity her.

Was Alec really unaware of the reason his brother had ended things with her? She hoped so. Because she liked motivating that smile of his and she hoped to do so again—very soon.

Alec returned the wave Mrs. Stone gave him as she headed next door to the dress shop, a smile on her lined face and her bandaged dog cuddled in her arms. He couldn't help smiling himself as he slipped back inside the clinic and shut the door. His first client! Albeit one he hadn't felt right about charging. Still, he hoped his time and care with Frances would prompt the dog's owner to share her positive experience with others.

He really had Isobel to thank for Mrs. Stone coming into the clinic. And he'd thank her the first chance he got. Being cooperative business owners was proving to be far better and more helpful than being rivals.

Whistling to himself, Alec selected another muffin to eat. He didn't want to leave the clinic on his first day, even to grab lunch. What if another customer came by in his absence?

The early afternoon stretched painfully by, though, and no one else dropped in. Alec itched for something more to do, besides polishing off nearly all of Isobel's muffins, pacing the floor and reading a copy of the newspaper. His earlier excitement at treating the little cocker spaniel waned with the time.

When he'd finished reading all of the news stories, he moved to the advertisements and announcements. One about the upcoming May Day festival caught his eye. In addition to a town picnic and a band performance, the festivities would include a *Ride for a Bride*. Alec had heard of such a race, in which a young lady rode away on her horse toward a predetermined location while the hopeful grooms chased her. The first young man to reach the girl won her as his bride. More often than not, the town preacher married the couple right then and there.

"Not my kind of thing," he said, shaking his head in amusement. Sounded like a foolhardy risk to him. What if the girl didn't like the young man who won? What if she'd been hoping for another victor?

The notice didn't say which of Sheridan's young ladies would be participating, but there was still a week to go until the festival. The other parts of the event sounded fun to him. Maybe he'd attend and not just for the pleasant entertainment. It might be a good venue to introduce himself to the local ranchers and farmers who would be there.

He'd just folded the paper and set it aside, when the door to the clinic clattered open. "Are you the doctor?" a matronly woman asked, her hand gripping that of the boy beside her. When Alec didn't respond right away, she gave the room a frantic perusal. "The sign outside says you're a doctor."

"I am." Alec stood and moved quickly toward the door. What sort of livestock or animal emergency had her so upset? "How can I help you?"

Palpable relief replaced the tension in her expression. "I'm afraid my son has broken his nose. He and some boys were tossing a ball around after school, and well, you can see he was hit."

Sure enough, the kid held a red-stained handkerchief to his face. Disappointment cut through Alec at the woman's misguided perception of his doctoring skills, though he did feel badly for the boy. He'd had a similar experience playing ball with Whit once. And his nose had been broken as a result.

"I'm a doctor, ma'am, but I run a veterinary clinic."

The woman lifted her eyebrows in confusion. "A what?"

"I doctor livestock and other animals."

She glanced down at her son, her brow crinkled with hesitation. "I see."

"If you want, I could still take a look at his nose," he offered. "If it's broken, though, you're going to want to see the...other...doctor in town."

Her face brightened. "That would be wonderful. Thank you."

Alec turned to the boy. "I'm Doctor Russell. What's your name?"

"Willy," the kid said, though the name came out slightly muffled from the hanky.

Nodding, Alec crouched down to eye level. "Can I look at your nose, Willy?" The boy looked from him to the woman.

"It's all right, son. Let the man have a look."

Willy lowered the handkerchief. Gently, Alec felt along the boy's nose before sitting back. "Good news. It isn't broken."

"Oh, I'm so glad," the mother exclaimed. Even Willy looked relieved before he pressed the cloth to his nose again.

"Looks like you already know what to do." Alec gave the boy a smile and stood. "Keep that cloth against your nose until the bleeding stops. And be sure to tilt your chin up as best you can." He pantomimed the action and Willy did the same. "You've got it."

Looking to the woman, he added, "Holding something cold against his nose will help the swelling go down. He'll likely have a bruise, but no broken bones to worry about."

"Thank you, Doctor Russell." The mother smiled fully at him.

He crossed to the counter and grabbed the last muffin from the plate. "You're welcome. And because you've been quite brave, Willy, here's a muffin to take home with you."

"That's kind of you." The woman jiggled her son's hand. "What do you say, Willy?"

Willy pushed aside part of the hanky with his wrist, revealing a smile. "Thank you."

"Glad to be of help."

The pair departed, leaving Alec alone again. He was grateful he'd been able to help the boy. On the other hand, he'd been hoping for a chance to demonstrate his veterinary skills.

Alec let himself through the door to the apothecary and set about rearranging his tools and medicine bottles. He decided to keep the clinic open a little later, on the off chance someone came by around suppertime. Finally, the gnawing hunger in his stomach couldn't be ignored. He moved to the door and flipped the sign from *Open* to *Closed*.

As he crossed the room, his gaze went to the photograph of his family on the wall. Would his father or Whit have been more successful on their first day of a new business? Probably.

Discouragement settled heavily on his shoulders as he exited the clinic through the back door. Though he'd done little physical labor that day, he still felt tired, his steps heavy on the outside staircase to his apartment.

Was he fooling himself to think he could accomplish

all that his father had asked of him? The stakes were higher now. If his business failed, he would not only lose his father's respect and his right to the other half of his inheritance, but Alec would also lose the half he'd invested to start his clinic.

"You look rather glum for someone who just opened their clinic."

Alec glanced across the way to find Isobel standing on her stairs, outside her apartment door. "I can't say it's what I hoped it would be," he admitted. "But I appreciate you bringing Mrs. Stone over."

"You're welcome." The warm smile she shot his way helped to push back his disappointment. "She loves that dog of hers and was quite worried." Isobel lowered her chin, her gaze on the ground below. "You were very kind to both of them."

Leaning his shoulder against the doorframe, he did his best to hide the smile her compliment provoked. "Are you saying I might have what it takes to run a clean, quiet, stylish and *caring* clinic?"

"Perhaps I am," she said with a chuckle as she looked at him again. "I think you convinced Mrs. Stone of that."

He blew out his breath. "Too bad she was the only one."

"You didn't have any other customers?" Alec appreciated how mildly surprised she sounded.

He bent forward and rested his forearms on the railing. "Not if you don't count the boy with a bloody nose whose mother thought I was a people doctor. However, I'm happy to report her son does not have a broken nose."

"Oh, dear." Isobel shook her head. "I'm sorry, Alec."

Hearing her call him by his Christian name sent a flicker of remembered pleasure through him. She'd once called him Alec, and perhaps her doing so now meant they were indeed becoming friends again.

"I guess I expected more people to stop by."

She curled her hands around her railing, her expression compassionate. "It isn't easy to open a business and even harder when it seems no one knows or cares about what you hope to accomplish."

"Exactly. Did you feel that way in the beginning?" Even though she nodded, he still couldn't imagine the successful Isobel Glasen having no customers coming into her shop or doubts about her business. Although he had sensed some insecurity about creating her own dress designs. "What about your first day? Did you have any clients?"

When she smiled, it was soft and filled with wistfulness. "Aunt Jo came, of course, and she'd persuaded two of her friends to join her. Unfortunately, that was it."

"Really?" Was she telling him the truth or downplaying her experience to spare his ego?

She gave a decisive nod. "I mean it. I was certain when I went to bed that night that the shop would be a complete failure and I'd wasted my inheritance to open it."

"I won't say I can't relate to that," he murmured as he straightened.

Isobel brushed a strand of hair away from her eyes. "Be that as it may, I soon discovered that's the way most businesses begin. It takes time for people to see that they need or want what you're offering. And it takes more time to grow and establish a regular clientele, too."

Her words floated across the evening air. Alec breathed them in, feeling them settle inside him. The reassurance she offered rekindled his hope.

"Thank you, again, for your help today, Isobel."

She stepped back from the railing. "My pleasure. You'll get there with your clinic and with having more customers. I know you will."

"How come you sound so confident?" he half-teased. "After all, if what you say proves true, I'll be seeing far more animals than I did today. And they'll be right next door to your fancy dress shop."

The impish look she gave him before she turned to unlock her door had his mouth twitching at the corners. "I wouldn't say I'm necessarily confident. I am optimistic, though. And I've seen your stubborn side." She glanced at him when he laughed. "Besides, I'm still holding out hope that my customers will find your place every bit as fancy as mine. At least as far as animal clinics go."

"Ah." He nodded with amusement. "Now that would be a success."

Isobel smiled once more. "See you tomorrow, Alec."

"See you tomorrow," he echoed.

He let himself inside his apartment and turned on the electric lights. He felt far less morose than he had earlier. Isobel's perception and encouragement had given him much needed insight into an otherwise disappointing day. He might have only had one client so far, but he also had Isobel as his advocate. And that felt as satisfying and significant as a full clinic surely would.

Chapter Six

"Oh, Issy! Come quick!"

Isobel dropped the gown in her hands and hurried out of the back room, afraid of what she'd find. She'd only opened the shop a few minutes earlier. Had Stella noticed something amiss that she hadn't? Isobel might have been the tiniest bit distracted since talking with Alec on the stairs the night before.

Her heart had gone out to him when she'd seen him standing there, looking more solemn than she'd ever seen him. And that same heart had thumped with more than compassion when he started to smile again and they'd exchanged some teasing banter.

There was nothing out of place when she entered the shop's main room. Nothing except for how pale Stella looked. "What's wrong?" Isobel asked her.

"I have either the most horrible news or the most flattering." Stella slumped into one of the armchairs, her coat and hat still on. "I can't decide which it is, and I didn't sleep a wink last night for debating it."

Relieved everything in the shop was still in order, Isobel fought the urge to return to the gown she'd just abandoned. But Stella was clearly too frazzled to concentrate on sewing at the moment.

"Tell me what's happened."

Stella's shoulders drooped. "The council has been arguing about which young lady to ask to participate in the *Ride for a Bride* race."

"Ride for a Bride?" Isobel repeated in confusion.

The girl lifted her head to peer at Isobel. "Didn't I tell you about that?"

"I don't think so."

A bit of color returned to Stella's face as she straightened. "Between seeing Franklin more regularly and working on my May Day dress, it must have slipped my mind." She clasped her hands in her lap. "Someone proposed the idea to the city council to host a *Ride for a Bride* race during the festival."

"But what sort of a race is it?"

"Basically a young lady rides a horse along a set route," Stella explained, "and the town's eligible bachelors ride after her. The first man to reach her wins the race and her hand in marriage."

"Just like that?" Isobel couldn't keep a doubtful huff from escaping her lips. "They're supposed to get married?"

It didn't sound very romantic; it sounded fraught with potential issues. What if the young lady didn't fancy the man who won? Or what if the would-be groom didn't know something about the potential bride that would drastically alter his feelings for her later on?

"Typically there's a preacher on hand to marry the couple before the day's over." Stella's tone held none of the skepticism Isobel felt.

She fought a shudder at the notion of an instant wedding. "Has the city council resolved their arguments about the young lady?"

"They did, just yesterday." Her assistant regarded her with tear-rimmed eyes. "It's to be me, Issy. Papa told me last night."

Doing her best not to gape in shock, Isobel dropped down into the other chair. She hadn't been wrong in thinking Stella's parents were growing more anxious about her. But to volunteer their daughter for such an event? It seemed rather drastic to Isobel.

"Y-you're to be the bride? Is that what you want, Stella?"

The girl shrugged. "I don't know. At first I was thrilled, thinking how wonderful it would be to have Franklin ride in the race. He's an excellent horseman. And if he won, I'd get to marry the man I love."

"But?" Isobel prompted.

Stella glanced at her lap. "But what if Gerald or another of my old beaus takes part, too? What will I do if one of them wins instead?"

"That's wise, to consider that possibility."

Burying her face in her hands, the girl groaned. "What do I do, Issy? I don't want to let Papa down, but I don't care for anyone else the way I do Franklin."

Isobel chose her next words carefully. "Do you know if Franklin returns your feelings?"

"I think so," Stella said as she lowered her hands.

Perhaps more questions would help the girl sort out her quandary. "Is he an honorable man?"

"Yes."

"Is he a man of faith?"

Stella nodded emphatically. "He is."

"Does he treat you with respect?"

Her face softened. "Very much so. He's always been a gentleman with me."

"I'm guessing I don't need to ask if you find him handsome," Isobel said, giving Stella a small smile.

"He's quite handsome," she replied, smiling back.

"Have you talked to him about the race?"

The girl dipped her head in another nod. "He told me he'd ride in a race like that if the girl he admired was participating. Then he asked me if I'd thought about volunteering."

From all Stella had voiced, it sounded to Isobel as though the couple had genuine feelings for each other. That realization brought her relief. She cared about Stella and didn't want to see the girl hurt.

"Why don't you see what his reaction is when you tell him you're going to be the bride in the race?" Isobel patted her hand. "My guess is he'll be as excited as you were at first. Which means he'll do everything in his power to be the winner."

"You're right." Stella pulled back her shoulders, her chin rising. "I'll tell him this weekend."

Isobel climbed to her feet. "Can the bride-to-be refuse to marry the winner?"

"I suppose so." Stella stood, as well. "But with all the hoopla that comes with a race like this, I don't think she'd dare back down. I wouldn't. The whole town would likely be upset, not to mention the groom-to-be."

Another shudder wound through Isobel. Even at her age, she'd never attempt to find or force a match by participating in such an event. Besides, she'd look ridiculous riding a horse, since she didn't know how.

"I think you're quite brave, Stella," she said, linking her arm through the girl's.

Stella gave her arm a squeeze. "Thank you. But I'm not as brave as you, Isobel."

"What do you mean?"

The girl waved her free hand at the shop. "Opening this place all by yourself, wanting to expand it, feeling content with being unmarried. That's braver than anything I've done or could do."

She knew Stella meant the words to be complimentary. However, Isobel felt a slight sting at the last item on the girl's list. She was content, yes, but Stella made it sound as if Isobel had never wanted to marry. Or that she didn't want that now. Nothing could be further from the truth. While Isobel recognized that finding a good man like her aunt had would likely not happen for her, it didn't stop her from wishing for it all the same, now and again.

"Will you come?" Stella asked. "To the May Day celebration now that I'm going to be in the race?"

Normally Isobel avoided the large town gatherings that brought ranchers and their families to Sheridan from the outlying communities. Doing so meant she was less likely to run into her former fiancé Beau Doyle as she had in the past. She wanted to support Stella, but she wanted to see Beau even less.

As Isobel hesitated with how best to answer, someone entered the shop behind them. "Morning, Isobel."

She released Stella's arm and turned. "Good morning." Seeing Alec again so soon was a surprise—but not an unpleasant one if the quickening of her heartbeat was any indicator. "Doctor Russell, I don't think you've officially met my exceptional assistant, Stella Ivy."

"Nice to meet you, Miss Ivy." He gave Stella a polite nod.

Stella smiled coyly at Isobel before turning her attention to Alec. "A pleasure to meet you, doctor. I'd love to hear all about your new clinic next door, but I'd better get started on the day's projects. Don't you think, Issy?" With that, the girl disappeared into the back room, looking far too eager to leave them alone.

"Are you here for your suit? If so, I'm afraid it's still not ready."

Alec shook his head. "No, it's not about the suit. I have an idea I'd like to run by you."

"All right." Her curiosity increased when Alec put his hands in his pockets and glanced about the room as though slightly embarrassed. "What is it?"

Clearing his throat, he met her gaze straight on. "I was thinking this morning about attending the May Day festival and passing out leaflets about the clinic." He pulled a wrinkled paper from his pocket and handed it to her.

Isobel read through the words he'd written on the paper. The message was short and concise but also persuasive. "I think this is well worded, Alec. And an excellent idea." His relief was palpable as she passed back his paper.

"You think so?" His eyes narrowed slightly as he regarded her. "You're not just saying that?"

It was her turn to shake her head. "No," she said with a light laugh. "I'm not just saying that. Handing out a leaflet like that at the festival is a wise business idea."

"Thank you." Alec put away the paper. "You're going to the festival, aren't you?" He chuckled before she could respond. "What am I saying? Of course you're going, what with all those women and families attending. I'm guessing you'll have a bunch of new clients by the time the festivities are over."

She turned slightly to face the back of the shop, hoping to hide the blush creeping into her cheeks. Of course, she ought to go. If she wanted to expand her business, which she still did, then she had to think in broader terms about finding more clients, as Alec was doing. Whether she saw one of her former fiancés or not. And what better way to find new customers than to interact with the women attending the celebration? She could even wear a new gown that showcased the upcoming summer fashions.

"Yes, I'll be there," Isobel said, facing Alec again. "What's more, I'll be sure to have your suit finished by then."

He smiled, renewing the rapidity of her pulse. "That'd be great, Isobel. If anyone asks about its fine craftsmanship, I'll send them your way."

"Likewise, if any men are looking particularly bored

while their wives and I talk dresses, I'll hand them over to you."

His smile increased along with the warm feeling inside her. "Who would have thought two business owners like us, the animal doctor and the dressmaker, could actually help each other?"

"Indeed."

Some of her enjoyment faded at the reminder of what their relationship was and what it wasn't. She liked talking with Alec and certainly hoped to continue to help him with his business, but they would never be more than fellow business owners and friends.

In spite of the sobering thought, Isobel couldn't deny a stir of excitement at the idea of actually attending the festival this year. The town had been hosting it for years, but she hadn't gone since she'd first come to Sheridan. Not only would she have a chance to possibly find more clients, but seeing Alec at the event would be nice, too.

"I appreciate you listening to my idea," Alec said, his tone sincere, "and reading through what I wrote."

Isobel trailed him to the door. "It's only your second day and already you're showing evidence of a born businessman."

Pausing with his hand on the doorknob, he looked back at her. The intensity in his gaze as he did so had the strangest effect on Isobel's senses. A tingle ran up her back, while at the same time goose bumps riddled her arms and heat infused her cheeks.

"That means a lot to hear you say. Especially coming from someone as successful in business as you've been."

She couldn't wield her tongue to reply so she simply nodded. The moment he exited the shop, though, and she had the door closed, she called out, "Stella? I've decided to attend the May Day festival."

A cry of delight sounded from the back room before the girl came out, beaming. "Issy, that's wonderful! What do we need to do to be ready?"

"I'm going to finish Alec's suit and the dress you're currently working on. Because you need to complete your May Day dress." Isobel sailed past her, a smile settling on her lips when Stella blinked in surprise. "After all, every would-be bride needs an exceptional gown, don't they?"

Her assistant gave a dazed laugh and hurried after her. "What about you, Isobel? What will you wear?"

"A brand-new dress of my own."

The people of Sheridan sure knew how to throw a party, Alec mused as he rode his horse down the main thoroughfare of the festival grounds. Children played around a maypole adorned with brightly colored ribbons. Wooden booths and tables offered attendees a variety of food and trinkets. A large banner strung between two poles announced the *Ride for a Bride* event, and the grandstand nearby was likely where the mayor would give his welcoming speech.

Dismounting, Alec tethered his horse to the makeshift hitching post. He'd chosen not to borrow a buggy from the livery to avoid the likely snarl of wagons and carriages. For now, he left the leaflets he'd had printed inside his saddle bag. He'd pass them out after he'd looked around.

His veterinary clinic had been open an entire week, and yet things hadn't been any busier than his first day. Mrs. Stone had returned to show him a happy, active Frances. She'd also insisted on reimbursing Alec for his help with a plate of freshly made scones. A group of schoolchildren had brought in a bird with a broken wing, which Alec had done his best to mend. There'd even been several farmers and ranchers who'd stopped in to ask about his skills, but he hadn't yet had a paying customer. He missed his busy days on the dude ranch. There he'd done more than look out for the health of the horses and cattle; he'd repaired roofs and fencing, worked the land and taken guests on horseback rides.

Still, Alec refused to let discouragement eat at him. He often reminded himself of Isobel's encouraging words from last week, and he spent longer on his knees praying at night too. Each time he questioned the Lord about his plans, he felt a sense of rightness at seeing them through, at least until his birthday. By then he'd know if his clinic had become a real success or not.

Alec wandered about the crowd, looking for Isobel. She'd told him she would be here. A sign bearing the HC Bar brand on one of the display tables caught his eye and drew a smile from him. "West," he called out as he approached.

His best friend circled the table and greeted him with a hearty handshake. "Good to see you, Alec."

"What are you selling?"

West waved to Vienna and Hattie, who were seated

on chairs behind the table. "Vienna made some pies and created the small bouquets of May Day flowers to sell. Figured anything we offered would help get word out about the dude ranch."

"Hello, Mr. Alec." Hattie smiled up at him.

Alec doffed his hat to her and Vienna. "Howdy, ladies. May I say how lovely you look in your blue gingham dress, Miss Hattie?" The little girl giggled at the compliment. "How are you feeling, Vienna?"

"Tired but well." She exchanged a smile with West as he stepped behind her and placed his hand on her shoulder. Then she turned her attention to Alec again. "You're looking very doctor-like in that suit."

He took the lapels of his jacket in his hands. "Thank you, ma'am. This is a one-of-a-kind suit designed by Miss Isobel Glasen herself." She'd brought the finished product over to him the night before, and Alec had been impressed with how well it fit and how he was able to comfortably move around in it.

"I didn't know Miss Glasen designed clothes," Vienna said.

Would Isobel be upset with him for saying something? Alec hoped not. "She's actually quite talented at it, but she's convinced herself that the women here don't want something created by her." He pushed aside one side of his jacket to show off his waistcoat. "She ingeniously designed this suit so I can look professional while working with animals."

"Sounds like she has a champion in you, Alec." Vienna and West shared a glance.

Alec had no trouble deciphering its meaning. His

happily married friends were eager to see him follow a similar path. They didn't know that he and Isobel could never be more than friends. He was holding out for a girl who hadn't been blind to him in the past, and Isobel seemed completely content with her present life.

"I made some leaflets to hand out about the clinic." He pointed his thumb in the direction from which he'd come. "I'm going to get them and start passing them out. But if there's any pie left over later, I want to buy one."

After the three of them bid him goodbye, Alec headed back toward his horse. He didn't fault Vienna and West for wanting to see him get married and soon. He wanted the same thing. Now that the clinic was open, maybe it was time for him to concentrate on the other tasks he'd been given by his father.

Rather than filling him with any degree of excitement, he felt mild trepidation. He might not have his brother or a friend around as competition this time, and yet he couldn't help wondering if there actually was a girl out there who would see him for himself.

Chapter Seven

Isobel gave the tethered horses a wide berth as she went in search of Stella. She'd arrived later than she'd intended to the May Day festival, after putting the finishing touches on her outfit. The dove-gray blouse featured swaths of rose-print material that peeked through on the bodice and sleeves. A red waistband around the ivory-colored skirt matched the red collar of the blouse and completed the ensemble. Isobel felt pleased with the end result and hoped other women would like it well enough to order something similar.

It wasn't her own design—a fact that typically didn't bother Isobel. However, sewing Alec's suit and seeing how perfectly it fit him had filled her with a unique sense of pleasure and satisfaction. One she used to feel whenever she created a dress of her own.

"Isobel!"

She turned toward the female voice and smiled when she saw Maggy Kent striding toward her through the milling crowd. Maggy held her sleeping baby in her arms.

"Hello, Maggy."

Isobel hadn't seen her friend in several months, though Isobel didn't feel slighted. Maggy had likely had her hands full with the ranch, her baby girl and her detective agency.

"I was hoping you'd be here today," Maggy said as she came to stand beside Isobel. "How are you? How's business these days?"

Isobel's gaze moved to the slumbering baby. A tiny ache unfurled inside her. How she longed to cradle a child of her own. And yet such an experience would never be hers.

"I…" She cleared her throat. "I'm well, thank you. The dress shop is doing well, too. I'm actually hoping to expand in the near future." As a fellow businesswoman, Maggy would understand Isobel's hopes for the shop.

Sure enough, a full smile graced her friend's face. "Isobel, that's fantastic. How do you plan to expand?"

"I'd hoped to purchase the building next to mine, but I didn't have the money in time." She lifted her shoulders in a quick shrug. "Now I'm thinking of maybe converting my second-floor apartment into more space for the shop."

To Isobel's surprise, she no longer felt regret at voicing the change to her original plans. Did that mean she no longer minded that Alec had come to town and set up his clinic? The answer came easily. Somewhere over the last two weeks she'd changed her opinion about him, his business and her lost opportunity to expand next door.

Maggy shifted her daughter within her grasp. "Did someone else buy the building?"

"Yes, a veterinarian. His name is Alec Russell. He's a good friend of West McCall's." Isobel glanced around, wishing Alec were nearby, so he could talk with Maggy too. "If you and Edward ever have need of someone to doctor your horses, he's very skilled."

Her friend nodded. "I'll be sure to tell Edward." A sudden gleam in Maggy's blue eyes worried Isobel. "Is this veterinarian married? Did he bring his family here with him?"

"Uh, no. He isn't married." She needed to change the subject before Maggy got any ideas about matchmaking. "Liza is getting so big."

Motherly love radiated from Maggy's expression as she smiled at her baby. "She's almost nine months old." Maggy lifted her eyes to Isobel's again. "I haven't taken very many detective cases since she was born, but I'd like to do more this summer. Which means I'll probably need some new dresses. My others are too small and the ones I wore when I carried her are too big."

"Stop by the shop the next time you're in town," Isobel said, "and we'll come up with a new wardrobe for you."

Maggy nodded. "I'm not sure if it's more humorous that I require a new wardrobe or that I'm almost looking forward to the process this time." They shared a knowing laugh.

Isobel could well recall how uncomfortable her friend had felt the first time Maggy had come into the dress shop to procure a wardrobe to fit her role as Edward's fiancée. She'd lacked confidence in her appearance and in what to wear. But once Isobel had shown her which colors complemented her auburn hair and blue eyes, Maggy had warmed to the idea of wearing dresses.

The recollection gave Isobel an idea, one that brought an equal measure of excitement and doubt. If anyone was willing to try it, though, it would be her unconventional friend Maggy Kent.

"How would you feel if I designed the new dresses for you?"

Maggy furrowed her brow in apparent confusion. "Isn't that what you did before?"

"Not exactly," Isobel said with a smile. "I typically copy the design for a gown from the latest fashion magazines or catalogues. This time, though, I would create a design of my own. One that complements your individual figure and preferences."

Her friend's eyes lit with understanding. "So I'd have a set of dresses that were meant just for me?"

"Precisely."

"I love that idea, Isobel."

She blew out her breath, thrilled and relieved at Maggy's excitement. "Really? You're all right with me designing your dresses?"

"Absolutely."

Overjoyed at the prospect of designing gowns again, Isobel stepped forward and, mindful of the baby, gave her friend a side embrace. "Thank you, Maggy."

"You're welcome," she said as Isobel released her. "I'll come by the shop in another week or so."

"I'll be ready."

Maggy glanced over her shoulder at the display booths. "Since Edward is likely still talking horses with some of the other ranchers, I'm going to visit with Vienna. She and West are selling baked goods and flowers. Do you want to come with me?"

"I'd love to, but I promised Stella I'd find her first thing when I got here." The girl was probably wondering why she hadn't seen Isobel yet. "Tell Vienna hello from me."

"I will."

Isobel waved goodbye to Maggy, then resumed her course toward the *Ride for a Bride* banner. Stella would likely be nearby. A tremor of exhilaration shot through her at her clever idea to design dresses for Maggy. Perhaps this was another possible way to expand her dress shop—not through the use of space but with what she could offer some of her less conventional clients.

The possibility was too thrilling for her to contain. Glancing around to be sure no one was watching, Isobel allowed herself a little skip. Then she smoothed her blouse and recommenced her ladylike strides. That didn't mean she had to stop smiling, though. Coming to the festival had been a wonderful idea, and she'd been here less than an hour. She couldn't wait to see what the rest of the day would bring.

Isobel found Stella pacing in the shade of a small barn, its walls obscuring the girl from the prying eyes of the festival crowd. With her strawberry blonde hair curled and pinned atop her head, Stella made a lovely bride-to-be in a pale blue blouse and dark brown split skirt. She'd told Isobel the day before that her plan was to swap her riding clothes for her new dress once the race had ended and a winner had been declared. A saddled horse stood nearby, ready to carry her mistress across the prairie where Stella would ride until someone caught up to her.

"Morning, Stella."

The girl spun around. "Isobel, you're here!" The profound relief in her tone and expression had Isobel wishing she'd located Stella sooner.

"I'm sorry I didn't arrive earlier." Isobel motioned to her outfit. "I was finishing up some sewing before coming to the festival. And then I saw Maggy Kent and we started talking…"

The horse flicked its ears and shifted its weight, causing Isobel to back away a few steps. "It's all right," Stella reassured. "Charger's just nervous."

"How are you feeling?"

Stella folded her arms as if chilled, though the temperature was far from cold, even in the shade. "I go from excitement to terror and back again." She resumed marching back and forth across the dirt as though either emotion was too intense for her to keep still. "What if Franklin doesn't win? Or what if he does?"

"Do you want to marry him?" Isobel asked, giving the girl and the horse more room.

"Of course. He told me he can't wait to win the race and be my husband."

Isobel sensed a note of hesitation behind Stella's words. "Are you certain?"

"Oh, Issy, I don't know." Stella stopped moving and lowered her chin. "I like him very much. I may even love him, but I'm not sure I want to marry anyone just yet."

Taking the girl's hands in her own, Isobel waited until she looked up. "Stella, you don't have to do this. You can refuse to be in the race. Perhaps if you told your father how you're feeling."

"I can't." A look of near panic filled her green eyes. "Everyone's counting on me. Papa, Mama, Franklin, the whole city council. Not to mention everyone waiting to watch the race."

Her horse tossed its head and let out a whinny as if protesting, too. "It's all right, Charger." Stella released Isobel's hand to rub the horse's nose, but the animal still acted uneasy. "Maybe he'll calm down if I walk him around."

"If you feel like you can't back down," Isobel said as Stella untied the horse, "then maybe wait and see who wins before you decide if you want to get married today or not."

Stella nodded and began walking the horse around the patch of shade. "That's a good idea." Charger lifted his head, his muscles rippling in agitation. "He can sense the crowd and doesn't like all the people. But Papa insisted I ride him because he's our fastest horse."

After another few moments the creature still hadn't calmed. "Maybe I should get on him. He might feel less nervous that way."

Stella went to put her foot in the stirrup, but she set it down almost immediately. "Isobel?" she hissed, one hand rising to her heart. "I... I feel like I'm going to faint." Indeed the girl's face more closely resembled sun-bleached wood than it did its normal rosy color.

"Oh dear." Isobel hazarded a step forward. "What

can I do to help?" She hated seeing Stella so anxious, and yet she couldn't fault the girl for not wanting to back out.

Stella straightened slowly. "Would you mind just sitting on Charger while I catch my breath?"

"Um…" Isobel eyed the horse warily. It looked much larger now that it was untethered. "I suppose so." She'd be fine. All she had to do was sit in the saddle until Stella regained her composure and her confidence.

With help from Stella, Isobel managed to mount the horse, even in her dress. She swallowed hard as she pulled her skirt farther down her calves. The ground looked far away. To occupy her shaky hands, she lightly clutched the reins between her fingers. At least that was something she knew how to do.

"Are you feeling any better?" she asked Stella, knowing her own uneasiness was rapidly increasing with every second she sat on the horse. But she would endure the worrisome minute or two for Stella's stake.

The girl had let go of the horse's bridle and stood there with her eyes shut, her shoulders rising and falling with slow breaths. "I'm starting to feel less faint. I think Charger's feeling less afraid, too."

"Is he?" Isobel kept the remark to a murmur so as not to bother Stella as the horse took several steps forward. "Not yet, Charger." Isobel pulled back on the reins, though she could feel the horse's resistance to remaining still.

On the other side of the barn, the clamor of the crowd grew louder. It must be nearly time for the race to begin.

Stella had told Isobel that the firing of a pistol was the signal to go.

"I can do this, can't I?" Stella opened her eyes. Already the color had returned to her cheeks.

Isobel gave a decisive nod. "You certainly can."

"Right." She dipped her chin, her gaze resolute as she took a step toward her horse. "I can—"

The rest of her words were drowned out by the sudden blast of a gun. Charger reared, causing Stella to leap back. Isobel pressed her knees into the horse's sides and clung to the reins in terror until all four of the creature's hooves returned to the ground. But before Stella could calm the horse, the animal bolted forward, carrying Isobel away.

"Isobel! Come back!"

Stella's worried cries mingled with Isobel's scream. They were the last things Isobel heard before the horse's thundering hooves masked all other sounds—except for the rush of the wind and the pulsing of her own heartbeat in her ears.

Alec heard the signal of a gunshot as he went to pull the leaflets out of his saddlebag. Some festival event must be starting, he guessed. As he removed the stack of papers, he heard a feminine scream of terror. Was someone hurt or in danger? He glanced around, but no one else looked concerned.

Movement out of the corner of his eye caught his attention. He turned in time to see a horse galloping wildly in the opposite direction of the crowd. The young woman on its back clearly knew little about riding—

she was bouncing around in the saddle like a kernel of corn inside a hot pan. But there was something familiar about her.

The animal was moving too fast for him to get a good look at its rider's face, but Alec felt certain he recognized Isobel. The young lady's dark hair and stylish clothes solidified his suspicions. Isobel, who if memory served him right, had never learned to ride, was careening across the prairie on the back of a frightened horse.

Tossing the leaflets to the ground, Alec untied his horse and threw himself into the saddle. It took him more painful seconds than he cared to waste navigating around the other horses and milling people. Once he reached the open prairie, though, he urged his horse into a full gallop. He noted a few other riders off to his right moving in the same direction, but Alec ignored them. If anyone was going to rescue Isobel, it would be him. Not just because they were fellow business owners or friends but because he figured a familiar face in the midst of such a terrifying experience might be calming.

His horse moved swiftly and smoothly across the uneven ground, making Alec grateful he'd picked this mount for making house calls. Although the probability of an animal emergency requiring him to push a horse this hard or this fast to get there in time wasn't likely.

Up ahead Isobel's horse veered to the right. Isobel slid dangerously to the side but then managed to correct herself. Alec leaned lower across his horse's neck. He had to get to Isobel before she or her horse were seriously injured.

Please let me reach her in time, Lord, he intoned silently. *Protect her, please.*

The thought of something happening to Isobel stole the moisture from his mouth. The headiness he usually felt when riding a horse at a full gallop was smothered by icy fear for Isobel's safety. Alec tightened his jaw with determination. He would reach her—he had to.

Isobel's horse had begun to slow but only slightly. Alec wondered what had scared the creature so badly and why Isobel had ended up in the saddle in the first place. The distance between the two horses was narrowing. As Alec drew closer, he cupped one hand around his mouth and hollered, "Keep holding on, Isobel." He wanted to give her fair warning that he was coming up alongside her, so she wouldn't startle and let go of the reins before he could slow her horse.

She must have heard him, or at least the sound of his voice, because she turned far enough around for him to get a clear view of her face. There was no mistaking those features, edged with obvious fear.

"Just hold on," he yelled again. Alec thought he saw her nod before she faced forward again.

He pressed his horse for one final burst of speed that lessened the gap between the animals to a few yards. They were nearly there. Keeping a firm grip on his own horse, Alec drew as close as he dared to Isobel's mount and reached out his hand. He snagged the other horse's bridle. With muscles burning in his right arm, he held on tight and guided his mount into a hard turn to the left. The other creature was forced to slow as it followed their lead.

Keeping a firm hand on the bridle, Alec led both horses through a series of turns until they slowed to a walk and finally stopped altogether. Only then did he dare peek at Isobel.

He'd never seen her face so white or her amber eyes so wide. Her shoulders and arms were visibly trembling, along with her chin. Alec wasn't sure if she was stoically fighting tears or in a state of shock. Possibly both. Most of her hair had tumbled loose from her normal bun.

"Isobel?" he asked in a low voice. He had no intention of inciting a repeat of her harrowing ordeal by spooking her or her horse. "Are you hurt?"

She shook her head back and forth. The repetitive action caused more of her hair to fall free of its pins. Alec had never known her hair to be anything but impeccably in place, but he found he actually liked seeing it down around her shoulders.

"Do you want me to help you get down?" he asked.

Again Isobel communicated her answer with a wordless motion—this time with a nod. She still hadn't released the horse's reins, though.

When he felt the fight leave her horse and the animal dropped its head to the grass, Alec released its bridle and dismounted. He gently uncurled Isobel's fingers from around the reins before placing each of her hands on his shoulders. "All you need to do is slide off the saddle. I'll help you to the ground."

Isobel nodded again. As she slid from the horse, Alec caught her around the waist and gently set her on her feet. He waited until she looked as if she could stand on her own before he released her. A quick look in the direction they'd come confirmed they were alone. The other riders must have seen him catch up to Isobel and had turned back.

"Th-thank you," she said, the words hardly more than a whisper. "For h-helping me."

Her ladylike composure, especially after such a frightening ordeal, made him want to gather her into his arms. But he wasn't sure she'd welcome that. "I'd say you don't need riding lessons anymore." He offered her an encouraging smile. "Not after handling that so well."

Instead of prompting an answering smile as he'd hoped, Isobel bolted away from him and the horses. A moment later he saw her bend forward and retch into the grass. The clear evidence of her fear had Alec moving swiftly toward her. She would likely be mortified at what he'd just witnessed, but he wasn't going to stand by without attempting to comfort her.

Sure enough, she didn't look at him as he came to a stop beside her, her cheeks flushed. Alec withdrew a bandanna from his trousers pocket and held it out to her.

"With how fast that horse was going," he said in a gentle, teasing tone, "I'm surprised he isn't sick, too."

Isobel accepted the bandanna from him. Though she still wouldn't meet his gaze, her blush of embarrassment was fading. She dabbed the cloth against her mouth.

"Probably more fun that you bargained for, huh?"

Her eyebrows arched. "Fun? If that is someone's idea of fun, then I'll pass."

Alec shifted his weight. He wanted to help her, not upset her further. "You did really well, Isobel," he said, trying again. "You didn't panic and you held on, which is exactly what you needed to do."

A whimper spilled from her lips as she turned those luminous amber eyes toward him. "I was so...terrified."

The sight of her standing there, devoid of her usual confidence and poise, did something funny to Alec's heart. He took her by the elbow and softly drew her to his chest. When she didn't protest the intimate gesture, Alec placed his arms around her. She held herself rigid for a moment, then with a quiet sob, she relaxed against him.

"Of course you were scared." He slowly rubbed her back, noting the pleasant, flowery scent of her hair. "Anyone would be, especially when you've never ridden a horse before."

She shifted within his grasp. Would she step away? Alec realized he didn't want her to, at least, not yet. There was something wonderfully familiar about holding Isobel in his arms, though he'd never embraced her before. He tried to tell himself it was only because he was offering her comfort, same as he would a friend or a sister if he'd had one. But the contented happiness filling his chest didn't match that of friendship or brotherly affection. No, this ran deeper and more closely matched what Alec had once felt for her.

Half reluctant, half relieved, he broke away first. "You feeling better?" he asked, his hands moving from her back to her arms.

"Yes." She gave a slow nod. "Thank you."

A tear still graced her cheek. Alec absently reached up to brush it away. Isobel's skin felt soft beneath his finger, and the way she was gazing up at him with those wide eyes had his heart thumping faster.

Alec cleared his throat and lowered his arm. He couldn't fall for her again, not after she'd made it clear years ago which Russell brother she preferred and which she saw as only a friend. "You ready to head back?"

"Do I have to get on that horse again?"

He chuckled. "You rode pretty far out of town, so it'd be a long trek back on foot. Whose horse is it, anyway?"

"It's the Ivys' horse," Isobel answered with a visible shudder as she looked at the animal. "Stella was supposed to ride in the *Ride for a Bride* race, but she was feeling nervous. She asked if I would sit in the saddle until she was ready."

"That was rather charitable of you, especially since you don't ride."

The first smile he'd seen since catching up with her lifted the corners of her mouth. "I'm not feeling particularly charitable toward her or that horse right now."

"Can't say I blame you." Alec laughed again. "Maybe a slow ride back will help." He couldn't say he'd mind. It was nice talking with Isobel alone, without the distraction of clients or their businesses to interfere.

She appeared a little less certain, prompting disappointment in him. And another reminder to keep his past feelings for her from resurfacing.

"Actually, I'm wondering...that is, if you don't mind..." Isobel glanced away as if uncertain. She took a minute to straighten her blouse and pin her hair back up into its usual style. Then, lifting her chin, she met his gaze. "Might I ride with you, Alec? I don't think I can get back on Stella's horse."

She wanted to ride back with him? Appreciation swallowed up his regret and the misunderstanding that she was eager for their time together to end.

"I think we can arrange that." His smile increased when he saw a blush tint her cheeks.

After tying the other horse to his, Alec stood next to the stirrups and cupped his hands together. Isobel placed her foot in them, then swung herself onto the horse. When she was situated, he climbed up behind her. She leaned back against him as Alec nudged the horse forward.

The pleasant contentment he'd felt earlier wound through him again, though Alec did his best to squelch it after a minute. It wasn't as if Isobel had asked to ride with him for any other reason than practicality. But, as he guided them back toward Sheridan, he couldn't entirely ignore the feeling of satisfaction growing inside him. The sun shone through the scattered clouds, and a breeze ruffled the grass.

Glancing down at Isobel, he offered a short but heartfelt prayer to the Lord for watching over them both. An experience that had started out frightening had become just the opposite. Once they got back to the festival, this moment would be over. Until then, Alec would simply enjoy the chance to sit beside Isobel and the gratitude he felt at having been the one to help her.

Chapter Eight

Alec clearly wasn't the only one who'd been concerned for Isobel's welfare. A nice-sized crowd met them when they returned to the festival. Instead of relief, though, the mood in the air was one of anticipation. A cheer rose up as they rode closer. By the time Alec had the horses stopped, he and Isobel were surrounded by people, all talking at once. The two of them managed to exchange a confused look before someone helped Isobel to the ground. Alec was assisted onto his feet on the opposite side of the horse.

His confusion escalated as men and women clapped him on the back and shoulders and called out, "Congratulations." It seemed an odd way to acknowledge his rescue of Isobel from the runaway horse, but perhaps these situations were a regular occurrence at the town's social events.

"Alec! Over here."

He recognized West's voice and felt instantly relieved. Maybe his best friend could offer some insight into the crowd's strange reaction. Moving slowly through the press of people, he finally made it to where West stood beside his wife, holding Hattie.

"You're a sly one," his friend said, grinning. "You didn't even say you'd entered. Looks like you get your own marriage of convenience." He leaned closer to add, "Or has this been growing into something more these past two weeks?"

Alec shook his head, his bewilderment expanding. He studied his friends' expressions—West appeared amused, Vienna pleased. Neither of them looked the least bit worried over what might have happened to Isobel if he hadn't reached her in time.

"What are you talking about?"

Vienna motioned to the crowd. "The race, Alec. You won."

"What race?" He removed his hat and swiped at his damp forehead with his jacket sleeve. The temperature felt much warmer now that he wasn't racing across the prairie and was hemmed in by so many people.

West glanced at Vienna, then back at Alec, his expression less certain. "The *Ride for a Bride* race. The one you entered without telling us."

"The *Ride for a…*" He let his words trail out as his mind began to sort out the details of what he'd seen and experienced since taking off after Isobel.

She'd been riding a horse that belonged to Stella, the same Stella who'd been chosen as the bride-to-be in the festival's main event. He recalled hearing a gunshot right before he'd caught sight of the horse racing away from the crowd. There'd even been several other riders coming behind him, all intent on reaching the girl on the horse. Could it be that the other horsemen hadn't been on a rescue mission as he'd been but hoping for a chance to win the race? A race that was supposed to end with the marriage of the girl to her victorious pursuer?

"You didn't know." West's tone held no levity this time.

"I…" Alec swallowed hard, apprehension bleeding through his earlier good mood. "I saw her on the horse and remembered she didn't know how to ride. I couldn't let her get hurt."

"So you bravely went after her," Vienna said, laying a kind hand on his arm. "I'm sure you can explain that to the officials."

His panic spiked as he jammed his hat back on his head. Did Isobel know what they'd gotten themselves into?

As if he'd voiced his thoughts aloud, he saw Isobel coming toward him through a break in the mass of people. Or rather, she was being steered in his direction by Maggy Kent and her husband. Isobel's amber eyes were as large as they'd been when Alec had caught up to her, and her face had drained of color once more.

Her friends guided her to stand directly in front of him. Unlike on the prairie, Alec sensed no friendly ease between them now or any remnant of the closeness he'd felt when he had held her in his arms. The awkwardness that had pervaded their first few encounters after he'd come to town coated the air around them.

"I guess we…" He felt as if everyone was listening to his words.

Isobel pressed her lips together and nodded slowly. "We won, apparently."

"I didn't know they'd count that as…completing the race."

A bit of relief flashed in her gaze. Had she wondered if he'd known was he was doing? "I didn't, either."

"What do we—"

His question was cut off by the sudden appearance of a group of men. Alec guessed they were the city council. "Mr. Russell, is it?" a man with round spectacles asked.

"It's Doctor Russell," Isobel murmured.

Before Alec could acknowledge her correction with a brief smile, he found himself being guided forward by two of the councilmen. A glance over his shoulder showed that Isobel was being shuffled along, as well.

"We were thrilled to learn one of our newest business owners won our race." The man with the spectacles gestured behind them. "And for our lovely dressmaker, Miss Glasen, to switch places with Miss Ivy? Well, that was a most welcome and delightful surprise." He added in a lower voice, "I know some thought Miss Glasen would never marry at her age. But then, that's the benefit of hosting a race like this."

Irritation heated Alec's neck at the spinster remark about Isobel. She wasn't less of a person for being unmarried. On the contrary, she was a successful, talented, beautiful woman who happened to be older in years than others. "Look, sir, regardless of what—"

His defense of Isobel was interrupted as the council deposited them onto the grandstand where the man waved for the crowd to quiet down. Alec noted the pastor of the church he'd been attending standing to one side, a Bible in his hands. Uneasiness churned in his empty stomach as he shot Isobel a look. He had to do something before they ended up married—something Alec felt certain neither of them wanted.

Isobel stood frozen beside Alec on the festival platform, a hundred pair of eyes staring back at her. While she'd hoped the women in town would see her new clothes and request some for themselves, this was not what she'd had in mind.

The mayor was explaining how she had swapped places with Stella to ride in the race. Isobel's face burned with a blush. If only one of those flash thunderstorms would roll in at this moment, making everyone scatter for cover.

What would her clients think of her now? The way the mayor talked, it was as if she'd *wanted* to be the bride in the race. As if she were so desperate to marry she had to trick a groom into taking her as his wife.

Her wandering gaze found Stella's in the crowd. The girl looked every bit as uncomfortable as Isobel felt. "I'm so sorry," Stella mouthed, her pale face taut with tension.

At least God, Stella and Alec knew the truth of why Isobel was standing here, whether anyone else did or not.

Thinking of Alec, she glanced at him. His posture remained as wooden and rigid as hers. He did believe her, didn't he? That she hadn't meant to be the bride in the race he'd apparently won? The shock in his blue-gray eyes suggested he did. He also looked stunned at the bizarre turn of events.

The mayor kept blathering on about the race and the council's decision to host it, but Isobel stopped listening the instant she caught sight of the pastor waiting beside the grandstand. Her heart leaped into her throat, just as it had while riding Stella's runaway horse. She and Alec wouldn't have to go through with a wedding, would they?

Isobel felt pressure against her hand and looked down. Alec's fingers were now wrapped around hers. Almost immediately a wave of calm washed through her, lapping at her apprehension. A similar feeling of peacefulness had spread through her when Alec had held her as she'd cried.

She had felt so humiliated that he'd seen her retching out her terror into the grass. But he'd made that joke about how the horse ought to be sick, too, and she hadn't felt as mortified after that. Then he'd offered her his bandanna to wipe her mouth and wrapped her securely in his strong arms. The kind gesture and warm embrace had calmed her thoroughly until her tears ran out. After that, no matter how hard she'd tried to believe otherwise, her pulse refused to acknowledge Alec as only a friend. Though she hadn't been held like that in a very long time, Isobel could remember how it felt. The erratic thump of her heartbeat and the fluttering sensations in her stomach were the same. Except that made no sense. It wasn't as if she and Alec were courting.

A bite of disappointment had mingled with relief inside her when he'd finally released her to arm's length.

Only then she'd gone and asked if she could ride back to Sheridan on his horse. Isobel had hoped to keep her strange reaction to him in check, but after he'd climbed up behind her, she'd been overcome by exhaustion, having spent all her strength trying to stay on the horse and praying for protection. So she'd gratefully leaned back against Alec.

Now he was offering her comfort yet again. She lifted her gaze from their hands to his face. He gave her a grim smile, then leaned close. "You don't want to go through with this, right?"

Of course she didn't. Although Isobel couldn't stop a traitorous seed of longing from sprouting inside her. If she were to marry, she wouldn't mind it being to someone as caring and funny as Alec. Memories of his brother and the fateful conversation that had ended their engagement marched through her mind. No, she and Alec could never marry.

"I don't, no," she said, removing her hand from his. She couldn't allow herself to rely on him or his strength. Eventually he would have a wife and family of his own to protect and comfort.

Alec studied her a moment before nodding. "Then we're agreed."

"Ladies and gentlemen," the mayor was saying. "I'll now turn things over to Pastor Jonas."

Isobel swallowed a gasp. Were they too late? Before the clergyman could step onto the platform, however, Alec moved to stand next to the mayor. "May I say something, Mr. Mayor?"

"Yes, yes, of course."

The crowd went surprisingly quiet, save for the mewling of a baby and the noise of some children playing along the periphery of the group. "Ladies and gents," Alec said in a voice that carried without being overly loud. "While we're all grateful to the city council for their enthusiasm and efforts regarding this race…"

Isobel barely managed to bite back an unladylike snort. She could think of two people here who weren't feeling so grateful.

"And to the Ivys for the use of their exceptionally fine horse…"

Stella blanched at that and ducked her head. Once they were done, Isobel would need to let the girl know she didn't hold Stella responsible.

"Isobel—Miss Glasen—and myself are of the same mind as to the outcome of the race." He threw her a look and she nodded for him to continue. "Unfortunately, that means we won't be needing your services today, Pastor Jonas."

A collective groan rose up from the crowd. "So you aren't gettin' hitched?" someone called out.

"Nope," Alec answered. "Sorry, folks, but there isn't going to be a wedding today."

The mayor frowned, his crestfallen expression mirroring those of the rest of the city council. "You sure you won't change your mind? You make a lovely couple." The other men nodded their agreement, save for Mr. Ivy. Isobel guessed his regret had far less to do with her and Alec and more to do with his daughter still being unwed.

"We're much obliged to you for planning such a wonderful festival, though." Taking her elbow in his hand, Alec led her down off the platform and off to the side. "You all right?"

Isobel pushed an errant strand of hair back behind her ear. "Yes. Thank you for what you said up there."

"They really wanted to see somebody married right then and there, huh?" He pulled his hat off and ran his finger over the brim.

Now that she no longer had dozens of people staring at her, Isobel managed a light laugh. "They certainly did." She motioned to the dispersing crowd. "Are you going to stick around for the other events?"

"Probably," he said with a shrug. "I still need to pass out my leaflets. That is, if I still have any." He shot her a sheepish smile. "I dropped them when I took off after you."

A flicker of pleasure rose inside her at his words. He'd cared more about helping her than about the advertisements he'd likely paid good money to print. "I appreciate all of your help, Alec."

"Glad to be of service." His gaze shone with sincere warmth. Plunking his hat back on, he added, "Besides, it's not every day you win a race after rescuing a pretty lady."

The compliment, whether teasing or not, quickened her pulse. "Well, I'd better go." Though where, she didn't know. She only knew if she kept talking with him, kept gazing into those blue-gray eyes, emotion would start to erode all the logical reasons why she couldn't like him as more than a friend.

Isobel glanced around and was relieved to see Stella

coming toward them. "I ought to talk to Stella and let her know none of this was her fault."

"That's a good idea." He tipped the corner of his hat to her. "I'll see you around, then. Bye, Isobel."

Nodding, she waited for Stella to reach her. "Oh, Issy," the girl exclaimed, looping her arm through Isobel's. "I'm so sorry. Had I known Charger would bolt like that, I never would have suggested you sit on him…"

Isobel did her best to reassure and listen. But her thoughts kept moving from Stella's apology to Alec, her gaze drifting in the direction he'd gone.

If she were free to love anyone of her choosing, if she could have a family someday, if she'd never been engaged to Whit, would she have wanted to marry Alec right now, as the city council had intended?

The answer bumped softly about her mind, as inspiring as it was terrifying. If there were no obstacles to her and Alec's future happiness, then yes, she would have married him, right then and there.

But since that isn't possible, Lord, she silently prayed as she followed Stella toward the festival booths, *help me choose to feel gratitude for his friendship instead of disappointment over what can never be.*

Whatever happened in the future, she would always cherish those minutes alone with Alec on the prairie. Not only for how nice they'd been but for the subsequent hope they'd brought to her—a hope that she might yet find a similar man who would love her unconditionally.

Chapter Nine

For two days following the festival, Alec had a rather steady stream of customers. At first he attributed the influx to his leaflets. But after a while he realized most of the people coming into the clinic weren't there to ask questions about their animals—they wanted to talk about the race. Nearly all of them offered congratulations to him for winning as well as their compliments on how well he handled a horse.

If that had been the end of the conversations, Alec wouldn't have minded the felicitations. After all, the more people he knew, the more likely someone would remember the clinic in the future and want to pay for the services he offered. But a good majority of the townsfolk had more than salutations to offer. They were full of curious questions about Alec and Isobel. Why hadn't they gotten married at the festival? Had Alec known Isobel was going to swap places with Stella Ivy? Had they shared a fondness for each other before the race? Were they secretly courting now?

Alec fielded the inquiries as best he could, but he didn't like the personal nature of the questions. Several times he considered closing the clinic early just so he wouldn't have to keep repeating his vague answers.

When a farmer came by late Saturday afternoon, saying he had a question, Alec figured the man must be another curious attendee from the festival. To his surprise, the farmer wanted to know the best treatments for hoof rot. Alec nearly hugged the burly man in gratitude. It was a blessed change to talk about something other than the race, and he welcomed the opportunity to finally put his medicinal skills to use. He promised to mix up a fungicide that the man could come get after the weekend. And because Alec was so relieved to be doing veterinarian work, he planned to only charge the fellow for the price of the ingredients.

As they had since the race, his thoughts drifted to Isobel. He hadn't seen her since the festival. Was she dealing with similar questions from her clients? Or was he the only one fielding the townspeople's reactions to what had happened?

By Sunday morning, Alec felt more than a little grateful the clinic would be closed for the day. He dressed in his new suit and set out for the church. He hadn't walked far when a couple stopped him to ask if they were correct in supposing he was the winner of the Ride for a Bride.

Alec stifled a groan and forced a somewhat polite smile. "That would be me."

"But where's your intended?" The woman glanced

around with a puzzled frown. "Isn't she accompanying you to church today?"

"No, ma'am." He inched past them a step. "She's not actually my intended, though I'm sure she'll be at church."

The woman's brow wrinkled further. "So, the two of you aren't getting married?"

"That's correct." Alec took another step toward the church.

"Oh, that's because you're courting." She exchanged a knowing smile with her husband.

Wrestling his annoyance into submission, he offered them a stiff shake of his head. "I'm afraid we're not courting, either. If you'll excuse me."

He tipped his hat and hurried on. But his progress was blighted twice more by churchgoers eager to engage him in a similar line of conversation. When he finally did arrive at the church, he was late enough that the only available seats were in the back pew. Alec could see Isobel sitting near the front beside Stella and her family. As the congregation rose to sing the opening hymn, he noticed several people ogling Isobel before glancing around as if looking for him. Alec cringed and lowered his head, keeping his gaze locked on the words in the hymnal.

While he didn't like all the attention, he couldn't entirely fault the residents of Sheridan for their keen interest. It wasn't every day a town held such a public matrimonial event. And seeing that they'd expected a couple to get hitched that day, or announce their intentions to do so in the future, then the outcome of the race must have been sorely disappointing.

If only he could make some sort of public statement, letting everyone know that he and Isobel were not a couple. Perhaps Pastor Jonas would give him time to say something after the service. Of course, that might not stop the questions. It might even increase them, since people would probably want to know why he and Isobel *weren't* interested in being a couple.

Alec sat back down with the rest of the congregants and bowed his head for the prayer. But his mind was less focused on the words and more on his current situation.

Would the people in town be satisfied with anything short of a marriage or courtship between them? Not that Alec minded the notion of being with Isobel. On the contrary, he'd always enjoyed talking with her and that pleasure had only increased the last few weeks. But neither of them wanted more than friendship from their present relationship. He didn't know Isobel's reasons for that, but his own were clear. He'd fulfill his task of finding and proposing to a woman of his own choosing who would clearly choose him in return.

An uncomfortable thought pushed its way forward as he attempted to listen to the pastor's sermon. If the people of Sheridan were so convinced he and Isobel were supposed to be together, how would they feel when they did see him courting another woman? Would their opinion of him, and his business, be soured as a result? Alec had no plans to start courting anyone until the clinic was bringing in a steady stream of paying customers.

But even then, would people still think he should be with Isobel because he'd won the race?

What do I do, Lord? he petitioned. *I want to win the trust and respect of these people. Yet how can I when they've got it in their heads which young woman I should be with?*

He found himself studying Isobel again, at least, what he could see from this angle. Beneath her hat, her coiffed hair looked nothing like it had after he'd come to her aid on the prairie. He liked that he'd gotten a glimpse at her more vulnerable yet courageous side. A side of her that wasn't so concerned about looking prim and proper.

Could her reputation suffer if he courted someone else? Could doing so bring an increase of the townspeople's pity for her spinster position? Alec frowned. Isobel didn't need pitying—she was an amazing woman who didn't deserve to have herself or her business tainted because of unmet expectations with the *Ride for a Bride* race.

Too bad the two of them couldn't just court each other for the sake of their reputations. At least until all the talk died down.

Alec whipped his chin up, his heart pumping faster with eagerness. Why couldn't he and Isobel court each other for the time being? If people in town heard they were courting, the gossip from the race and the curious questions would likely stop. The townspeople would eventually grow tired of the topic, especially if they saw him and Isobel frequently stepping out together. At that point, the two of them could quietly let it be known they hadn't suited each other, and they'd each be free to court whomever they wanted without repercussions.

It was a brilliant plan, one that would benefit them both. Now all Alec had to do was help Isobel see the wisdom of it.

No matter how hard she tried to concentrate on Pastor Jonas's sermon, Isobel couldn't fully ignore the constant stares or the whispered conversation between a mother and daughter seated behind her. They were speculating whether she and Alec were courting in secret and how they hoped an announcement regarding their engagement would be forthcoming.

Isobel discreetly rubbed at her throbbing temples. She'd hoped for a reprieve from the persistent gossip during the service, but that was not proving to be the case. It wasn't the first time she'd been talked about, either. Her broken engagement to Beau had set tongues wagging, too, even a year later when her former fiancé married another woman. The painful recollection tightened her lungs, forcing her to take several long, deep breaths.

Glancing around, she tried to determine if Alec was seated nearby, but Isobel couldn't see him. Had he been forced to manage the same tittle-tattle as she had? Likely not. Men weren't interested in discussing such topics, were they?

Yesterday she'd finally given up answering the endless flow of inquiries and allowed her clients to conjure up their own conclusions. Stella had done her best to try to explain that Isobel hadn't purposely switched her places for the race. But it was clear the townspeople weren't interested in the truth; they wanted to cling to their romantic theories about what had happened that day.

Normally Isobel would have been thrilled with the influx of new female clients, but more of them were interested in satisfying their curiosity than their wardrobes. There had been a few new orders, and she still had the opportunity to design dresses for Maggy to look forward to. Beyond that, though, her attendance at the festival had proven to be more of a hindrance than a help. Except for the time she'd spent with Alec. Isobel wouldn't wish that away, no matter how fierce the gossip.

At last the congregation rose to sing the closing hymn. Isobel shared a hymnal with Stella, who leaned in to whisper, "He's at the back."

"Who?" Isobel asked, frowning.

Stella lifted her eyebrows, signaling some secret meaning. When Isobel stared blankly at her, the girl rolled her eyes. "Doctor Russell."

"Why would I need to know where he is?" Isobel kept her voice low, though anyone watching her would still see the blush on her face. Had Stella succumbed to all the talk, too?

It was her assistant's turn to frown. "I thought you might want to know, so you can avoid running into him on your way out."

"Oh." There was wisdom in that. If she and Alec were seen talking, who knew what the congregants would begin saying? "Thank you."

Stella offered her a grim smile. "You're welcome. I'm only sorry to be the cause of all this trouble for you."

"You aren't and you weren't," Isobel said with sincerity. "People love a romantic tale. It'll be old news soon." At least, she hoped so. She wasn't sure how many more days she could endure in the limelight.

After the closing prayer, Isobel fiddled with her gloves and repositioned her hat, to allow Alec time to leave the building ahead of her. The Ivy family bid her goodbye as she finally climbed to her feet. A peek toward the back of the church showed her that Alec hadn't exited. Instead, he stood at the back wall as if waiting for someone.

Bother, she thought as she bent to collect two hymnals and set them in their proper places on the pew shelf. How much longer would she need to stay busy before he left? She found a stray button on the floor that appeared to have come from a boy's coat. Isobel picked it up and set it on the pew. Perhaps the child's mother would notice the missing button and come back to collect it.

Isobel looked around, but there was nothing more to tidy up around or beneath the bench. Even so, she smoothed the front of her dress and flicked a piece of dirt from her skirt to give Alec another few moments. However, when she glanced toward the door, she saw he hadn't moved from his spot. Isobel pressed her lips over a grumble. What was he doing? Did he want her to leave first?

She exited the pew, nodding to a family who were still gathering their children and belongings. Keeping her gaze straight ahead, she moved at a steady pace down the aisle. If she ignored Alec, then maybe that would quell the gossipmongers for a few blessed minutes.

But as she drew alongside him, he stepped into the aisle and looked directly at her. "Good morning, Isobel."

"What are you doing?" she demanded in a quiet voice, though she didn't bother hiding her exasperated tone. "We can't be seen talking."

He furrowed his brow as he studied the nearly empty church. "Why not?"

"Because I haven't had a moment's peace since Thursday." Isobel peered around to make certain no one was paying attention to them before she continued. "If we're seen conversing after services, it will only start their tongues wagging all over again."

She started past him, but the man clearly hadn't heard a word she'd said. Rather than let her pass, Alec settled his hand on her elbow and bent close to whisper, "I have a solution."

"A solution?" she repeated. He wasn't making sense. Or maybe it was the way her pulse sputtered at his nearness that didn't make sense.

Throwing a look over his shoulder, he guided her a few steps toward the door. "Let's talk about it outside."

"But we can't." She pulled back on his gentle grasp to indicate she wasn't leaving the building with him.

His amused smile didn't help her already erratic heartbeat. "Because?"

"You're not listening. We can't be seen together, Alec." How could she help him understand how much she wanted the gossip over? "That's what I'm trying to tell you."

Alec's expression softened. "Believe me, I get it. I've had a whole procession of people come through the clinic since the festival, but most of them just want to talk about that race."

"Truly?" Perhaps he did understand. Isobel stopped resisting his hold on her arm. "I wouldn't have thought ranchers or farmers would be interested in such talk."

He shook his head. "Me, neither. But trust me, Isobel. I have an idea that should temper their flapping tongues—be they male or female."

Even without knowing his plan, she didn't need to ask herself if she trusted him. Alec had proven his trust-worthiness when he'd come to her aid and hadn't teased her about it afterward.

"All right," she conceded with a sigh. "Into the lion's den we go."

Chuckling, he led her out the door and down the church steps. Isobel knew the instant they'd been spotted together. A vibrating hum, like the drone of bees, emanated from those still visiting outside the church house. She kept her chin tilted upward as Alec guided her to a patch of shade along the side of the building, but she still hated the unabashed glances and the mur-muring lips.

"What is this idea of yours?"

Alec released her arm, causing a flicker of disap-pointment to shoot through her. "We court each other."

"We what?" Isobel stared at him in confusion. Surely she'd misheard.

But no, he repeated nearly the same words. "We're seen around town courting each other."

"How does that help the problem, Alec?" She rubbed at her forehead, feeling the return of her earlier headache.

He took a step closer to her. His eyes were lit with the same enthusiasm she'd seen whenever he talked about his profession or the ranch in North Dakota. "It helps because it takes away the problem." Tipping his head, he indicated the other church members who were still eyeing them with open curiosity. "They're all wondering if we're courting or not, so we give them what they want."

"Is that really—" Isobel closed her lips over the rest of her protest. Isn't that what she'd always tried to do in business? Give her customers what they wanted? "I suppose that makes sense. You really think that would silence the gossip, though?"

Alec gave a confident nod. "It'll take the mystery and speculation out of what we're doing or not doing. Without that, it'll eventually become old news."

"Wouldn't it be living a lie?"

With a shake of his head, he pocketed his hands. "No, because we really will be courting. At least until all the talk goes away."

"What then?" A part of her could see the wisdom in such a plan and the other part of her found the whole scheme, including the idea of courting another Russell son, to be completely audacious.

Alec squinted up at the sky from beneath his hat. "I figure if we let a few people know we didn't suit, the news will get around. Then we're free to court whomever we like."

Isobel swallowed the grimace that rose to her lips. Alec would likely have admirers, but she was under no delusions about herself. There wouldn't be suitors waiting at her door, eager to be her beau. Even if there were, they wouldn't stick around once they learned of her deficiency. Just as Whit and Beau hadn't.

A grieving ache filled her chest at the reminder of her two disastrous engagements. Of course, she and Alec would never reach that point, even if she agreed to walk out with him to silence the rumors. And yet, a courtship between them would have to be believable to be effective. Could she be that vulnerable again with a beau, especially in public, after having her heart broken twice in the past?

She glanced at the dispersing group of church members again. Several threw meaningful smiles her way before they moved toward their wagons and buggies. The idea of enduring such attention for another week, if not longer, transformed the grief inside her to smothering anxiousness. She simply wanted to make, sell and possibly design beautiful dresses and expand her shop. She didn't want people's scrutiny or pity.

Could this arrangement be a solution to more than one of her concerns? Courting Alec, even for a time, would bring her temporary relief from others' uneasiness regarding her unmarried status. Their unwanted sympathy had only grown more pronounced since things had ended with Beau. It was why Isobel kept mostly to her shop and apartment. But did she want to be seen around town on the arm of another suitor again?

Not that Alec would be her suitor in any true sense of the word. A courtship with him would be no different than a business arrangement between two mutually benefiting partners.

Looking at him again, Isobel couldn't help comparing him to Whit. Both brothers were handsome. But having come to see more of Alec's open temperament and humor the last while, she had to admit she thought him the more attractive of the two.

Why he hadn't he married, as his brother had? Did Alec also carry hidden wounds when it came to matters of the heart? Isobel couldn't tell for certain, though she doubted he'd been rejected in the same way she had. Perhaps bachelorhood was his choice.

"What do you think?" Alec asked, interrupting her musing. "Will you agree to court each other for the sake of our sanity?"

A hopeful smile accompanied his questions and invited a similar response from Isobel, but she squelched it for a moment. She couldn't appear too eager. Instead, she maintained a level gaze with him. The eagerness faded from Alec's face as she regarded him silently.

"I'll do it," she said, letting her smile shine through at last.

Alec's eyes widened, then he grinned. "This is going to work, Isobel. I know it." The look he gave her made her feel as if she'd singlehandedly filled his clinic with clients. One day some fortunate girl would be the daily recipient of this warm look.

"When do we start?"

He lifted his eyebrows. "How 'bout now?" He held his arm out to her. "Since we're courting, I probably ought to walk you home from church. If that's all right with you, Miss Glasen."

Why did the offer of his arm and the way his eyes were dancing with pleasure make her hesitate? Isobel pulled in a calming breath. She could do this. As Alec had said, this agreement would work. All she had to do was go along with it.

Releasing her breath, she tucked her arm within Alec's. "I'd like that, Doctor Russell."

Chapter Ten

"Wait a minute." The whir of the sewing machine stopped as Stella spun in her chair to face Isobel. "You're closing the shop early tonight? But you never close early."

From where she stood in the doorway of the back room, Isobel did her best to maintain a blasé expression. "I have to tonight because…" She threw a glance over her shoulder at the shop when she heard someone enter. Her morning clients were here. "Because I'm having dinner with Doctor Russell," she finished in a rush as she stepped back, intent on greeting her customers.

Unfortunately, she'd underestimated Stella's curiosity. Instead of returning to her sewing, the girl hurried out of the back room, her green eyes lit with interest.

"You're having dinner with the doctor?"

Isobel cringed at the volume of Stella's voice. "Yes," she murmured.

"Issy?" Stella kept pace with her as Isobel moved toward the pair of women standing by the counter. They didn't even bother to look as if they weren't listening. "What aren't you telling me? Are you two courting?"

Though she kept her head up and her hands clasped demurely in front of her, Isobel barely managed not to flinch at the question or the astonished look the other two women exchanged. She had agreed to Alec's plan, and it would only work if word got out. However, she hadn't anticipated anyone learning that they were courting less than twenty-four hours after Alec had walked her home from church.

"You're courting someone, Miss Glasen?" The younger of the two women lifted her eyebrows. "Is it the doctor who won the race?"

Isobel forced a pleasant smile. At least she hoped it appeared pleasant. "Yes, Doctor Russell and I are... courting...each other." Is that how one would say that? It had been too many years since she'd last had a suitor. Even then, she hadn't gone around discussing it or explaining it to everyone.

Stella squealed and clapped her hands. "Why didn't you tell me sooner?" Thankfully she didn't wait for Isobel to respond. "Oh, this makes everything that happened at the festival all right. Maybe you were meant to get on Charger instead of me, so the doctor could win the race and your heart."

"Maybe," Isobel echoed with a hollow laugh.

She longed to tell Stella the truth—that this courtship would only last as long as it took the gossip to die off; there would be no winning of hearts between her and Alec. But she couldn't say anything when her clients were eagerly listening. She didn't want to spoil Stella's evident relief, either. Since the festival, the poor girl had been almost morose over the race. The return of the vibrant, optimistic Stella was reason enough for Isobel to wait a few weeks before explaining the unromantic, businesslike nature of her courtship with Alec.

"Such a handsome young man." The oldest of the pair offered Isobel a knowing look. "What sort of medicine does he practice, dear?"

"He's a veterinarian." Isobel motioned to the two armchairs. "If you'll have a seat, ladies, I'll get those dresses for you."

The two women sat, then the younger one inquired, "Is Doctor Russell from around here?"

"He actually hails from Pittsburgh, but he spent a number of years in North Dakota." She trailed Stella toward the back room to collect the gowns the women had ordered.

"Isn't Pittsburgh where you're from, Miss Glasen?" one of them called out after her.

The innocent question made her freeze. No one in Sheridan, save for her aunt and uncle and Alec, knew about her past relationship with Whit. But now that she was courting Alec, would word slip out about her failed engagement to his brother?

Isobel squeezed her eyes shut, grateful her back was to her clients. It wasn't difficult for her to imagine the overabundance of pity she'd receive if people ever learned about Whit, especially once things ended between her and Alec.

Perhaps she broke if off with the older brother be-

cause she had secret feelings for the younger. Or worse. *Poor Miss Glasen. Why can't she keep a suitor?*

Would she now have to field questions about her past and why it hadn't worked out with either of her former suitors? She gripped the doorframe for support. Why had she agreed to sit on that horse in the first place?

A lack of confidence that she hadn't experienced since Beau broke their engagement pressed heavily on her now. She'd worked so hard to be successful with her shop, to make a name for herself as a woman entrepreneur and a skilled dressmaker. But it would never be enough if she was only ever seen as worthwhile as someone's sweetheart or wife or mother. She wanted to be valued simply for herself. It was a truth her parents had taught her—she was of worth because she was God's child. In moments like these, though, Isobel struggled to hold fast to that truth.

Please see me through this newest difficulty, Father. Let something good come from it. It was the same prayer she'd been offering since the festival, but today she added another line. *And help me remember I'm of value whether I'm courting someone, engaged, married or alone.*

Opening her eyes, she took a steadying breath. There were plenty of courtships and engagements that ended with the couple parting ways. Hers weren't so different.

"I am from Pittsburgh," she finally said, glancing back at the women. Better to be as truthful as she could. "Doctor Russell and I knew each other there, but it wasn't until he came to Sheridan that we became reacquainted."

The younger lady offered her a dreamy smile. "Did he come here for you?"

"No." Isobel shook her head. "He is close friends with the McCalls, who own the HC Bar dude ranch. I believe that's why he chose to set up his clinic in Sheridan. I assure you that I had nothing to do with it."

The older woman nudged her companion. "Or so he says."

Isobel fought a groan as she entered the back room and gathered up the required dresses. She wasn't sure which was worse—last week's tittle-tattle about the race or this newest gossip about her and Alec courting. She wasn't one for quitting or backing out of a decision, though. There were far more challenging situations in the world than spending time with a kind, handsome doctor to squelch the local talk.

She'd stitched her dress, so to speak, and now she would wear it. And who knew? Isobel thought as she presented the finished gowns to her customers. She might actually find the prospect of a courtship with Alec, however temporary, to be enjoyable.

Pausing on the bottom step of the staircase leading to Isobel's apartment, Alec adjusted his tie and ran his hand over his jaw, grateful he hadn't nicked himself with the razor. The nervousness in the pit of his stomach reminded him of the first time he'd overseen the birth of twin colts—by himself. It wasn't that he hadn't ever courted a young lady before. But he could count on one hand the number of times he'd done so, and he felt sorely out of practice.

It's only Isobel, he reminded himself as he started up the stairs.

This was really just a means to an end, and it wasn't as if he didn't already know Isobel. She was a fellow business owner and friend.

But she's also Whit's former fiancée.

That reminder had him lowering his arm before he could knock on her door. Would Isobel be comparing him to Whit throughout the dinner? Alec didn't think she was still pining for his brother, but she might be hard-pressed not to catalogue their similarities and differences. And there were plenty of differences, especially when it came to success in business and family. Alec couldn't compete, even this far away from Pittsburgh.

Maybe his plan to court Isobel wasn't such a brilliant one, after all.

Then he recalled how her eyes had shone with gratitude after the race. She'd been thankful to him, not his brother. Alec, not Whit, had been the one she'd seemed to enjoy talking with lately and the one whose business she'd been championing.

Straightening his shoulders, he knocked on her door. Isobel answered immediately, making him wonder if she'd been waiting for him nervously or with anticipation. She wore a cream dress dotted with red flowers, and her cheeks were attractively flushed. Her lips rose in a soft smile, likely prompted by his silent stare.

Right then, Alec didn't care about being compared with anyone, including Whit. He, and he alone, had the good fortune of being with Isobel this evening.

"Hello," he said, offering her his arm.

Isobel shut and locked her door, then slipped her arm through his. "Hello." Her chuckle sounded more uneasy than joyful.

"It feels different, doesn't it?" He hoped she appreciated the honest admission. "Like we need to be formal?" She nodded as they started down the stairs, but she still looked uncomfortable. Once they reached the street, Alec stopped.

"I don't want this to be awkward for either of us, Isobel. So let's just say we're neighbors and friends attending dinner at the same time."

Relief relaxed her expression. "I think that sounds wonderful."

"Where would you like to go to dinner?" Alec guided her around her building. "There's the Sheridan Inn. I've heard it's good."

Her fingers tightened on his arm. "Would you mind if we tried a different restaurant?"

"Bad food?"

Isobel shook her head, her gaze lowered. "More like bad memories."

Alec wanted to ask what she meant, but he wanted to respect her desire for privacy, too. So he remained silent as they continued to walk slowly away from their apartments.

"That probably sounds silly," she said with a wince. "To not eat at a place because of the past."

"Not really. I think we all have places that stir up sad memories."

She shot him a grateful smile. "It would be impolite of me to explain it further to a suitor. But seeing as we're simply going to dinner as friends tonight, I don't mind telling you."

He waited as she drew in a slow breath and exhaled. "Six years ago, I met a rancher. We began courting, and after a month we became engaged."

It took a great deal of effort for Alec not to gape at her. Isobel had been engaged after Whit? What had happened? He could hardly believe another man had been as daft as his brother in letting her go.

"Because we were engaged," she continued, "we were allowed to join other ranchers and their wives for social dinners at the inn. However, when things between us…" She glanced away, but not before he caught the flash of pain in her eyes. "Suffice it to say, I haven't frequented the inn's dining room in a very long time."

Alec covered her hand where it rested on his sleeve. "I'm sorry, Isobel. I didn't know."

"How could you?" She lifted her chin to look at him. "Even as a friend, you don't know all of my secrets."

The instant the words left her mouth, she went white, as if she hadn't meant to say them. Alec couldn't help but be intrigued. But he also recognized a return of her earlier discomfort. It was time to change the subject.

"Do you like roast beef? The restaurant near City Hall is supposed to have excellent beef."

"I heard that too. Although, you should know…" Alec inwardly cringed as she paused. Had he unintentionally brought up another set of painful recollections with his suggestion? "I very much like roast beef, so I intend to eat every bite."

Isobel accompanied her teasing remark with a full smile, and this time the gesture held nothing but pleasure. Throwing her a grin in return, he kept his hand resting lightly on hers as they headed toward the restaurant.

The roast beef was as good as promised, and Isobel enjoyed every last morsel. But Alec's company was the most enjoyable part of the evening. He regaled her with funny or touching stories about his years in North Dakota and showed genuine interest in her answers to his questions about the beginning years of her dress shop and living in Sheridan.

Thankfully the flow of conversation moved easily between them because they were interrupted often throughout the meal. Just as the ladies who'd come into the shop today were eager to hear about their courtship, a number of the restaurant's other guests were equally interested to see them in public together.

Isobel didn't mind the attention so much tonight, though. The questions and the knowing glances were far more bearable with Alec experiencing them right alongside her. It also helped to share their own meaningful looks at how well their plan was working.

By the time they left the restaurant, the moon had come up, along with a brisk breeze. Isobel shivered as the cold seeped through the thin material of her long sleeves. She'd been too nervous and excited about the evening to remember to grab her coat so she could wear it on the walk home.

"You're shivering something fierce," Alec said, stopping on the sidewalk to look at her.

"Sorry. I forgot my coat."

He removed his suit jacket and placed it on her shoulders. "You can have mine."

"Thank you." Isobel nestled into the material. "Are you going to be all right without it?"

"If you promise to take my arm again, I'll be fine."

The teasing smile he gave her brought a quiver of feeling to her stomach. She willingly linked her arm with his, grateful for the added warmth of his nearness. Dispelling the chill in the air wasn't her only reason for walking closely at his side. But Isobel didn't want to analyze the other reasons just yet. Instead, she wanted to simply enjoy the walk back to their apartments, on the arm of her friend.

"Can I ask you something?" Alec glanced at her, but the shadows made reading his expression difficult.

Her heartbeat sped up. Would he ask her what she'd meant earlier about him not knowing all of her secrets? Isobel had been embarrassed, then concerned at letting such words slip out.

"Go ahead," she managed in a fairly steady voice.

He faced forward again before he spoke. "Was the real reason you were against the clinic just because of the noise and the animals?"

"Oh." Isobel expelled a relieved chuckle. This was something she could speak of without fear. "No, that wasn't the only reason."

"Did it have to do with my brother?"

A hint of tightness in his tone made her glance at

him, though she still couldn't see his face well enough to ascertain what he was thinking. Not for the first time, she wondered what he thought about her and Whit's broken engagement. With whom did he place more of the responsibility for things ending—her or his brother?

"Seeing you did remind me of Whit, at least at first." She tilted her face toward the moon, remembering the first moment she'd gone next door and found Alec working there. "But the real reason I was upset had nothing to do with you setting up an animal clinic."

She felt his gaze settle on her. "What did it have to do with, then?"

"I've wanted to expand my shop for some time now and had hoped to buy that building."

Alec guided her across the street. "Had I known, I would've tried to find another location." She caught a glimpse of the sheepish smile he threw her way. "No wonder you didn't seem too thrilled to see me that first day."

"I was surprised to see you," she amended, "and yes, disappointed about the building. I don't regret you buying it, though."

The truth of those words resonated through her. She hadn't been keen on the idea of having Alec nearby, but in the nearly three weeks since his arrival, she had come to appreciate having him next door.

They stepped up onto the opposite sidewalk. "You're sure?" He sounded unconvinced. "Because it seems like I've brought you a fair share of trouble since I got here. First with the building and my clinic, then with that race."

"You're not the source of any trouble for me, Alec." Except, perhaps, for the moments here and there when her pulse raced at being near him or seeing his smile. But those were still hers to recognize and keep in check. "I'm not angry about the building or your clinic. And as far as the race goes, it was me who agreed to sit on top of that horse. Besides…" Isobel nudged him playfully in the side. "I thought you said that was a thorough and successful horseback riding lesson. You aren't taking that back now, are you?"

He laughed, the deep, happy sound rumbling through her. "No, ma'am. I stand by what I told you. You were a true horsewoman that day."

It took effort not to let his words weaken her knees or her resolve to view this courtship as a business agreement. After all, this was Alec, not a real suitor.

"Coming from a man who worked with horses for a living, I'll take that as a compliment." She kept her voice light, in spite of the delight she felt at his remark.

"As you should." He nudged her back. "What will you do about expanding your shop now?"

Isobel glanced at the darkened store windows as they walked. "Once I have the money I need, I may convert my living quarters into more shop space. Though I'd have to find a new home if I do that."

A measure of sadness uncurled inside her at the thought of actually living elsewhere. She loved her cozy apartment in the center of town. Not only did she find the hum of city activity energizing, but she also felt less alone here. There was also the convenience of living above her shop. Would she be able to find another place close by?

"That would give you twice the space you have now," Alec said, drawing her back to their conversation. "But is there another way to expand without giving up your home?"

Isobel wanted to believe his question stemmed from a desire to keep her as a next-door neighbor. But she dismissed the thought as fanciful. More than likely he was speaking from a practical perspective rather than a personal one.

"I've thought of one other way, but I'm not sure I can make it successful." She lowered her gaze to the sidewalk, feeling suddenly vulnerable at admitting more of her aspirations aloud. "I would like to design dresses again. In fact, I'm going to be creating some for Maggy Kent."

Alec ground to a stop. "You're going to design dresses?"

"Yes," she answered hesitantly. The dim light still made it difficult to gauge his reaction.

She didn't expect him to laugh, though. A flush spread over her cheeks. She'd hoped Alec wouldn't think her foolish for wanting to pursue such a path. After all, he'd been the one to remind her of her neglected dream the other week.

"I knew it!" The note of triumph in his voice was unmistakable, even if she couldn't determine his expression. "I knew you still wanted to do that."

So he didn't think her unrealistic. He was happy for

her, championing her, even. Elation replaced Isobel's embarrassment.

"Of course you should do it," he continued, his voice rising in volume. A young couple across the street appeared to be watching them. "It's going to be more than successful, Isobel. You are going to be—"

She pressed her fingers against his mouth, ending his boisterous speech. "Shh. Only you and Maggy are aware of this, and I'm not ready for the whole world to…"

The rest of her statement faded to silence when she became fully aware of Alec's masculine lips beneath her hand. She couldn't recall ever touching a man on the mouth before. The planes and angles were likely similar to her own, and yet they felt intriguingly different beneath her fingertips.

As the quiet stretched between them, she felt the corners of his mouth rise in a smile. Heat bathed her face again as she lowered her arm to her side. Thankfully the shadows that obscured Alec's expression would hide her mortified one.

"I-I'm sorry." She shook her head at her stammering, breathless words. "I shouldn't have done that…it's just that you were making such a commotion."

To her surprise, he scooped up her hand and threaded his fingers through hers. "You don't have to apologize. I *was* making a commotion, and neither of us needs more attention than we already have." She guessed he was still smiling as he added, "I can't say that it was an unpleasant way to be silenced, though."

Isobel couldn't hold back her own smile. "I do appreciate your enthusiasm." She hoped he knew how much. Other than her parents and her aunt, no one had encouraged her to design dresses—until now.

Looping her arm back through his, Alec guided her toward their apartments again. Neither of them said anything until they reached her staircase, but Isobel found the stillness far from uncomfortable.

"Thank you for dinner," she said, turning to face Alec on the landing as she handed back his jacket.

He nodded. "My pleasure."

The warm sincerity behind his reply induced a smile from her and melted any lingering consternation she still harbored.

"Would you permit me to call on you again, Miss Glasen?" he asked more loudly as he glanced around. He was likely hoping they'd be overheard, to help solidify their courtship plan even more. "Say, the night after tomorrow?"

Her smile deepened. "Of course, Doctor Russell."

"I'll be looking forward to it."

After bidding him good-night, Isobel entered her apartment and shut the door. She'd thoroughly enjoyed the evening with Alec, and she was also looking forward to seeing him again soon. *Only as a friend and temporary beau*, she reminded herself. But it still took several minutes before she could stop smiling, and it was even longer before she felt certain her head and heart were properly aligned once more.

Chapter Eleven

On Friday evening, more than a week after winning the infamous race, Alec dined at Isobel's. Or, rather, on her outside stairs. Giving the attention they were still receiving, they'd agreed that dining alone inside her apartment would cause another spike in the amount of rumors already circulating—and that was something they didn't need.

The number of people wandering into the clinic had remained steady, though now the farmers and ranchers yammered on about his courtship. Still, he felt encouraged that there'd been as many questions about animal care and remedies this week as there'd been about him and Isobel. Hopefully these same people would become regular customers, willing to pay for his veterinary services.

"That was delicious, Isobel."

She extended her hand to take his empty plate. "Thank you," she said, adding his plate to hers. "I don't fancy myself an expert in the kitchen, but when I came here, Aunt Jo taught me how to make a proper corn-bread and baked beans."

"Are you close with your aunt?" Alec had instantly liked the woman after meeting her the other week. Jo-anna Clawson radiated inner strength and confidence, much like Isobel.

Rising to her feet, she nodded. "After she left Pitts-burgh years ago, we wrote each other regularly. I knew when I left home myself that I wanted to live close to her again." The corners of her mouth lifted in a wistful smile. "She and I have quite a lot in common, although, she's far more fun-loving than I am. When I first ar-rived in Sheridan, she was relentless about encouraging me to have more fun and be impetuous."

"You're not interested in having fun?" Even as he voiced the question, he couldn't recall ever seeing Iso-bel doing what he'd deem as fun or spontaneous—not back in Pittsburgh or here in Wyoming.

Her chin rose a notch. "I like to have fun," she coun-tered. "Just in more cautious ways."

"I see." He chuckled, but that only seemed to get her dander up further. "I didn't mean any offense, Isobel. Everyone is different."

Her gaze moved to the street. "I learned as a girl the importance of caution. I suppose it's a way of looking at life that isn't easily changed, no matter how much one would like to."

Curiosity piqued, Alec considered asking her what she meant. But the lines on her forehead and the pen-sive set of her mouth told him that she wasn't ready to share more. Maybe one day she would.

"Can I wash those dishes for you?" he offered.

She shook her head, her preoccupied look disappearing. "No, that's all right. I'll get us dessert and clean the dishes later."

Since her hands were full, he jumped up to open the door for her. Isobel gave him grateful smile and entered her apartment. Alec settled himself on the staircase again, pleased that she wanted to keep talking with him.

That was what he enjoyed the most about being with Isobel—conversing with her—especially without interruption. Thankfully there'd been no interruptions tonight as there had been both times they'd dined at the restaurant this week. Alec appreciated her clever sense of humor, too, and how she wasn't timid about sharing her opinions.

But if he was honest with himself, talking with Isobel wasn't the only thing he liked about being with her. He also enjoyed having her arm tucked inside his as they walked or the way she'd pressed her fingers to his mouth the other night. Was that wrong, though? He leaned forward on the hard step, his elbows on his knees. Surely it was all right for him to be attracted to the woman he was courting, even if it was for expediency's sake.

"Doctor Russell?" A wrangler on horseback stopped beside the staircase.

Heat crept up his neck, though he knew the horseman couldn't surmise his thoughts. "That's me. Can I help you?"

"Mr. Kent is hoping so."

Isobel exited her apartment right then, carrying a

plate with a slice of pie on it. "Oh, hello, Franklin. I'm afraid Stella has gone home for the night."

"Unfortunately, I'm not here to see Stella, Miss Glasen." He tipped his head at Alec. "I'm here at the request of Mr. Kent. He'd like Doctor Russell to come to the ranch as quickly as possible."

Concern tightened Alec's gut as he stood. The situation at the Kents' ranch must be rather dire if Edward had sent one of his men all the way to town to collect him. "What seems to be the trouble?"

"One of the mares has a real bad case of colic." Franklin turned his horse around to face the direction he'd come. "Mr. Kent has been trying to help her, but the usual treatments aren't workin'. Will you come look at her?"

Alec locked gazes with Isobel. He hated to cut their evening short, but he couldn't refuse the man's request, either. A serious case of colic could kill a horse.

"It's all right," she said with an understanding smile. "The pie will keep for another evening."

Gratitude and relief that she wasn't angry emboldened him. He lifted her free hand and pressed a quick kiss to the back of her palm.

"Thank you, Isobel. I'll see you tomorrow."

Pink filled her cheeks, but she didn't look offended or upset. "I'll be praying for you and the horse."

Alec squeezed her hand, then hurried down the stairs. "I've got to grab a few things from my clinic and get my horse from the livery," he told the wrangler. "You go ahead of me and let Mr. Kent know I'm coming."

"I will." The words were barely out of his mouth before Franklin spurred away on his mount.

Inside the clinic, Alec located the medicine he needed. He placed everything inside his doctor's satchel. This would be his first time carrying his bag and making a house call since his arrival in Sheridan. He chose not to bother changing out of his "courting" clothes and instead hurried on foot to the livery stable. The owner had his horse saddled in record time, and Alec soon left the buildings behind him.

Adrenaline and uncertainty had his heart pounding along with his horse's hooves. How sick was the horse? Would Alec be able to help or would it be too late? Isobel's words about praying for him had Alec doing the same. He asked for guidance with his actions and for the horse to live, if possible.

After a time, he passed the drive that led to the McCall's dude ranch. Alec was getting closer to his destination. Finally, he reached the side road that led to the Kent's ranch. Alec turned his horse to the left and kept going. He'd been to the Running W once before, when Maggy and Edward hosted West and Vienna's wedding party. Once he'd crossed the bridge and headed up the drive, he reached the house in less than a minute.

They were ready for him. Franklin appeared and grabbed his horse's bridle as Alec dismounted in front of the porch. "They're inside the stable there," the wrangler informed him.

Alec walked quickly toward the stable that stood beside the large ranch house. Through the open doors, he saw Edward Kent and two other wranglers gathered in front of one of the stalls. The place was devoid of animals, save for the mare.

"Doctor Russell," Edward said, extending his hand as Alec drew near. His grim expression spoke volumes. Alec shook the man's hand. "Thank you for coming."

He nodded and eyed the horse. The poor creature pawed at the ground, then turned to look at her flanks—both signs of colic. "Tell me what happened."

"Her pace started slackening this morning, and she kept trying to lie down and roll." Edward crossed his arms over his chest. "I recognized the signs of colic right off and so we gave her a bit of laudanum and walked her around. When that failed to help, I crushed up hot coals, added them to some table salt and dissolved the mixture in water." The rancher shook his head. "However, you can see that hasn't helped her, either."

Alec had used both remedies on horses at the ranch in North Dakota. Now that he had his own clinic and apothecary, though, he had access to more treatment methods. Hopefully what he had inside his doctor's bag would prove effective in treating the distressed horse.

"West McCall spoke very highly of you when we were in town for the festival, which is why I thought to send for you." The rancher's distress and affection for the animal was evident as he returned his gaze to the mare. "Is there anything more you can do for her?"

"There is. I have some chloride of lime with me," Alec explained. "But seeing that your other treatments didn't work, I'd like your permission to try something that's been known to work better than the chloride of lime."

Edward directed a frown at him. "What is it?"

"Spirits of turpentine. It's potent, but when administered in the correct dose, it's also very successful in relieving colic."

The rancher studied him for a long moment as if taking his measure as a veterinarian. Alec maintained his own level look in return. What he was suggesting was risky, but he also knew it might be the only thing to save the horse at this point.

"I trust you to do what is best for her," Edward said at last, stepping back from the stall to make room for Alec. "What do you need from me?"

Buoyed by the man's confidence, he set down his bag, removed his jacket and began rolling up his sleeves. "I need a clean spoon and someone to hold the horse's head."

Edward left to collect a spoon from the kitchen, while Alec pulled the medicine bottle from his bag. The mare hadn't stopped moving in an agitated manner inside its stall. A fresh wave of compassion and resolve moved through Alec. This was what he'd been trained for, what he hoped to do for other animals and their owners here in Wyoming.

The two wranglers hadn't spoken yet, apparently deferring conversation to their boss, but their concern for the horse hung heavily in the warm, pungent air of the stable. Alec could easily identify with their worry.

"Hang on, girl." He stood and reached a hand out to the mare. She sniffed it, then tossed her head. "We're going to get you feeling better soon."

After Edward returned, Alec poured less than an

ounce of the spirits of turpentine onto the spoon. The rancher grasped the horse's head to keep it still, while one of the wranglers followed Alec's instructions to pull aside the horse's bottom lip. Alec's heartbeat sped as rapidly as it had earlier. Slowly and carefully, he brought the spoon to the horse's gums and tipped the liquid into the space behind the creature's back teeth. He watched the horse swallow, then he nodded for the two men to release the animal.

The mare reared in protest at being handled in such a manner, but none of the men were close enough to be hurt by the action. "Once the colic is completely gone," Alec said, handing the spoon back to Edward, "you'll need to give her a quart of raw linseed oil."

The rancher dipped his head in acknowledgment. "We'll do that. How long before the treatment will take effect?"

"I'd like to give her twenty, thirty, minutes." Alec returned the medicine to his bag and straightened. "Then we'll see if there's any change."

Edward turned to the two wranglers. "Thank you for your help, boys. You may head to the bunkhouse now. I'll stay with Doctor Russell."

Once the hands departed, the rancher set two stools in front of the mare's stall. Alec took a seat on one and Edward the other. The sounds of the horse's movements filled the quiet of the stable for a few moments.

"I understand you worked at the same dude ranch as West," Edward said, removing his hat and wiping his sleeve across his forehead.

Alec figured he'd worked up a few beads of sweat

himself in his eagerness to help the horse. "I did, though my friendship with West goes back even before that."

"Did you always wish to be a veterinarian?"

Smiling at the memory of his boyhood aspirations, Alec turned to watch the restless horse. "Ever since I learned there was such a thing as an animal doctor, I wanted to be one. What about you? You always want to be a horse rancher?"

"Ever since I heard one could do such a thing here in America." He threw Alec a smile. "How is your clinic doing?"

Alec shifted on the stool. It wasn't easy to admit the truth to a man as respected and successful at his business as Edward Kent. "It's been slow going so far. I'm hoping all the people stopping in to talk about the race or about me and Miss Glasen will eventually want my help with their animals."

"I see." Edward nodded with apparent understanding, then gestured toward his horse. "If this treatment of yours works, I promise to put in a good word for you with the other ranchers in the area."

"Thank you," Alec replied with sincerity. A favorable recommendation from Edward would surely go a long way toward increasing business.

Their conversation turned to talk about Edward's other horses and their care. The rancher was interested in what measures he could take to possibly prevent colic in the future. As they talked, Alec continually returned his gaze to the mare. Was it his imagination or had the horse's troubled movements begun to slow?

"Does she seem calmer to you?" Edward asked.

Alec stood, hope thrumming through him. "I was thinking the same thing."

The rancher rose to his feet and the two of them approached the mare. Edward ran his hand down the horse's nose. Instead of responding with distress or aggression, the mare lowered her head and nuzzled the man's shirt.

"Would you look at that?" Edward gave Alec a full smile. "This is the most docile she has been all day. I believe your spirits of turpentine has done the trick, doctor."

Letting out his breath in relief, Alec gently rubbed his hand across the horse's right flank. A shiver rippled the horse's muscles, and she glanced back at his hand.

"She's still uncomfortable, but she seems to be through the worst of it." Alec collected his jacket and drew his arms through the sleeves. "When you think the colic is fully gone, give her the linseed oil."

Edward patted the horse again, then turned to Alec. "What do I owe you, Doctor Russell?" Alec named the price. "Sounds fair. While I collect your payment, I'll have Franklin bring your horse around."

Alone in the stable, Alec picked up his bag and offered the horse his own affectionate rub on the nose. "Glad you're feeling better, girl." He sent a prayer of gratitude heavenward and exited the building.

A few minutes later, he sat astride his horse, the cash from Edward tucked securely into his pocket. "She should be fully back to normal in another day or two. Let me know if she isn't."

"I will." Edward extended his hand to him, and they

shook hands again. "I can't thank you enough, Doctor Russell. As I said earlier, I plan to let others know it, too."

With a wave, Alec set off down the drive. It would be past dark by the time he returned to Sheridan. And though he felt tired after his frenzied ride to the ranch and the tense situation of treating the sick horse, he couldn't help grinning. Maybe his clinic would be a success, after all. Either way, he now had his first paying customer.

True to her word, Isobel had prayed for both Alec and the sick horse after placing his uneaten pie back inside the tin and laying a towel atop the dessert. How were things going? she wondered as she prepared for bed. Was the horse faring any better? Knowing Alec, Isobel was confident the animal would receive the very best care.

She awoke the next morning, eager to know how things had gone. Fortunately she didn't have to wait long for the answer. One of the first people to walk through her door after Isobel opened the shop was Maggy Kent.

"Did you hear about our horse?" Maggy asked, breezing into the room with all the vivacity of a spring gale. She didn't wait for Isobel to respond before she continued. "The poor mare had colic, and your Doctor Russell helped her."

Isobel ignored the part about Alec being hers in favor of an empathetic statement. "I'm relieved to hear that, Maggy. The horse is doing better, then?"

"More than better." Maggy took a seat in one of the chairs. "She's as active today as a young colt. Edward is so grateful he asked me to go next door, after I'm finished here, and thank Doctor Russell again. We'll both certainly be recommending his services to the other ranchers and farmers around here."

Genuine happiness for Alec's success brought a smile to Isobel's face—almost as if he were actually hers. She mentally shook the thought away. Alec was hers in that he was her friend. And she was pleased to hear *her friend* may have secured more business for himself after last night.

"Are you ready to see what I've come up with?" Isobel gathered up the stack of fashion magazines she'd earmarked.

Maggy pulled a face, but her blue eyes were sparkling. "I'm afraid saying yes might ruin my detective reputation."

"Nonsense." Isobel laughed. "If anything, it will enhance it. You'll be a well-dressed detective with a set of gowns that are uniquely yours."

"I'll admit I like the sound of that," her friend said with an impish smile. "If I'm going to wear a dress every day, then I want it to suit me and my life."

Isobel dipped her chin in a nod. "Exactly what I had in mind." She opened the first magazine to the page she'd marked and placed the publication across Maggy's knees. "If we alter the color and the design of either of these dresses, I think they would fit you perfectly."

Excitement and confidence bloomed inside Isobel as she showed Maggy each of the ideas she'd come up with and how to make them unique. Maggy asked plenty of questions and voiced her opinions, which made her the ideal client to begin designing for. Isobel didn't want to impose her designs on someone; she wanted them to catch the vision of uniquely tailored garments and share in the process of coming up with those designs.

She wasn't sure how much time had passed when the shop door opened and her aunt entered. "Aunt Jo!" Isobel set aside the magazine on her lap and stood. She didn't think her morning could get any better, but her aunt's surprising visit added to her already good mood.

"Hello." Joanna embraced Isobel, then turned to Maggy. "A pleasure to see you again, Mrs. Kent."

Maggy offered the woman a warm smile. "It's wonderful to see you, too, Mrs. Clawson."

"Have a seat, Aunt Jo." Isobel cleared the chair of magazines and pieces of fabric.

Joanna sat in the chair Isobel had vacated. "What are you two planning?"

"Isobel is going to design some new dresses for me."

Her aunt raised her eyebrows in surprise, though her expression conveyed delight. "Oh, Issy, that's wonderful. When was the last time you designed a gown?"

"It's been a long time," she admitted. "But I figured Maggy would be game to let me experiment with the new dresses she needs."

Maggy nodded. "Not only am I game, but I'm actually excited now."

"What brings you into town, Aunt Jo?"

"You." Joanna gave Isobel a look she couldn't fully interpret. "I wanted to see how you're faring."

Isobel chuckled in confusion, though she was touched by her aunt's thoughtfulness. "I'm well." She motioned to the scattered periodicals and fabric. "Better than well. I'm going to be designing dresses again."

"I also wanted to ask you about something I overheard the other day."

Worry slithered through Isobel. Had her aunt heard the rumors about Isobel and Alec? If so, she wanted to tell Aunt Jo the truth. Isobel shot a glance at the back room where Stella was still working. "What did you hear?"

Looking slightly uncomfortable, Maggy rose to her feet. "I'd better head to next door to thank Doctor Russell."

"It's all right, Maggy. You don't have leave yet." She didn't mind her friend staying for this conversation. Ever since word had spread about her courtship, Isobel had longed to share the truth of it with someone other than Alec. Now she had that chance, and she fully trusted that Maggy and her aunt would be discreet with what she shared. "Whatever Aunt Jo has heard is likely already common knowledge."

"Then you and Doctor Russell are courting?" Isobel couldn't tell if Aunt Jo was more astonished by the news or more hurt at not having learned it from her niece first.

Maggy's eyes widened. "You and Doctor Russell are courting?"

"Yes, they are," Stella cheerfully called out from the back room. "For almost a week now."

Her face heating, Isobel shook her head. "It isn't like that," she explained in a soft voice.

"I still don't understand." Joanna regarded her with

a mixture of concern and confusion. "I heard you two are courting because of something to do with the May Day festival."

Isobel sat in Maggy's empty chair and swiveled to face her aunt. "It's a rather long story. Suffice it to say, Stella was supposed to participate in the *Ride for a Bride* race. Through a mix-up, though, I rode off on her horse instead."

"You?" There was no mistaking her aunt's amazement. "But you don't ride."

From the corner of her eye, Isobel caught her friend's surprised expression. "I didn't know that," Maggy said. "You must have been terrified."

"I was…"

The memory of that harrowing ride flashed through her mind. But seconds later, it was replaced by the recollection of Alec, coming to her aid and offering her comfort. He'd been every bit a real hero that day. She blushed at the notion, though neither her friend nor her aunt could know what she was thinking.

"Anyway, Alec—Doctor Russell—stopped the runaway horse." Isobel lowered her gaze to her hands, remembering how tenderly his hands had held her. She cleared her throat to continue. "Neither of us knew that in coming to my rescue, he actually won the race. The city council wanted us to marry right then, but…" She lifted her eyes to her aunt's. Of all people, Joanna Clawson would know Isobel's reasons for not agreeing to marry Alec. "We both knew that wasn't what we wanted."

Maggy chimed in. "Because you wanted a real court-ship instead."

"Not exactly." She dropped her voice to a whisper, though Stella wasn't likely to overhear her now over the hum of the sewing machine. "There was so much fuss after the festival. People asking Alec and me if we were going to marry or if we were secretly courting. He came up with the idea that if we courted for real we could stem the tide of the gossip until it died down."

Her aunt frowned. "Then what?"

"Then we'll let it be known we don't suit…" Isobel fiddled with the cuff of her sleeve. "And we'll be free to go on with our lives."

Her friend's amused laugh had Isobel peering up at Maggy. "While it's a sound plan in theory, you only have to look at me, Isobel, to know the heart makes its own rules."

Mild panic threaded through Isobel at the reminder. Maggy and Edward had staged an engagement a few years ago, which had eventually led to their union as husband and wife.

This was different, though, Isobel reminded herself. Her courtship with Alec was about practicality. It could never lead to the same result the Kents now enjoyed. "It really is a means to an end. Once people are no longer interested in our courtship, everything will go back to the way it was."

Maggy didn't look convinced. "Please don't say anything to anyone, Maggy," Isobel implored.

"I won't. I promise." Her friend moved toward the door, and Isobel stood to follow her. "Think about what

I said, though. Sometimes the thing we don't want is the very thing we need."

Isobel managed a smile. "That's wise advice."

"Let me know when the dresses are ready."

Her smile deepened. "I will. I'm looking forward to making them."

After bidding Maggy goodbye, Isobel shut the door and moved to tidy up the mess they'd made. Her aunt's troubled countenance stopped her.

"What's wrong, Aunt Jo?"

It was Joanna's turn to look toward the back room. "I'm worried about you."

"I'll be fine." She lowered herself into the other chair again. "Honest. Another few weeks and this will all blow over."

Her aunt reached out and clasped her hand. "Does Alec know why his brother ended your engagement?"

"I-I don't think so." Isobel swallowed hard. "He's never mentioned it."

"I don't want to see you hurt again."

She lifted her chin. "I won't, because it isn't going to develop to that point."

"And if it does?" Joanna pressed, her tone gentle. "Will Alec care that you can never have children?"

Tears blurred the stack of magazines and swatches of fabric. "Most likely, yes." After all, he came from the same family as Whit. Alec's brother had been shocked and saddened when Isobel had told him that she'd never be able to give him a family of their own.

"I don't bring this up to hurt you, Issy." Joanna

squeezed Isobel's hand. "I only want to caution you about this courtship plan."

Isobel didn't fault her for her apprehension, especially since Aunt Jo was unable to have children, as well. But that didn't stop Isobel's alarm from growing. Was she wrong to have agreed to Alec's plan? Should she tell him she no longer wanted to continue with their pretend courtship?

She blinked to clear her view of the room. How she loved this shop and wanted it to remain successful. If that meant staying the course by courting Alec Russell, then so be it. Besides, as a lady, she would not go back on her word.

"I know what's at stake here," she reassured, giving her aunt's hand a squeeze in return. "I appreciate you looking out for me, but I don't plan on repeating the past when it comes to the Russell men."

Neither Maggy's predictions about love nor Joanna's about getting hurt would prove true. Instead, Isobel would see this courtship arrangement through to its end—with her heart still intact.

Chapter Twelve

Alec surveyed the calendar nailed to the wall of the clinic. In three more days, it would be June. Only two months left to fulfill his commitments to his father. Thankfully Alec no longer felt worried about the viability of the clinic.

Edward Kent had made good on his promise to recommend Alec as a qualified veterinarian. The three weeks following his treatment of the rancher's colicky horse saw nearly the same number of people wandering into his clinic as the weeks before, but now they were there for their animals' care and well-being—not solely for gossip. Alec had also made two more house calls to nearby ranches, one for a foundering horse and the other for an arthritic goat.

Now his days were wonderfully busy as he prepared medicines, answered questions and treated the occasional animal in the clinic. And while not overflowing, the cash box tucked beneath the counter of the apothecary no longer sat empty, either.

His evenings were quieter but no less enjoyable, especially those he spent with Isobel. Twice a week they dined at the restaurant, and on the weekends they went for evening strolls or ate dinner together on Isobel's outside staircase. On Sundays Alec had the pleasure of sitting beside her during church services.

Their courtship strategy seemed to be working well. There were still plenty of people eager to ask them questions about their relationship and future plans, but he and Isobel were interrupted less often in their comings and goings as a couple.

His other task—that of finding a wife and settling down—was less appealing to him the longer he was in Sheridan. But he'd need to meet that provision if he wanted the rest of his inheritance.

If only he could find a young lady as easy to be with as Isobel. They never lacked for things to talk about. The other day she'd even asked him for business advice, regarding whether she ought to design dresses for more people or continue to focus on expanding her shop through more space. It had been a proud moment for Alec, knowing Isobel saw him as a real business owner and not a novice any longer.

In moments such as those, he found it hard to remind himself that they were only courting temporarily. Of course, he hoped they'd always be friends. But if he let his old feelings for Isobel resurrect themselves, wouldn't he be right back in Whit's shadow all over again? He was carving out a life and business here that was all his own. Shouldn't that apply to the person he gave his heart to, as well?

After locking the clinic's door, Alec made his way to the back of the building. He still had ample time left before his birthday to find another young lady whom he'd like to marry. Someone with no ties to his—or his brother's—past. For now, he was content with his arrangement with Isobel. Once they both agreed that the talk about them was as good as gone, they could end things and he'd be at liberty to turn his full attention toward meeting someone new.

Since he and Isobel weren't eating together that night, he prepared himself a simple supper. The warmth from the stove drove him outdoors to enjoy the early summer evening. Alec took a seat outside on his staircase and balanced his plate on his knees. Before he'd taken more than a couple of bites, he heard a scuffling sound at the side of the steps followed by a soft mewing. Curious, he set aside his plate and stood. He leaned over the railing to find a small gray cat peering up at him.

"Well, hello there." Alec smiled at the cat. "Are you hungry?"

The feline gave another plaintive meow as if answering him.

He chuckled and turned to grab his plate. He moved slowly down the stairs, but even that action sent the cat skittering away from him. Sitting back down, Alec settled in to wait, knowing the skinny creature would be hard-pressed to ignore the tantalizing smell of his meal—no matter how modest or bland it might be.

Sure enough, a minute or so later, the cat crept back toward him. When it was still a few feet away, Alec extended a piece of meat toward the animal. The cat froze, its eyes on his hand. Then it began to tentatively inch its way forward. At last it grabbed the morsel from his fingers. Alec sampled another bite himself before offering the cat a second tidbit. This time the feline didn't cower. Instead, it eagerly accepted the food.

The poor thing looked half-starved, but beyond that, Alec couldn't see any that it suffered from any other physical ailments. The more scraps he fed it, the closer the creature came. Finally, it rose and rested its front paws on Alec's knee.

"Feeling better with something in your belly?" he murmured, running a hand down the cat's back. "I feel that way, too." The feline was a girl and looked to be older than a kitten, though not yet fully grown.

Alec kept alternating between eating and sharing bites with the cat until his plate was nearly empty. Setting it on the ground, he let the feline finish off the rest. "I'll be back with something to drink."

Inside his apartment he filled a dish with water. The cat was still licking his plate clean when he returned outside, so Alec placed the bowl next to the plate. Once no trace of his meal remained and the cat had drunk some of the water, she rubbed against his pants leg as if expressing her thanks.

"You're very welcome." Alec scratched the tiny gray head. The cat shut its eyes and purred in response. "Too bad you can't stay here." The other animals that came into the clinic would likely scare the little thing away.

A sudden loud noise from next door sent the cat ducking behind the staircase once more. Alec glanced at Isobel's apartment, trying to figure what he'd heard.

A *thwack* accompanied by a human screech had him jumping to his feet. He hurried over to her staircase. The muffled sound of a chair smacking the floor met his ears as he bounded up the steps to the door.

Was Isobel in trouble? Alec paused before the door, uncertain if he should barge in or not. He opted to try knocking first, but if there was no answer, he was entering her apartment uninvited.

He gave the door a hard knock. "Isobel? Are you in there?"

"Yes," she answered, though her voice sounded breathless and upset.

Alec reached for the handle. "Can I come in?"

"Not yet. But when I say, I want you to fling the door open."

Frowning, he studied the worn wood in front of his face. The situation was growing more bizarre by the second.

"Alec, did you hear me?"

He nodded, then realized she couldn't see him. "I heard you. Open the door when you say."

"Yes, please."

Alec wrapped his fingers around the handle in preparation. His confusion and curiosity mounted as he heard another *thwack* from the other side of the door followed by an audible grumble of frustration.

"Open the door, Alec," she suddenly cried. "Open it now."

He twisted the handle and threw the door open wide, bracing himself for whatever might come flying out. But the only thing he saw was Isobel, gripping a broom between her hands. Her dark hair fell around her face and shoulders, and her amber eyes were narrowed in determination. Instead of a stylish dress, she wore a faded yellow robe over what looked to be a long white nightgown.

"There it goes!" she exclaimed as she pointed at his shoes.

Glancing down in bewilderment, Alec saw a mouse dart past him and down the steps. It reached the street in seconds, only to have the cat give chase.

"I've been trying to shoo that thing toward the door for ten minutes." She breathed a puff of air that dislodged a lock of hair from her cheek. "But every time I poked at it, it would scurry in the opposite direction."

Alec opened his mouth to respond, then shut it just as quickly. The sight of Isobel's unfettered hair and the way the yellow of the dressing gown enhanced the color of her eyes left him momentarily speechless. Adding in the fact that she'd efficiently driven the mouse out of her apartment on her own, he couldn't recall in that moment why he didn't want to court this beautiful, strong, resourceful woman for the rest of his life.

"Are you…all right, Alec?" She studied him in turn, her brow furrowed with evident distress.

He mentally shook himself. "I'm good. Great, even." He ran a hand over his jaw in an effort to ground himself in the present. "Do you get mice often?"

"Not usually." Isobel visibly shuddered. "But I don't like finding even one that's made its way in here."

He couldn't blame her—he didn't necessarily like

mice, either. "I'm impressed with your effective herding skills." He nodded at the broom.

Color rose into her cheeks. "Thanks for coming over when you did." She drew the lapels of her wrapper closer together with her free hand. "And for opening the door. How did you know something was wrong?"

"I was sitting on my steps, eating supper, when I heard some strange noises."

Her blush deepened, but then so did the playful spark in her eyes. "I've found that extricating mice isn't a noiseless process."

"I can't say I don't agree with you there." They exchanged a laugh.

Isobel fell back a step and set the broom against the wall. "I'd better return to my sewing. I had no idea when I designed those dresses for Maggy that she'd love them so much she'd tell others."

"I could have told you that." He hoped she'd sense the sincerity behind his teasing. Alec had felt downright proud of her these past few weeks—as if she actually were his sweetheart—as she'd courageously designed dresses for Maggy Kent and accepted orders for several more unique gowns. "How many other women are you designing for?"

She pursed her lips in thought, drawing his attention to their attractive bow shape. "Two, for now. Mrs. Stone, whose dog you helped, and Lola Winchester. Mrs. Winchester also mentioned that she might be interested in having dresses designed for her older daughters, too."

"I'd best let you go then." Alec didn't want to keep her any longer with all she had to do. He was grateful for the chance to talk, however briefly, on a night he hadn't expected to see her. "If there are any more mice, let me know and I'll gladly be your doorman."

Her lovely laugh pealed across the evening air. "I'll remember that. Though I hope there won't be. I've considered putting out traps, but I don't like the thought of finding a dead mouse waiting for me when I came up from the shop."

"Hold on," Alec said, an idea forming. "I think I have another solution."

Isobel's eyebrows rose in question. "What is it?"

"Give me a few minutes, and I'll be back."

With a shrug, she started to close the door. "Just knock when you're ready."

Alec descended the steps to the street. There was no sign of the stray cat, but he figured he knew how to coax it back. After grabbing a few more morsels of supper that were stuck to the pan, he returned outside and sat on his stairs again.

"Here, kitty," he called softly as he held out the food. "Come here, kitty."

He didn't have to wait long. The feline appeared up the street, then it scampered past Isobel's place and up to Alec.

"How would you like a new owner?"

The cat eagerly snatched up the tidbits Alec offered, as if it hadn't eaten already. Once his fingers were empty, Alec scooped up the feline and cradled it to his shirt. Instead of protesting, the creature nestled against him. He carried the cat into the clinic, where he located a brush. Alec brushed the gray fur until it was shiny and free of knots. A quick examination confirmed his earlier assessment—the cat was hungry and skinny but in good health otherwise. Nothing that regular meals and a warm place to sleep wouldn't fix.

He held the cat in his arms and retraced his footsteps to Isobel's door. She answered his knock right away, but the expectancy in her expression dimmed when she saw what he held in his arms.

"A cat?"

Alec nodded. "Hear me out, and if you still don't want her, you don't have to keep her."

"All right." She folded her arms over her wrapper. "I'm listening."

"This little thing found me tonight, and I gave her some food. What she really needs, though, is a good home and you need a mouse catcher."

Isobel frowned. "What do I feed it? And where is it to go when I'm at the dress shop?"

"She can eat most of what you do for meals," he explained, "and during the day, all you have to do is let her outside to explore and find her own snacks until you come back in the evening."

Was he wrong in thinking her skeptical look had softened? "Is she healthy?" Isobel put out a tentative hand and the cat slipped its head beneath her palm. It began to purr as Isobel stroked its head.

"My prognosis after looking her over is that she is fit as a fiddle."

A chuckle escaped Isobel's lips. "She is rather small, isn't she?"

"She'll grow, though my guess is she'll never be an overly large cat."

Isobel lowered her arm to her side and pushed out a sigh. "I've never owned a pet before, Alec."

"Never?" Even in the city, his family had owned horses and a number of birds.

She shook her head. "What if she doesn't like it here, with me?"

"I can't see any reason why she wouldn't." Any person or animal would be blessed for knowing Isobel. "Do you want to hold her?"

Hesitation radiated from her before she held out her hands. Alec passed her the cat, hoping the thing wouldn't scratch or bolt. His fears were unfounded, though. The feline snuggled into Isobel's arms as if she belonged there. Isobel ran her hand along the cat's head and back, and soon soft purrs filled the air.

"A proper cat needs a proper name," Isobel said after a few moments, bringing her gaze to rest on Alec's.

The quiet appreciation glowing in her eyes sent a zing of emotion through his chest. She'd not only accepted his gift, but she was grateful for it, too. "You'll keep her, then?"

"I'd like to, yes." She smiled down at the cat. "What if we call her...Duchess?"

Alec wasn't sure if she had inadvertently used the word *we*, but it brought a smile to his face nonetheless. "I think Duchess is a great name."

"Goodnight then, Doctor Russell." Isobel lifted the cat's paw in a wave. "Thank you for helping us."

He pantomimed tipping a hat to the pair of them. "Night, ladies."

As he moved down the stairs, he heard Isobel's door click shut. She now owned her first animal and Duchess had a real home. Happiness filled him as he returned to his own apartment and went to work tidying his small kitchen.

A sobering thought pushed back at his joy some time later. His past feelings for Isobel hadn't stayed buried as he'd hoped. Seeing her earlier after she'd expelled the mouse, talking with her now and giving her that cat had stirred the dormant ashes in his heart. And Alec feared it wouldn't be long before they became a tiny flame he wasn't sure he wanted to snuff out a second time.

Isobel absently rubbed Duchess's soft fur as she carried the cat through the kitchen to the sitting area. She sat in the chair drawn up to the sewing machine and placed the feline on her lap. Duchess continued to purr at the attention.

Alec had given her a cat. Isobel's lips curved upward as she stared unseeing at the dresses and cut pieces of fabric that adorned the settee, the armchair and the mannequin. It had been years since a man had brought her any sort of gift. And while the pleasure of owning her first animal made this present particularly special, that wasn't the only thing on her mind.

She kept recalling the admiration in Alec's eyes after he'd opened the door for the mouse. "It isn't how a friend would look at you," she mused aloud to the cat. Then again, the way her pulse had tripped in response as she'd gazed back had certainly stemmed from more than friendliness, too.

"What am I doing, Duchess?" she whispered in confusion.

Isobel gazed at the half-finished and nearly finished gowns that surrounded her. This had been her life for so long, and for the most part she loved it. But spending regular time with Alec the past three and a half weeks had ironically made her aware of the loneliness deep inside her that had been growing for some time. She had Aunt Jo and Uncle Evan, of course, but they didn't live nearby. Even Stella, whom Isobel considered a close friend, went home to her own family every night.

Then Alec had stumbled back into Isobel's life, and she found she now looked forward to those evenings when she would see him. Apart from her aunt and uncle, she had also discovered she could simply be herself around Alec. Perhaps it was because he was simply himself with her, too. He certainly frequented her thoughts more than any other person now.

"Still, that's to be expected, isn't it? I mean, we are courting, even if it's only temporarily."

Duchess snuggled her head against Isobel's palm, seeking another rub. With a soft laugh, she obliged. Her merriment faded quickly, though. How did she make sense of the kaleidoscope of emotions Alec inspired in her?

"I don't know the answer to that, Duchess," she admitted aloud as she lifted the cat and stood. "But I must figure it out sooner rather than later." She buried her face in the gray fur, the vibration of the cat's purr humming against her cheek. "Because if Alec is somehow vying for my heart, I'm afraid he might be succeeding."

The next day Alec looked up from examining the goat in front of him to find West coming through the front door of the clinic. He waved at his friend, then turned back to the farmer. "She looks much improved, Pete."

"She is to be sure, doc. And I can't you thank you enough for helping her."

Alec smiled as he stood. "Glad to be of service." He waved away the few dollars Pete extended toward him. "Consider this a follow-up visit to my house call the other week."

"Appreciate that. Come on, Gladys." The farmer tugged on the goat's lead rope and guided the animal out the door.

"The place looks busier every time I come in," West said with a grin as he crossed the room.

Alec shook West's hand and nodded. "If things remain steady like this, I think the clinic may actually make it."

"You had no doubts from me."

He appreciated the statement of confidence from his best friend. "What brings you to town today? Picking up a new group of guests for the dude ranch?"

"Nope, I just dropped off a group at the train station. I was also picking up the phonograph we ordered last month. Vienna thought the guests might enjoy listening to some music in the evenings."

"Speaking of things being busy..." Grabbing the

broom, Alec commenced ridding the floor of animal hair. "Sounds like your ranch is even more popular this year than last."

His friend took a seat on one of the benches. "It is, and we feel truly blessed for that."

"How are Vienna and Hattie doing?"

"They're doing well. In fact, that's the reason I'm here." West leaned forward and rested his elbows on his knees. "They've both been asking when you can come to dinner again."

Alec paused in sweeping. Between things with the clinic and spending time with Isobel, he hadn't returned to the HC Bar in nearly six weeks. "Tell them I'd love to come."

"How about tomorrow night at six o'clock?" West asked as he rose to his feet.

"I'm taking Isobel to a restaurant for dinner tomorrow night."

His best friend wouldn't be surprised by Alec's plans. The last time West had come into the clinic, curious about the rumors he'd heard in town, Alec had been more than happy to tell his friend the truth. He had explained his courtship with Isobel was more of a business partnership, and he'd been grateful when West had acknowledged the validity of their plan.

"Could you come to our place, instead? Vienna specifically asked if the two of you would come to dinner."

Alec studied his best friend's face, but West's expression appeared innocent, even hopeful. Was there more to this request? "Wouldn't you rather be alone as a family after a week of ranch guests?"

"What we'd like," West countered with a chuckle, "is for you and Isobel to join us."

Though still wary of their motive, Alec finally nodded. "I think that should work. I'll talk to Isobel to be sure, but I'd say plan on the both of us."

"Wonderful. I'll let Vienna know."

Alec set aside the broom and followed West to the door. "You know nothing's changed between Isobel and me. We're still just friends."

"I know." West grinned. "See you tomorrow night, Alec."

Instead of smiling himself, he frowned as he watched West through the clinic window. He couldn't quite decide which bothered him more—that his friends seemed to be up to something or that his words about himself and Isobel only being friends had sounded rather hollow, even to his own ears.

Chapter Thirteen

Clutching the side of the buggy with one hand, Isobel maintained at least two inches of distance between herself and Alec on the seat. It wasn't that she hadn't grown accustomed to sitting next to him or walking at his side. But the narrow confines of the carriage and the fact that they were joining his closest friends for dinner made this evening's outing feel more intimate. Surely that was the reason for the tension roiling in her middle. After all, she was already acquainted with the McCalls. So why the nervousness?

Isobel inwardly shook her head at the silent question. This was more than nerves. Tonight she felt exactly as she had before meeting Whit's family for the first time. Except that made little sense. She and Alec weren't a real couple, not as she and his brother had been, and he'd reassured her twice that West and Vienna understood that.

"Almost there," Alec murmured as he turned the buggy off the main road and drove beneath the HC Bar's archway.

Neither of them had spoken much on the ride from Sheridan to the dude ranch, beyond discussing each other's days and how well Duchess was adjusting to living with Isobel. Did that mean Alec also felt a bit apprehensive about this dinner? The possibility, however unlikely, eased some of Isobel's worry.

"I hope Hattie likes the doll clothes I made." She grabbed the wrapped parcel on her lap to keep it from sliding toward her feet.

Alec glanced at her, and the first hint of a smile tugged at his mouth. "She'll love them. That was real sweet of you to make those for her."

"I had plenty of scraps of fabric left over," she said with a casual shrug. Inside, though, Alec's approving praise felt as warm and wonderful as the shaft of sunlight parting the clouds ahead of them.

All three members of the McCall family were waiting for them on the porch. After parking the buggy, Alec climbed out first to help Isobel exit. By then, Hattie had moved closer.

"Hello, Miss Isobel." She dropped a little curtsey, her green eyes shining. "I like your dress. It's real pretty."

Isobel had to swallow past the lump in her throat to speak. "Thank you. Yours is lovely, too."

Despite the obvious differences in their hair and eye colors, she felt as if she was watching a younger version of herself. Isobel had also practiced ladylike manners and had been fascinated with her mother's friends' gowns. Like Hattie, she'd been loved by caring parents and had a bright-eyed view of the future. A future that she'd hoped would include having a family of her own someday.

The memories elicited a wave of sorrow she hadn't felt in a long time. She missed the happy, less cautious girl she'd once been—before the harsh possibilities of life had changed her.

How many fun things had she missed experiencing— such as learning to ride a horse—because not doing so might save her from inheriting the condition that plagued her aunt? Her parents had clung to the hope that caution and restraint would eventually encourage her monthly bleedings to finally start. But years had passed, and her situation remained the same.

Isobel blinked back a sheen of tears. There was nothing wrong with mourning what might have been, but she'd also experienced plenty of compensating blessings. Her parents had loved her unconditionally, and she wasn't without loving family nearby now. The dress shop had also brought her much fulfillment and was the realization of her childhood passion for sewing and dressmaking. Her dreams of designing were at last being fulfilled, too. And soon she'd have enough money to expand her shop.

Glancing over her shoulder at Alec, who stood talking with West and Vienna, she added his renewed friendship to her list of blessings. She also had Stella, Duchess and these friends right here.

"I brought you a small gift," she said, crouching down in front of Hattie.

The little girl's mouth lifted in a full smile and she bounced from foot to foot. "What is it?"

"Open it and see." Isobel handed her the parcel.

Hattie tore open the paper and gasped at the tiny dresses tucked inside.

"They're for your dolls, so I made several different sizes."

Her face lit up with excitement. "Thank you, Miss Isobel." She raced over to her mother, Isobel following more slowly. "Mommy, look, they're dresses for my dolls!"

Vienna picked one up and fingered the tiny collar. "These are exquisite, Isobel. How long did you spend on them?"

"I started sewing them last night."

Looking at her, Vienna smiled. "I think you need to sell doll clothes as well as dresses in your shop."

Isobel shook her head, though she had enjoyed making the tiny dresses. It was something else she hadn't done in years. "I enjoy sewing women's dresses a bit more, but if your dolls need a wardrobe for the winter, Hattie…" She offered the girl a conspiratorial smile. "You let me know. I haven't made a doll's cape and muffler in ages and it would be fun to do that again."

"I'm sure she'll take you up on the offer, won't you, Hattie?" The girl gave another vigorous nod in answer to her mother's question. Then Vienna motioned them toward the house. "Please, come in. Dinner is on the table."

West nodded to Isobel. "We're happy to have you here, Miss Glasen."

"My pleasure."

And she meant it. Most of the frantic flurries in

her stomach had subsided. At least, until Alec gently gripped her elbow, staying her from following the family onto the porch.

"Did I just hear Isobel Glasen use the word *fun*?"

He bit back a laugh as she gave him a haughty look. "Why, yes, you did, Doctor Russell."

"But you told me you don't like having fun."

He'd been turning over that conversation in his mind for several weeks now as he'd tried to think of something that would change Isobel's views about having fun. Her agreement to take in Duchess had been a good start. And yet, Alec wanted to help her see that there was a time and place for spontaneity as well as for caution.

"I happen to find making dresses, whether for dolls or people, to be quite fun."

The McCalls were probably wondering what had detained them. Alec led Isobel up the porch steps toward the front door, but he wasn't finished yet. "As someone who also loves what I do, I agree that a job done well can be fun. I'm talking about other things, though."

"Other things?" She visibly swallowed as if he'd suggested having fun meant eating something distasteful or breaking the law.

This time he let his laugh escape. "I'm not saying you do something illegal or immoral, Isobel."

"Then what are you saying?"

He released her arm to hold the door open for her. "I'm issuing you a challenge to have more fun." When she opened her mouth to likely protest, he hurried to

add, "In a safe, calm way, of course. I'll think of some
things that sound fun and then we'll try them."

"Who gets to determine if your suggestions are actually fun or not?"

Alec followed her inside. "You do. But only after
you've tried the suggestions."

Her eyes narrowed, though he had little doubt she
would back down. Isobel might be properly cautious
but she was also fiercely determined.

"All right. Challenge accepted."

"Alec? Isobel?" Vienna called from the direction of
the dining room.

Isobel threw him an imperious look. "We're coming, Vienna."

Despite her lingering reluctance over Alec's challenge, Isobel found the dinner with the McCalls delightful. The food tasted scrumptious, confirming what
she'd heard about Vienna's exceptional cooking. Conversation flowed easily, too, and before long, Alec and
West were trying to best each other with tales of their
boyhood antics and from working together in North Dakota. By the time she helped Vienna clear the plates and
utensils to the kitchen, her cheeks hurt from laughing.

"Thank you for having us." Isobel set the dishes she'd
carried onto the sideboard. Why had the word *us* slipped
so easily from her lips?

Vienna smiled. "We're so glad you both came. We
enjoy having Alec over, especially Hattie. But it's always nice to have another woman here."

"Have you known Alec long?"

With a shake of her head, Vienna leaned back against the sink. The slight bump beneath her dress attested to the news she'd shared at dinner that she was expecting. "I only met him last year when West and I traveled to North Dakota to visit the dude ranch there. I knew right away, though, what a good, honest man he is. You two knew each other back in Pittsburgh, correct?"

Isobel didn't want to talk about the past tonight, but she didn't want to be rude to Vienna, either. "Yes, I became acquainted with his family a number of years ago, before coming to Sheridan."

Vienna looked as if she meant to ask something else, but Hattie, thankfully, rushed into the kitchen. "Mommy, Mr. Alec is going to do a trick. Come see."

"We don't want to miss that, do we, Isobel?" Vienna said with a laugh as she allowed her daughter to tug her toward the door.

No, she didn't want to miss this. Isobel returned with them to the dining room. Alec glanced at her as she walked in, a smile teasing his mouth. Hattie sat in the chair that faced his.

"All right," he said. "If everyone's ready, we'll begin." He lifted his hand and showed them the penny he held between his fingers. "What's this, Hattie?"

"A penny."

"Would you like to see it disappear?"

The little girl nodded, her excitement palpable.

"Then watch closely."

Quicker than Isobel could follow, Alec had his hand in a fist, the penny no longer visible. "Okay. Count to three, Hattie."

"One…two…three," she called out.

He uncurled his fingers, and Hattie leaned forward. Isobel found herself leaning forward, too. But Alec's palm sat empty.

"You made it disappear!" Hattie looked in awe at him, then glanced at the table. "But where did it go, Mr. Alec?"

Alec rubbed his empty hand against his chin. "Now that's an excellent question, Miss Hattie." He slowly rose to his feet. "It never seems to land in the same place twice. Once it was under my boot." He lifted his shoe for the little girl to examine. "Another time it was in my shirt pocket."

Bending, he let Hattie pat his pocket. "Not there," she said with a frown.

"However, there is one place it likes to land the most." He straightened and walked toward Isobel. The teasing glint in his gaze gradually faded, changing to thoughtful admiration, as he drew closer. "That would be tucked behind a pretty lady's ear."

He reached up, his fingers grazing Isobel's earlobe. She drew in a swift breath as her heart quickened its usual rhythm. If this was his idea of having fun, she wasn't sure she was prepared to join in. Everything about this moment felt the opposite of caution.

"There it is," Alec murmured, his eyes still on Isobel's as he lifted the penny into the air beside her head.

"Yippee." Hattie hopped off her chair and clapped. "You did it, Mr. Alec."

He fell back a step, allowing Isobel the space and ability to breathe normally again. Then she caught sight of the perceptive look West and Vienna exchanged, and her face heated with embarrassment. What must they think of her and Alec? Acting far more familiar than mere friends.

"How did you get it behind her ear?" Hattie asked Alec.

Crouching down in front of her, he presented her with the penny. "A true magician never reveals the secrets behind his tricks."

"Hattie," her mother said kindly, "can you thank Mr. Alec for the trick and the penny?"

The little girl put her hand on Alec's shoulder, then bent forward to give him a kiss on the cheek. "Thank you, Mr. Alec."

His smile softened. "You're most welcome, Miss Hattie."

The tender exchange provoked a mixture of pleasure and pain for Isobel. Alec would make a wonderful father someday. She could easily imagine him entertaining his own children with parlor tricks and funny stories like the ones he'd told during dinner. But she could never be the woman to provide him with those children, even if the two of them had been courting to marry. A dull ache settled inside her chest at the reminder.

"Have you tried out the phonograph yet?" Alec asked as he stood.

Their host pushed back his chair. "It plays beautifully. Want to hear it?"

Alec looked to Isobel, and she eagerly nodded. Anything to push this ache from her heart and the memory of Alec's gentle touch to her ear from her mind.

After a minute or so, a sprightly tune filled the air. Alec chuckled. "It sounds like an orchestra is the next room."

"Dance with me, Mr. Alec."

He took Hattie's hands in his own and spun with her around the table. But Vienna shook her head. "You two can go outside. There's plenty of room in the yard and you can still hear the music from there."

Offering the crook of one arm to Hattie, Alec turned and extended the other to Isobel. "Will you join us outside, Miss Glasen?"

She hesitated. Wouldn't it be better to help Vienna in the kitchen than spend another charged moment with this wonderful, handsome, caring man?

"Go ahead, Isobel," Vienna encouraged.

She glanced at their hostess. "Are you sure? I can help with the dishes."

"No, it's fine. West can help me."

Was Isobel mistaken in thinking Vienna hurried her husband from the room? With both Hattie and Alec watching expectantly, she decided the best course of action would be to go along. She slipped her arm into Alec's, and the three of them headed outside, leaving the door ajar behind them.

Vienna had been right—the music could still be heard in the yard. Isobel took a seat on the porch, content to watch. Keeping their arms linked, Alec and Hattie swung each other around as they danced to the jaunty tune. Both were laughing, and Isobel couldn't help a small smile as she observed them.

When the song ended, Alec braced his hands on his

knees. "That was some mighty fine dancing, young lady. But I think I'll sit this next one out."

"Okay, Mr. Alec."

He dropped onto the porch beside Isobel as Hattie continued to dance by herself. Isobel admired the girl's lack of inhibition. Even without a crowd of onlookers, she wasn't sure she could dance like that without embarrassment.

With the next tune, the music changed, slowing in tempo. Isobel recognized the rhythm of a waltz. "Miss Glasen?" Alec turned toward her and held out his hand. "Would you care to dance?"

"What? Now?" she hedged. "I thought you were taking a break."

"I did."

Isobel glanced around them. Vienna and West were still gone, but Hattie eyed them curiously from where she stood swaying to the languid music. "This isn't an actual dance, though, with lots of people."

"Who says it needs to be an actual dance?" Alec climbed to his feet, his hand still extended toward her. "This way the dance floor never gets crowded."

Pressing her lips together, she stared at Alec's hand. She couldn't agree. If she did, it would only make things feel more real between them.

"It'll be fun." His blue-gray eyes sparked with challenge. "Consider this your first assignment."

Isobel scowled. She couldn't back down now—not after agreeing to his challenge earlier. "Fine," she grumbled. She rose slowly to her feet and placed her hand in his. Alec tugged her forward into dance position, and before she realized it, they were waltzing about the yard.

After a moment, she sneaked a peek at his face. "You dance quite well."

"Why thank you."

In fact, he moved more effortlessly and guided her with greater ease than she recalled his brother doing. Whit had approached waltzing as he did life—with driving energy—so that Isobel had often felt as if they were charging around the ballroom. With Alec, though, they were gliding, in spite of the uneven ground beneath their feet. The tension inside her began to ebb as she allowed herself to relax within Alec's arms.

"You still waltz beautifully," he said, his voice low.

Isobel lifted her chin and eyed him in surprise. "Still?"

"We danced the waltz once before." He studied something over her head. "It was the same night you and Whit announced your engagement."

How could she have forgotten? Isobel thought back to that night, though doing so brought a trace of pain. She'd danced with Whit. And then…yes, she'd danced with Alec. After that waltz, their father had stopped the music to announce that she and Whit were betrothed.

"I-I remember now."

They were no longer moving, though Alec still held her hand. The music had stopped. At some point, Hattie had gone inside, leaving the two of them alone in the yard.

"Isobel, there's something I'd like to tell you."

She swallowed, then offered a wordless nod. Would

he tell her that he was ready to end their courtship? She waited to feel relief. After all, this was what she'd wanted and planned for, wasn't it? But only sharp disappointment thrummed inside her.

"It was that same night, after dancing with you, that I realized something." Alec stroked the back of her hand with his thumb, sending ripples of feeling up her arm.

He wasn't ending their courtship yet. Unbidden relief flooded through her then. "What did you realize?"

Lifting his free hand, Alec brushed a strand of hair from her cheek. Isobel's breath came out in harried puffs. "Whit wasn't the only one who had feelings for you back then."

"You mean..." She stared in shock at him, certain she'd misunderstood his statement. Alec couldn't be confessing that he'd admired her in the past. He'd never given her any indication, nor had they spent much time together in Pittsburgh. However, a faded recollection niggled at her thoughts. She'd forgotten the times she and the two brothers had gone on outings together, usually with a servant in tow to keep things aboveboard.

The chuckle that escaped his mouth sounded as pained as it did amused. "I'd planned to say something that night, after our waltz, but then Father ended the dancing."

Isobel lowered her gaze to the ground. How could she have been so blind? She'd assumed Alec had tagged along because he had nothing else interesting to do— certainly not because he'd been interested in spending time with *her*.

"Did Whit know?" She didn't look up.

"No. He still doesn't."

"Then why tell me now?"

Alec tipped her chin upward with his finger, his eyes more blue than gray in this moment. "Because I felt you deserved to know, especially since we've been courting for a while now." He glanced at her lips. "And because I've been thinking that I'd like to…"

"To?" Isobel repeated softly. The sound of her pulse strummed in her ears as she leaned toward him.

He matched her stance. "To—"

"Miss Isobel, look at my dolly."

The little girl's voice sounded as loud and unexpected as a gunshot. Isobel jumped back, tugging her hand free. Whirling around, she faced the porch, hoping her face wasn't as red with mortification as it felt.

"Will you look at that?" she said in an exaggerated tone of cheerfulness. "The dress fits your doll exactly."

Hattie gave a happy nod, innocently unaware of what she'd interrupted. "I'm gonna try the others on her now." She spun on her heel and headed back into the house.

"I'll come with you and see if I can help with the rest of the dishes." Without looking at Alec, Isobel hurried after the little girl. She couldn't remain in the yard with Alec alone any longer. Not after nearly kissing him.

Chapter Fourteen

Alec jammed one hand into his pocket and raked the other through his hair. Someone had started up the phonograph again, and the cheerful melody mocked his frustrated mood. He hadn't planned to tell Isobel about his past feelings for her. He'd only wanted to dance with her—to show her that doing so, even in an empty ranch yard, could be fun. However, waltzing with Isobel had unearthed long-forgotten memories.

In that moment, there was no longer dirt beneath their feet or the evening prairie air surrounding them. Instead, he was once more leading Isobel across the polished wood floor of his family's gold-colored ballroom. The words Alec had meant to say that night had filled his mind and throat all over again.

He'd been prepared to risk Isobel's possible rejection and his brother's likely anger to share his feelings with her after their waltz. Except at the exact instant Alec had opened his mouth to speak, his father's authoritative voice had stilled the festivities. Bringing an end to the dancing and to his hopes for winning Isobel.

Alec could still recall how the engagement announcement had sliced through him with stinging surprise and disappointment. And while he'd been happy for his brother, he hadn't been able to stop himself from wondering what might have happened if he had spoken to Isobel sooner.

"Likely the same result as tonight," he muttered to himself. With Isobel walking away as she'd done just now, looking confused and troubled. Only this time Alec had shared more than his past feelings for her. He'd almost shared a kiss with her, too.

He started slowly toward the house, reluctant to face those inside. Maybe he ought to feel grateful for Hattie's interruption. After all, he didn't want to hurt Isobel with the false promise of a kiss. They were only supposed to be courting for a time, not deepening their friendship into something neither of them wanted. But his logical thoughts rang dull and flat in his head.

If he didn't know better, he'd say he was feeling every bit as confused and troubled as Isobel.

Stepping onto the porch, Alec did his best to push aside his convoluted thoughts. There was nothing wrong with sharing pieces of his past with Isobel, even ones she hadn't known before. What he did regret was that doing so, coupled with nearly kissing her, had placed them both in an uncomfortable situation. He was determined to make things right, though. To do all in his power to restore the earlier ease of their relationship and keep his past feelings for her in check. Otherwise, the impending buggy ride home, as well as the rest of their courtship, would be more awkward than a mail-order cowboy at a rodeo.

"There you are, Mr. Alec," Hattie said as he entered the dining room. She was lying on her stomach on the rug, dressing her dolls in the clothes Isobel had made.

He felt West's and Vienna's gazes on him as he joined them at the table. The only one who didn't look at him was Isobel. She continued to sit demurely in the chair across from his. "Such a nice night," he said. "Not too hot but not too cold."

"Would you like some coffee?" Vienna asked. At his nod, she poured some into a mug and slid it toward him.

Alec took a sip, his eyes on Isobel. The splotches of color that had taken up residence on her cheeks hadn't faded yet. "That was a delicious meal, Vienna."

"Thank you. You two are welcome to join us any-time." If either she or West noticed the strain clouding the air, they didn't let it show.

Desperate for a return to the pleasant atmosphere that had reigned earlier, he blurted out the first thought that came into his head. "Did you know Isobel has a cat now?"

"You do?" Hattie called out from the floor. "What color is it, Miss Isobel?"

She glanced at Alec, but he couldn't read her expression. "She's gray."

"What'd you name her?"

"Duchess." Her mouth creased a bit at the corners.

It was far from being an actual smile, but the sight still brought Alec a measure of relief.

West repeated the name. "I like it. How come you decided to get a cat?"

"It was actually Alec's idea. I've had some trouble with mice."

"Trouble she handled with all the fierceness of a commanding general," Alec said, recalling Isobel's ingenuity and courage. She didn't return the smile he sent her way, but she didn't seem displeased by his praise, either.

Vienna looked between them. "What do you mean?"

"The other evening I hear this noise coming from Isobel's apartment." Alec cocked his head as if listening. "I couldn't figure out what it is, but being concerned, I went over and knocked on her door." From the corner of his eye, he saw that Hattie was now sitting up, watching him. "Instead of saying she needed help, Isobel asked if I would open the door when she told me."

Warming to his story, Alec climbed to his feet and stepped back from the table. "So I gripped the door handle…" He pantomimed the action, even arranging his face in an exaggerated look of bewildered concern. Hattie giggled. "And I'm wondering what in the world I'm going to find when I open the door."

"What'd you find?" the little girl asked.

"Well, Isobel called to me to open the door and I threw it wide." He acted out throwing the door open. "I couldn't see anything at first, except for Isobel standing there, brandishing this broom like it's a sword." Alec jabbed the air a couple times. A peek at Isobel's face revealed there was more of a smile on her mouth now. Vienna and West were chuckling. "Then this mouse came skittering out of her house like he's being chased by a whole pack of felines."

Isobel gave him a rueful smile. "That isn't exactly how it went."

"I'm sorry, ma'am," he said, feigning a serious tone, "but I'm afraid the passage of time has altered your memory some. Because that is exactly how it went."

He turned to the rest of his audience to finish. "Miss Isobel singlehandedly shooed that mouse right out the door, using only her wits and a broom. Naturally I knew she could take on a whole legion of mice herself." Isobel visibly shuddered. "But to keep her from having to do so alone, I thought she might like the assistance of another mouse-fighter, Miss Duchess."

"I like your stories, Mr. Alec. They're funny."

"Hear, hear," West said, echoing his daughter's sentiments.

Alec bowed to them. "Thank you."

When he straightened, he looked at Isobel. Had she enjoyed his retelling of the story, too? To his relief, she no longer appeared distressed. Instead, she rewarded him with a full smile that momentarily made him forget what he'd been doing or that anyone else was in the room.

"You'll have to ask Mr. Alec to tell you the story about the race at the May Day festival." Her amber eyes sparkled. "I think his rendition would be quite entertaining."

Hattie hopped up. "Please tell us, Mr. Alec. Please!"

"It'll have to wait," he said as he stooped in front of her and tousled her blond hair. "Miss Isobel and I need to head back to Sheridan before it's full dark. But I promise to tell you the story next time."

Her face lit with a smile. "Okay."

Alec straightened and joined the rest of the group outside. He and Isobel thanked the family for dinner, then he helped her into the carriage. After waving goodbye, he guided the horse down the drive.

"Thanks for coming with me, Isobel."

The earlier tension between them had dissipated. But he still wasn't sure if he had been forgiven for the awkwardness he'd created by almost kissing her in the yard.

"I'm glad I did," she said after a moment. "It was…" Isobel paused and glanced away, though not before Alec caught a flicker of a smile on her lips. "It was actually quite fun."

He couldn't help a hearty laugh—both at her choice of words and the way they'd restored their comfortable relationship. They were still friends. Thankfully his earlier error in judgment hadn't changed that.

"Then I'd say we're on the right path, Miss Glasen," he drawled, throwing her a grin, "to help you keep having fun."

Had she known what she was getting herself into, Isobel mused two weeks later, she might have used a different word to describe the evening at the McCalls. Not that being there with Alec hadn't been fun. However, since their dinner at the HC Bar, he'd made a more concerted effort to introduce additional fun into her life.

Alec had taken her fishing, horseback riding—albeit very slowly—and to one of the nearby ranches to see a litter of puppies he'd helped deliver. The latter outing had been the most fun to Isobel. She'd loved cuddling the wiggling puppies as they licked her chin. Duchess, on the other hand, had taken a sniff of Isobel's dress and refused to come near her until Isobel had changed.

With the exception of dancing at the McCall's ranch, she'd quickly surmised that Alec's idea of fun involved animals. And though she didn't mind broadening her experiences with God's four-legged creatures, Isobel had decided to come up with her own set of fun activities for the two of them to do together. Alec had kindly offered no objections.

One evening they'd spent several hours in her shop, the door propped open for propriety's sake, so Alec could observe her process for coming up with a design for a dress. Another time she'd shown him how to use the sewing machine, a lesson that had resulted in far more laughter and entertainment than Isobel had anticipated. They'd also attended a musical performance, something Isobel had enjoyed when she first came to Wyoming but hadn't done in a long time.

The one thing they hadn't done was talk about their near kiss in the McCall's yard or Alec's past feelings for her, though Isobel hadn't forgotten about either. She was grateful things between them were as relaxed as ever. However, she'd also noticed Alec acted more like a friend than a suitor these days, though they were still courting. He only took her arm when they were in public, and he hadn't suggested they try dancing again.

Still, Isobel felt happier than she had in a long time. She was actually living life again, beyond her work, and she had Alec's encouragement and friendship to thank for it.

Humming a song from the musical concert, Isobel unlocked the shop's door one Saturday morning. She expected a full day ahead, given that the town's annual summer ball was one week away. A handful of women had already ordered new gowns to be sewn for the event, but Isobel knew from experience there would be plenty of others who'd bring in their older dresses at the last minute for slight alternations or new embellishments.

Stella had yet to arrive, so Isobel opted to bring some work into the main room of the shop while she waited for the girl. The lovely purple silk she was currently hand stitching would be worn by Maggy at the upcoming ball. Her friend had been so impressed with the dresses Isobel had designed for her that she'd commissioned a unique ball gown, too. Isobel had finished the other dresses she'd designed for Mrs. Stone and Lola Winchester, but that was only because Stella had expertly taken over their other orders for the dresses Isobel hadn't designed herself.

Finally, her assistant arrived. But instead of entering the shop with her usual cheerful greeting and vibrant energy, Stella slipped silently inside.

"Morning." Isobel set down her sewing. "Is everything all right, Stella?"

For a brief moment a smile touched the girl's lips, but it fell away when she shook her head. "Yes and no."

"What's happened?"

Stella sank into the armchair across from Isobel's. "I have something I need to tell you, Issy. I'm just not sure how to say it."

"I see."

Her heart sped up, though she did her best to look outwardly calm. Isobel had never seen Stella so subdued, and she found the girl's lack of drama and exuberance more worrisome than what Stella planned to say.

"I have news." The girl lowered her gaze to her lap.

Clasping her hands tightly together, Isobel waited for her to continue. The last time Stella had brought her news it had meant she was losing the building next door. Although that hadn't turned out to be as bad as Isobel had expected, what with Alec returning into her life, so perhaps this would be the same.

"Franklin asked me to marry him last night."

Isobel blinked in surprise. This wasn't the sort of news she'd anticipated. "How did you answer?"

"I told him I would be honored to be his wife." Stella lifted her chin, revealing eyes that sparkled with pure joy. "Which means I'm going to be married."

Taking the girl's hand in her own, Isobel gave her a full smile. "Oh, Stella. I'm so happy for you. He seems to be an honorable, good man."

"He is," the girl said, her tone full of happiness and hope. "Thankfully my parents think so, too. The wedding will take place next month, and I want you to design my wedding dress, Issy."

She squeezed Stella's hand. "Nothing would make me happier."

Relieved at the nature of the girl's news, Isobel gathered up the dress she'd been working on and stood. "Why don't I help you finish those other ball gowns this morning and then we'll take some time this afternoon to talk about what you'd like for your wedding dress?"

"That would be nice." But the words sounded less enthusiastic than Isobel anticipated. Stella hadn't moved from her chair, either.

"If you're worried I won't have time to design your dress," Isobel said, hoping to reassure her, "I'll work every evening after we close, so you can have the wedding dress you want."

To her shock, she caught the glimmer of tears in Stella's eyes. "It isn't that. And after you hear what I have to say next, Isobel, I'll understand if you don't want to make my dress."

"What do you mean?" Isobel's pulse tripped with alarm as she pressed the half-finished gown she still held to her bodice. "Why wouldn't I make the dress for your wedding?"

Stella visibly took a deep breath and rose to her feet, her gaze on Isobel. "Because once I'm married, I'll be living with Franklin in a little cabin near the Running W. We'd like to start a family right away." Her cheeks went pink. "So after next month, I won't be working here in the shop anymore."

Though she heard the words, they still took a moment to settle inside Isobel's head. Of course, Stella wouldn't keep working for her once she got married. Isobel had known this day would come at some future point, especially with how eager the Ivys had been for the marriage of their daughter. And yet...

The feel of silk against her fingers had Isobel glancing down at the dress she'd designed for Maggy. Reality pressed down on her in that instant, causing her heart to skip a beat.

Without Stella's help, Isobel would no longer have the luxury of focusing the majority of her time on designing dresses, as she'd done the last month. She would need to go back to copying dresses from the magazines, at least until she found a new assistant seamstress to help her. But what if the next girl up and left because of marriage, too? There were plenty of young single ladies in Sheridan, and yet those with the time and inclination to work for Isobel would likely be as inclined to wed as Stella, should the opportunity present itself.

Her dreams of designing and of expanding the shop were once again falling to pieces before her eyes. And Isobel felt powerless to stop it.

What was God trying to teach her this time?

She cleared her throat and managed a sincere smile for Stella. One that didn't reveal any of her inner anguish. Whatever happened, she had a business to run and a friend to reassure. There'd be time enough later to identify the emotions pressing hard against her ribs.

"I appreciate you telling me, Stella." Isobel prided herself on sounding composed. Not a trace of the lump inside her throat leaked into her voice. "And while I can't imagine not having you here to help anymore, I understand your decision, and I'm truly happy for you and Franklin."

With her typical liveliness now restored, Stella rushed forward to give Isobel a tight hug. "Thank you, Issy. I'm going to miss you. You've taught me so much."

Isobel embraced the girl in return and did her best to stay the tears that threatened to escape. Tonight, alone, she would let them fall. For now, she kept her chin up as she released Stella and stepped back. "We've got a lot to do before we can start putting together a design for your wedding dress, so let's get to work."

Alec flipped over the letter from his brother and broke the seal. He'd regularly communicated with his parents for years, but he hadn't received a missive from Whit in a long time. His brother hadn't even been the one to share with Alec the news about the birth of his daughter. Their mother had told Alec. So why would Whit be writing him a letter now?

He pulled out the single sheet of paper. Thankfully, the clinic was currently empty so he could read the letter right away instead of waiting until he'd closed for the day. The missive began with an update on Whit's family. The boys were happy to have a sister, although both had expressed their deep disappointment that baby Cecilia did very little but coo and cry.

Alec smiled at his nephews' sentiments. Apparently Whit had felt the same way about him for the first few months after Alec's birth.

Now that Jocelyn and Cecilia are able to travel, we feel a change of scenery is in order. Which brings me to my reason for writing in the first place. We are planning to come visit you there in the wilds of Wyoming. I've already written to West McCall to secure our stay at his dude ranch. Our family will be arriving...

A glance at the calendar revealed Whit and his family would be in Sheridan in less than a fortnight. Alec shook his head in surprise. He couldn't say he wasn't pleased with the news, though, especially at the prospect of meeting his niece.

The rest of the letter detailed the family's travel plans before concluding with Whit's enthusiasm at seeing Alec and his clinic. A tremor of uneasiness rocked through him at the thought. Would his brother be impressed with what Alec had accomplished here?

At the bottom of the page, a postscript had been added. As Alec read it, his apprehension hardened into a knot in the pit of his stomach.

After sharing our plans with Mother at dinner the other night, she expressed how much she would also like to see you. She discussed it with Father and today they told us that they'll be accompanying us. So get ready, little brother. Looks like the entire family is eager to see what you've been up to in Wyoming.

Alec sank onto one of the clinic benches, his breath coming fast and shallow. Impressing Whit would now be just the start. It was his parents, and particularly his father, to whom Alec really needed to prove himself.

The realization reawakened his old insecurities, giving them new life.

With his family here, would he feel he was being compared to Whit as a businessman, a family man and a son all over again? What would they think of his clinic? Alec's gaze swept the tidy room. It was far from the notable offices of his father and brother, with their wood paneling, expensive leather chairs and Turkish carpets. By comparison, his clinic looked rudimentary, even with the framed photographs on the wall. At least Alec was making a profit now. However, even if his family found no fault with his business, there was still the matter of his finding a girl and settling down. That was something he hadn't done anything about yet.

Rubbing his hand across his face, he leaned his head back against the wall. He would likely need to end his temporary courtship with Isobel before his family arrived. What would they think if they found out he'd been seeing Whit's former fiancée? Or that he hadn't yet found a girl who liked him first and foremost?

Courting someone—even someone his family had known in the past—would still be a fulfillment of his second task, though. Wouldn't it?

"No," Alec muttered as he shut his eyes.

It would be better to end things with Isobel beforehand. Their courtship agreement had been mutually beneficial. But continuing to court her as a means of satisfying his other assignment from his father would be selfish and dishonest. It would only benefit him and his pride, and it would be living an untruth, since he and Isobel weren't courting for real.

That reminder sent a slice of disappointment through Alec—as it had every time he'd thought about it lately. Which had been often.

When Isobel had caught her first fish, when she'd bravely agreed to ride a horse again, when she'd laughed as she'd held the squirming puppies, Alec had experienced a jab of regret at the temporary nature of their relationship. Watching her design a dress and listen with rapture to the musical performance they'd attended had only furthered those feelings of remorse—along with deep enjoyment.

If only they'd been courting for no other reason than mutual affection for each other. If only she hadn't been enamored with Whit first. If only she seemed to care for Alec as much as he'd begun to care for her again.

The creak of the door drew Alec's eyes open. Things with him and Isobel weren't meant to be, and he would do well to accept that fact. He climbed to his feet and slipped his brother's letter inside the envelope as a farmer strode inside the clinic, a chicken under his arm.

"Doctor Russell?"

It took him a moment to force his mouth upward. "Howdy."

"My prize hen here is ailing."

Nodding, Alec tucked his letter into his pocket and motioned to the bench he'd vacated. "Have a seat. I'll go wash up, then take a look at your bird."

Alec wanted his family to feel proud of him and what he'd been doing the past eight weeks. He wanted them to see his clinic as successful, to see how he'd become a businessman in his own right. Knowing how to accomplish that, though, was a different story.

One thing he knew for certain, he needed to talk to Isobel about their courtship. Just as he'd predicted weeks ago, the townsfolk were no longer interested in the comings and goings of the *Ride for a Bride* couple. Which meant he and Isobel didn't need to keep courting. When he saw her tonight, Alec would find out if she was in agreement about ending their temporary arrangement.

He probably ought to tell her, too, that the entire Russell family was coming to Wyoming, though he wasn't sure how she'd feel about the news. Alec had noticed a far more carefree quality about her of late, and he hated to think of that possibly coming to an end when she learned Whit and his family would be visiting. Would Isobel go back to being more serious and spending most of her time sequestered inside her shop or apartment as she'd done before they had begun courting? Alec hoped not.

Maybe he could keep challenging her to try new things—fun things—as a friend instead of a pseudo suitor, he thought as he dried his clean hands on a towel.

Although the friendship between him and Isobel wasn't likely to stay the same, not after he started courting another young lady seriously. And that's what Alec needed to do. No matter how depressing the idea was of not having Isobel as a constant in his life anymore.

Chapter Fifteen

Isobel sat on her outside staircase, her chin resting on her palm. With her other hand, she stroked Duchess's gray fur. The cat stood on the step below hers, eating some dinner scraps. Isobel had sent Stella home an hour earlier than normal. Then she'd closed the shop soon afterward, in an effort to finally be alone.

She'd managed to scrape something together for dinner, though she'd only eaten half a dozen bites. The grief inside her left little room for hunger. After eating, she had planned to sew. But the projects waiting for her inside her apartment felt more smothering than comforting, so she'd fled outside. Only now did she allow herself to give in to the emotion she'd kept in check all day.

Tears slipped down her cheeks, over her fingers, and into her cuffs, blurring her vision. She was sincerely happy for Stella and the girl's forthcoming wedding. And yet Isobel felt heartsore at the thought of putting her dreams for the shop on hold.

She wanted as few projects as possible left undone

by the time Stella left, so she wouldn't be overwhelmed when she was on her own again and needed to take time to find herself a new assistant. That meant designing dresses would have to wait—yet again—along with her plans to possibly expand the shop into her apartment. She didn't want to be searching for another seamstress and a new place to live at the same time.

The postponement of her plans wasn't the only thing she was mourning, though. Stella's marriage announcement had served as a painful reminder to Isobel of her own shattered hopes for the future. Her dear friend would soon be a wife and most likely a mother. Those were events Isobel longed to experience herself, even now, in spite of knowing their impossibility.

You can still be happy, Issy, her mother had often told her. *That's a possibility no one can take away from you. One that God will help you find, over and over again.*

"I'm trying, Mama," she whispered, her grief at losing her mother tangling with the grief she felt tonight. "But sometimes it's so very, very hard."

With her gaze riveted on the ground and her thoughts elsewhere, she didn't hear Alec's approach. Duchess clearly heard something, though, because the cat suddenly scrambled up the steps and ducked behind Isobel. She lifted her head to see what had caused the commotion and found Alec watching her from the bottom of the staircase.

Heat flooded Isobel's cheeks at being caught crying. She hurried to wipe the moisture from her face and gave him a thin smile. "Hello."

"You still want to go for our evening stroll?" His gaze bored into hers.

She'd forgotten all about their walk. "Perhaps we could go tomorrow night? I'm feeling rather tired this evening."

"Tomorrow night it is." Alec motioned to the staircase. "Mind if I pull up a step and sit for a bit, instead?"

Isobel wanted to deny the request, afraid if he lingered he'd read the obvious distress in her red-rimmed eyes and lackluster conversation. But the unspoken concern in Alec's expression soothed a tiny portion of her sorrow. Perhaps talking with him would help.

"You're always welcome to pull up a step." Scooting over, she patted the empty spot beside her.

Alec gave her a grateful smile as he sat next to her on the stairs. "How were things at the shop today?"

"Busy, what with the ball happening next week."

He leaned forward, his elbows on his knees. "Are you going? To the ball, I mean."

"I don't know. I haven't attended in a long time." That hadn't stopped her from half-wondering, half-dreading Alec would ask to accompany her.

Clasping his hands together, he glanced at her, his mouth twitching with a hidden smile. "It isn't your idea of fun, then?"

"I wouldn't say that," she admitted with a chuckle. "I like dancing." She blushed a second time as she recalled dancing with him—both in the past and in the ranch yard the other week. "Regardless, I don't even own a ball gown anymore."

"Yet you make new dresses for the event every year?"

Isobel nodded. "A handful of them. Most of my customers only order a new ball gown every few years. The rest of the time they bring in their old gowns for refitting or redecorating."

"So you enjoy dancing and you make ball gowns for others," he said, his tone light but confused, "but you haven't made one for yourself. How come?"

She pulled Duchess onto her lap. "I suppose I…felt like I didn't belong there."

Running her hand along the cat's back, Isobel looked between the railing slats in the direction of Alec's building. Memories of the last ball she'd attended marched painfully through her mind.

"I went to the ball a year after my former fiancé Beau ended things between us." The story slipped almost unbidden from her lips. "I'd worked long and hard on sewing that ball dress. I walked into the room that night, feeling as scared as I did brave, after my broken engagement. Everyone stared at me, but I figured it was only because I hadn't attended many town events."

She kept petting Duchess, the repetitive movement pushing back against the remembered humiliation. "Then I came face-to-face with Beau and his wife. I had no idea he'd be there. In that moment, I realized all the staring looks had been ones of pity." The cat hopped down, and Isobel grasped her empty fingers together. "I left right after that."

"And you haven't been back since?"

The gentleness in his question threatened to renew

her tears. "There are a lot of things I haven't done since my time with Beau...and Whit." She whispered the latter name, but the pained look that crossed Alec's face told her that he'd heard her. "I stopped designing dresses. I stopped attending social functions."

Her eyes stung and her throat filled with a lump, but Isobel couldn't seem to stop the tide of words. "I stopped wearing the color yellow, even though I love it, because Whit liked how it matched my eyes. I stopped arranging my hair down because Beau preferred it that way. I stopped living my life and meeting new people." Tears dripped off her chin. "Because it was too painful. I threw everything into making this shop successful and now..." Now she feared losing it, too.

Isobel didn't realize Alec had tugged her toward him until his shirt brushed her wet cheek and his strong arms enfolded her. She ought to be mortified, both at what she'd shared and at showing so much unfettered emotion.

Why had she told him things she'd never told anyone else, including Aunt Jo? When had her remorse over Stella's leaving and its effect on her business transformed into sorrow over other things in her life? But any embarrassment she might have felt vanished as she cried against Alec's chest.

Alec held her, his heart breaking with each of her quiet sobs. He'd known something was amiss the moment he'd walked up. And though Isobel had tried to hide the fact that she'd been crying, he'd seen the unmistakable evidence written on her face. Had thoughts of her former fiancés prompted those earlier tears?

The pain in her voice as she'd talked just now had torn him up inside until he couldn't sit there without offering her solace. Especially not after learning his brave, confident Isobel had been burying a wealth of hurt for years. The anger he'd once felt at his brother for Whit's part in Isobel's past returned, mingling with annoyance at her other suitor, as well.

How could either man have let her go? Why had they been so blind to the incredible woman that Isobel was? Would she ever be able to live her life again without the hurt?

The questions had barely finished running through his head when a sudden thought banked his resentment toward Isobel's suitors. He and Isobel were far more alike than Alec had realized. Both had been spurned by those they'd cared for in the past; neither had been seen for who they really were. But Alec hadn't stopped living his life as Isobel had because of the hurt.

Or had he...?

Wasn't that the real reason he hadn't settled down yet? Why he'd been more than content to focus all his time and energies into working at the dude ranch, while guarding his heart more than risking it? Opening the clinic and wanting it to be successful before he started courting had been another excuse. If he didn't seriously court a young lady, then he wouldn't be hurt once she up and decided he wasn't the man for her.

Alec shut his eyes, clarity bringing the sting of regret. Even his unconventional career and love of fun had become, in many ways, a mask to hide his deepest fear. A fear that no matter how many girls he courted, he would never meet one who didn't find something lacking in him.

When he could no longer hear Isobel crying, he opened his eyes and glanced at her bent head. He could see—and had seen—how brave and resilient she could be, in spite of the heartache she'd experienced. Could she see him just as clearly? He didn't know for sure, and yet she'd believed in him, again and again, since he'd come to Wyoming.

His business wouldn't be what it was now without Isobel's initial advice and encouragement. She'd also willingly placed her trust in him—after the horse race, with his courtship idea, and in the fun challenges of the past few weeks. Surely that meant she saw something in him that maybe Alec hadn't fully seen in himself.

And it was time for him to return the favor.

He nudged her chin upward and waited for her to look at him. When she did, the sight of those lovely eyes, framed by wet lashes, set Alec's heart pumping faster with anticipation and concern. How could he go through with his plan to tell her about his family's impending visit? Or that they needed to end their courtship? He couldn't, not yet. Surely there would be time to tell her that the rest of the Russells were coming before they arrived. In the meantime, he had a new plan. To bolster Isobel's confidence as she'd done with him.

"My mother taught me never to argue with a lady," he said in an earnest tone, "but I'm going to have to make an exception tonight."

Isobel leaned slightly away from him, her expression troubled. "Oh?"

"You might have stopped living your life at one point, Isobel. But that isn't what you're doing anymore."

Wiping her fingers across her cheeks, she studied him. "I'm not sure I understand."

"For starters, you boldly shared your keen business sense with a clueless veterinarian who desperately needed it. You also attended the May Day festival, which is a social function, I might add." He shifted toward her until their knees touched. "Then you courageously helped a friend by sitting on that horse and managed a frightening race across the prairie. You started designing dresses again, and you agreed to our courtship plan. Even when it meant being seen in public with a suitor all over again." Only now did Alec understand how difficult that must have been for her.

With one arm still around her shoulders, he took hold of her hand with his free one. "You've also accepted every fun challenge I've given you, while even coming up with a few of your own." Her lips bowed a little, bending their earlier tight line. "All of that isn't hiding out from life, Issy. It's living it."

"Issy?" she repeated, her eyes widening. "No one but my aunt and Stella has called me that for years."

The nickname had effortlessly and unconsciously escaped his mouth. "I'm sorry, Isobel. I didn't—"

"No, it's all right. I don't mind."

Happiness, born of something much deeper than permission to call her by her pet name, filled Alec's chest. But he wasn't sure he wanted to take the time to understand all that it meant. He still needed to share with Isobel the idea taking shape inside his head.

"So in an effort to keep living life, as you are right now, I have a proposal for you."

She lifted her eyebrows, clearly intrigued. "A fun challenge?"

"It could be," he teased. "Though it's also going to require a healthy dose of bravery."

"What is it?"

Alec let the merriment drop from his demeanor. He wanted her to know his invitation was serious and not extended out of jest. "Will you allow me to accompany you to the ball next weekend?"

"The ball?" Her brow furrowed, but she didn't refuse the invitation outright.

Taking that as a good sign, he continued. "Before you agree to come with me or not, I've got another request." He shot her a sheepish smile. "Make that two."

"I'm listening."

Would she be angry at him when she heard his wishes? Alec hoped not. He was asking because he wanted to help and empower her as she had him. "Will you wear a yellow dress and your hair down?"

Her sharp intake of breath made him flinch. Releasing his hold around her shoulders, Alec settled his other hand on top of their joined ones, desperate to help her understand. "I get your reasons for not doing that in the past. I do. But if you like yellow dresses and wearing your hair down, then I'll hope you'll choose to do both next Saturday. Not for me, Issy, but because you want to for you."

She regarded him for a long moment. Hesitation and interest played across her pretty features. Would she agree? Even if it she didn't, he still very much wanted to go to this event with her. To spend an evening waltzing with this wonderful woman around a ballroom.

"I don't know if I'll have time to make myself a new...yellow gown."

Was she agreeing? "Do you have an old one you could change up?"

"I might." Her gaze glittered with an impish light, all trace of her tears now gone. "I don't promise to wear my hair completely down, but I will do it different than normal."

Alec grinned as he pulled her onto her feet. His heart felt lighter than it had since before reading his brother's letter. "Does that mean you'll attend the ball with me?"

"Yes," she said, giving him a full smile. Not only was she not angry with him, she was once again proving her courage by accepting his invitation.

In that moment, Alec couldn't imagine ever meeting someone as lovely, inside and out, as Isobel. She was everything he'd hoped to find in his future sweetheart and wife, except she wasn't his—not permanently.

"I'll see you tomorrow at church." He released her and took a much-needed step in the opposite direction.

Acknowledging her goodbye with a wave, he returned to his apartment, feeling both nervous and excited for the upcoming ball. Should he take back his invitation? Alec dismissed the thought immediately. He would keep his commitment. Not only because he'd given his word but because talk of attending had brought renewed strength and vitality to Isobel.

In truth, he wanted very much to accompany her. What he wasn't sure about was how well his heart would survive the occasion. Especially when dancing with Isobel was likely to further the notion he finally forced himself to consider.

In spite of all the reasons not to, in spite of what his family might think, Alec was falling in love with Isobel Glasen all over again. She might not share his feelings, just as she hadn't in the past. But unlike last time, he didn't want to simply let her go.

Chapter Sixteen

Alec's belief in her bravery coupled with Sunday's sermon on courage as it related to Joseph of Egypt calmed some of Isobel's grief over the past and her concern for her shop's future. It also hadn't hurt when Alec had held her hand through the service—something he hadn't done before. Isobel was grateful for the brief but wonderful connection between them, especially since she hadn't seen Alec since then.

He'd told her after church that he wanted to spruce up the clinic by adding wood paneling to the walls of the waiting area. Isobel thought the place looked nice without it, but she couldn't fault him for wanting changes. She could well remember making similar updates to her shop that first year.

For her part, she'd been equally busy and unavailable for their usual dinners at the restaurant or their evening walks. She and Stella had worked past closing time the past four days on ball gowns and other commissioned dresses. Each night, Isobel had continued sewing in her apartment until her tired eyes refused to focus on another stitch. The ball was only two days away now, and she still hadn't figured out what she was going to wear to the event. There'd been no extra time to start sewing something for herself.

"Issy?"

Stella's voice broke through her thoughts as did the sudden silence in the back room as the whir of the sewing machine stopped. "Do you need to go?" Isobel glanced at the clock. They'd closed the shop early in an effort to get more done, but that had been over an hour ago.

"No. I just…had a question."

Isobel returned her gaze to the gown spread across her lap. It was Maggy's purple ball gown, and she was close to having it finished. "What is it?"

"How do you know if you're really in love?"

Lifting her chin in surprise, Isobel lowered her needle. "Are you concerned you don't love Franklin?"

"I do love him." Stella swiveled to face her, her expression troubled. "At least, I think I do. I just want to be sure."

"Before you marry him?" Isobel finished.

The girl nodded. "Have you ever been in love?"

How often had she asked herself that same question, especially after her broken engagements? Isobel pushed out a soft sigh. "I thought I was in love twice in the past. Until those two relationships ended."

"I'm sorry." Stella's tone conveyed genuine sorrow. "Is that why you haven't courted anyone else before Doctor Russell came along?"

Her conversation with Alec the other day flitted

through Isobel's mind. "I didn't want to get hurt again, so, yes, I haven't put much focus into meeting any eligible suitors."

"What of the other young men I thought I loved?" The girl glanced down at her lap, her demeanor uncharacteristically somber. "I didn't even think how hurt they might be by my choice."

Had Whit and Beau felt similar regret for the pain they'd elicited from ending things? Both were good, God-fearing men, not villains, however much their rejections had hurt Isobel. It was a perspective she hadn't considered before, but one she was grateful to see through Stella.

"Inevitably there's sadness and hurt whenever a relationship ends" she said, reaching out to pat Stella's hand. "I imagine several of those young men were disappointed by your choice. And you didn't set out to be cruel or unkind to any of them."

Some relief settled onto the girl's pretty face. "Do you love Doctor Russell?"

"N-no," Isobel choked out as she sat back. "Stella, there's something I need to tell you about Alec and me."

"What is it?"

It was Isobel's turn to lower her gaze. "We didn't begin courting because we cared for each other." She swallowed hard. "We did so to stop all of the speculation and gossip that came after Alec won the race."

She hazarded a glance at Stella and found the girl watching her with obvious confusion. "So, you aren't courting to get married?"

Isobel shook her head. "I imagine we'll end our arrangement soon, since most of the rumors have died down."

"But…" Stella leaned forward, her elbows on her skirt. "I've seen the two of you together, Issy. You don't look or act like a couple who doesn't care for each other."

"We do care for each other," Isobel countered. Her next words seemed to stick in her throat, as if reluctant to be shared. "Just not in the way you and Franklin do."

The girl frowned. "Is he a man of faith?"

"Of course."

"Is he honorable? Does he treat you with respect?"

Why did Stella's questions sound familiar? "Yes, he is and always has been a gentleman."

"Do you find him handsome?"

Isobel resumed her sewing. She'd asked Stella these same questions about Franklin before the May Day race. "I don't see how that is relevant to this conversation, but yes, Alec is handsome."

"Does he return your feelings?"

Isobel looked pointedly at her. "There are no feelings for him to return, Stella."

"But you like him as more than a friend, don't you?"

This unexpected turn in the discussion was proving to be exhausting, especially when it was veering closer and closer to the truth. How had they gone from talking about Stella's feelings to Isobel's?

"It's more complicated than that." When the girl made no reply, Isobel pushed out a sigh. "I was once engaged to Alec's older brother. After he ended things between us, I came here and opened the dress shop."

She could feel Stella's searching gaze.

"Do you still have feelings for his brother?"

"Not at all," Isobel said, whipping her chin up. "He's happily married now, and I realized a long time ago that we likely wouldn't have suited each other."

"Why not?"

Isobel shrugged. "He was very determined, which is what made him successful in business. But I wasn't the sort of person who could curb that drive when needed or to join it. Instead, I often felt overpowered and swept along by Whit's confidence."

"Is Alec like that?"

She couldn't keep a smile from forming. "Alec is confident but in a different way. He approaches life with optimism and humor, rather than sheer force of will."

Why did Stella look a bit smug? "Have you ever felt overpowered or swept along by him like you did with his brother?"

"No, I haven't." Alec had always been encouraging and kind. *Even back when I was courting Whit.* The remembrance deepened Isobel's smile.

The girl straightened and turned back to the sewing machine. "You never know, Issy. A pretend courtship can become something real if the two people care as much for each other as I think you and Alec do."

A seedling of hope sprouted at Stella's words, but Isobel did her best to uproot it. Alec hadn't voiced deeper feelings for her, even if hers no longer felt confined to friendship. Besides, Alec wasn't likely to be any more accepting than his brother had been about never being a father if he married Isobel.

"Love sure is complicated," Stella said.

Isobel laughed lightly. "It is. But if it's mutual, if your relationship is built on affection, honesty and faith, then you'll be all right."

"I like that." The girl glanced over her shoulder at Isobel. "Affection, honesty and faith. I think that's what Franklin and I have, Issy."

She smiled. "I think you do, too."

Did she and Alec? Isobel's smile drooped a little. She hadn't been honest with him about not being able to have children, but then again, they weren't really courting. If they were, she would need to tell him. That had been her mistake with Whit and Beau. Isobel wished now that she'd told them about her condition sooner, before agreeing to marry either of them.

"I finished making my ball gown last night," Stella said over the sewing machine's noise. "Do you have yours done?"

Isobel had told her about Alec's invitation to the ball. "I haven't had any time."

Fingering the pretty silk on her lap, she allowed herself a pang of regret at not having a new gown of her own to wear. She would just have to make do. The one yellow dress she presently owned was rather outdated.

She still couldn't believe she'd agreed to Alec's terms for attending the ball. And yet, as apprehensive as she felt at wearing yellow and arranging more of her hair down, Isobel couldn't deny a growing excitement inside herself, either. She didn't want to live so cautiously anymore.

"Speaking of time," she added, looking at the clock again, "you can go, Stella. It's nearly past suppertime already."

Stella stopped sewing. "I don't mind staying."

"I know you don't, but we both need to eat."

Rising to her feet, the girl began gathering up some of their unfinished projects. "What if I fix us some supper while you get started on sewing your ball gown?"

Isobel stood, as well. "That's thoughtful of you, but I need to finish Mrs. Kent's dress. Not one for myself tonight." She draped the purple silk over her arm.

"I can sew the finishing touches on Mrs. Kent's dress so you can sew your dress." Stella nodded at the gown Isobel held. "It would still be designed by you. I'd just be assisting in the completion of it."

Did Stella believe her help wasn't wanted on the dresses Isobel had designed? Of course she would, when Isobel had insisted handling all of the stages of those dresses herself. Isobel wasn't the only one with a talent for wielding a needle and thread, though. Her dear friend and assistant was equally skilled and could expertly handle finishing the uniquely designed gowns.

"You're right." Isobel offered her a warm smile. "I would very much love your help, Stella. And not just with Mrs. Kent's dress but with the others I designed for Mrs. Winchester's daughters that still need finishing."

Stella's eyes widened, then she threw her arms around Isobel. "Thank you! I can't tell you what it means to know you trust me like that."

"It's you I need to thank," Isobel said, her throat filling with emotion. "You've been more than a wonderful seamstress these past two years. You've been a wonderful friend, too."

The girl released Isobel and wiped at her tear-filled

eyes. "I'm a weepy mess already, and the wedding still isn't for another few weeks." Adding the purple dress to her pile, she moved toward the door. "I've got a lot to do, so after supper, I'll go tell my parents I'll be at your place until late."

"Don't forget I'm still planning to sew tonight, too," Isobel said with a laugh as she followed Stella out of the back room.

Stella shook her head as Isobel let them out the shop door and locked it behind them. "Not on any of these." She held the pile away from Isobel. "Like I said, you're going to work on your own dress."

"I don't—"

"Please, Isobel." They circled the building and approached the back staircase. "You've done so much for me. Let me help you in return." Nudging Isobel in the arm, Stella added, "Besides, a girl who hasn't been to a ball in years needs her own dress."

Isobel didn't have the inclination or the heart to argue with her. Not when she very much wanted to create something special for herself. "Are you sure?" she asked as she opened her apartment door. Duchess bounded up the stairs and slipped in with them.

"Absolutely." Stella set everything on the couch. "Will you sew a brand-new gown?"

Shaking her head, Isobel moved into her bedroom, calling back over her shoulder, "I think I have something I can work with."

She opened her wardrobe and pushed aside most of her dresses. Reaching out, she touched the yellow ball gown hanging there, with its billowing lace sleeves and clusters of flowers along the bodice, shoulders and skirt. She'd worn this dress the night she'd become engaged to Whit—the same night she'd waltzed with Alec. It had remained unworn ever since that evening, and yet, Isobel had been loath to part with it, especially since she'd designed the entire thing herself.

Removing the dress from the wardrobe, she carried it into the apartment's main room. Stella was already moving about the kitchen, preparing their meal.

"I'd like to wear this, though it needs some changes to help it look less dated."

The girl turned and gasped. "Oh, Issy. It's gorgeous, even just like that. Did you design it?"

"I did." Isobel ran her hand down the silk damask. Pulling out the dress tonight, she felt only pleasure, instead of pain, at having created something beautiful.

Stella beamed at her. "I know what you said about you and Alec. But after he sees you in this gown, I think there's a good possibility we'll have another wedding in town before long."

Isobel didn't reply but moved to sit at her sewing machine. However, unlike earlier, she allowed herself to embrace the hope that Stella's words might come true.

Twisting one way, then the other, Isobel eyed her hair in the bureau mirror. She'd gathered it back from her face. But instead of piling all of it into its normal coif, she had twisted and plaited it so half of her hair fell below her neck and brushed the back of her gown. Her eyes glowed with eagerness, their color highlighted by the soft yellow hue of her dress.

She had trimmed and resewn the lace sleeves, which now ended just below her shoulders. The flowers she'd left. However, she'd removed one cluster from the skirt and used it to adorn the right side of her hair. A smile tugged at her lips. How glorious it felt to wear yellow again and to have her hair styled in a different way. What had started out as acquiescence to Alec's challenge for the ball had now become something Isobel wanted to do—for herself.

A knock sounded at her door as she pulled on one of her long white gloves. Her heartbeat leaped in response. Alec was here to accompany her to the ball.

Forcing a steadying breath, Isobel approached Duchess's favorite chair and gave the cat a pat goodbye. Then she slid her other glove up her arm and swept through the kitchen. She could do this.

Isobel opened the door. Her eyes widened when she saw Alec, dressed in stylish evening clothes. She'd expected him to wear one of his regular suits to the ball. Instead, he wore a pair of pressed black trousers and a pristine white shirt and waistcoat beneath his black tailcoat. A white necktie completed the outfit.

A distant memory floated forward in her mind. Alec had dressed in similar attire the night he'd danced with her in Pittsburgh. She remembered now how handsome she'd thought him then. Tonight, he looked every bit as dashing. Especially as he regarded her with a serious yet tender expression on his face. One that released a swarm of flurries through her middle.

"You look absolutely breathtaking, Isobel." He offered her a sincere smile. "That isn't unique to just to-night, though."

Warmth spread through her at his compliment. "Thank you." She pulled the door closed behind her as she stepped toward him on the landing. "What about you? Where did you find evening clothes?"

Alec grinned and gripped the lapels of his coat. "That's my secret. Although, I've realized this week that a good veterinarian is worth his weight in ball-room attire, especially when a certain beloved cocker spaniel is involved."

"Ah, Mrs. Stone." Isobel locked the door and dropped the key into the purse at her wrist.

Chuckling without denying it, he offered her his arm. "Shall we?"

"Of course."

She slipped her arm into his, as she had dozens of times, but tonight it felt different. Perhaps it was the way Alec kept her tucked closely to his side as they began to walk. Or the affectionate light that filled his eyes when he glanced at her. Whatever the reason, tonight she felt as if they truly were courting.

The closer they came to City Hall, where the ball would be held, the more her delight became riddled with doubt. Could she walk into that room again? The same one in which people had gawked at her in pity and whispered behind their hands about her being jilted.

Sweat beaded on her forehead, and she tightened her grip on Alec's arm as they entered the building. They took their places at the end of the line of couples enter-ing the room designated for the ball. Through the open doorway, Isobel glimpsed the attractive decorations she knew Maggy and the other women from the ranchers' wives club had strung along the walls. The brightly lit room and festive décor couldn't still the churning in her stomach, though.

They moved slowly forward. Panic clotted in Isobel's stomach. What had compelled her to do this? To face the painful past so boldly? What if Beau and his wife were here tonight, just as they'd been last time?

She tugged on Alec's arm, pulling them out of line. "I don't think I want to do this," she whispered without looking at him.

He believed she was living her life again. And in some ways, she was. But tonight everything inside Isobel cried out to let caution dictate her actions.

"What's wrong?" he asked, his voice devoid of censure.

Isobel waved her free hand at the doorway. "What if Beau is here tonight? What if they all whisper and stare at me again?"

"Is that what happened last time?"

She gave a wordless nod, her throat too thick with dread to speak.

Alec led her several feet away from the gathering crowd. "After getting my own taste of being talked about and watched, I don't blame you for not wanting to repeat that experience."

"Would you be all right with leaving, then?"

Without a moment's hesitation, he nodded. "If that's what you want. You don't have to go through with this, Isobel. We can head right back out the door."

"But?" she prompted, sensing he had more to say.

His mouth curved up. "But I also know that a woman who owns a successful dress shop, who not only survived but thrived after two broken engagements, can absolutely walk into that ballroom and face whatever comes her way." He rubbed his thumb over the back of her gloved hand, his gaze solemnly earnest. "How fully or cautiously you live your life, Issy, is entirely up to you."

The statement echoed the one she'd recalled the other day from her mother. Both of them were right. Isobel turned to watch the people entering the ballroom. Why should she let her past experiences dictate the way she lived now? There was so much about her life she felt grateful for. Most of all that she hadn't married Whit or Beau. If she had, she likely never would have opened her shop or begun making her dream of designing gowns a reality.

She glanced at Alec again and felt her gratitude deepen. If she'd married either of her former suitors, then this wonderful, handsome man would not have become her closest friend.

Nearly since his arrival in Wyoming, Alec had encouraged, listened, teased and believed in her. He'd also brought a more lighthearted attitude and more fun into her cautious world. And yet, he seemed to think she'd decided on her own to more fully live her life, when in reality, it was his companionship and positive influence that had inspired her. For that Isobel would be forever thankful.

Even now, Alec had full confidence she could walk into that room and attend her first ball in years. But he wouldn't cajole or force her into doing it if she didn't want that for herself.

Which made her love him all the more.

Isobel stifled a gasp and hurried to look away to hide her embarrassment. Why had Alec and the word *love* joined together in the same thought? Her pulse beat faster with the truth. She did love Alec. And if tonight was one of the last times they would be together as a couple, then she wanted to enjoy every moment of it.

Turning to face him again, she lifted her chin and smiled. The nerves in her middle were losing the battle to the new emotions swirling inside her heart. "I'd like to go inside."

"You're sure?" A spark of approval flashed in his eyes. Or was it relief? Perhaps he'd been looking forward to this night, too.

Isobel gave a decisive nod and firmed her grip on his arm. "Shall we, Doctor Russell?" She swept her hand toward the diminishing line.

"Nothing would give me greater pleasure, Miss Glasen." His sincere smile and the absence of any teasing in his tone renewed the chaotic rhythm of her heartbeat.

No matter what happened after tonight, she would cherish this evening the rest of her days. Because it was likely the last time she'd dance with the man she was only now realizing she loved far more deeply than she had anyone in the past.

Chapter Seventeen

If Isobel's determination to go through with the ball hadn't solidified Alec's heart as hers, then waltzing with her twice certainly had. He was now twirling Mrs. Stone around the room. In spite of her age, the woman moved with the grace and poise of one much younger. Still, Alec wished he was dancing with Isobel again. Since they weren't engaged, he had to be content with both of them having other dance partners this evening.

That didn't stop him from watching her, though. He'd always thought Isobel beautiful, but tonight she glowed. Gone were the lines of concern and caution from her face, replaced by a relaxed confidence that enhanced her natural beauty.

Presently, she was dancing with one of the bachelor wranglers from Edward Kent's ranch. As Alec observed them, Isobel laughed at something the other man said, her amber eyes sparkling. Alec's chest tightened with an emotion that could only be labeled jealousy. But what right did he have to be jealous? He and Isobel might be courting in the eyes of those assembled, but it wasn't real or permanent. Sooner or later they would end things, and she would likely receive attention from other men.

The regret inside Alec increased, along with a measure of confusion. They weren't meant to be. Isn't that what he'd learned from the past? If he and Isobel were truly meant to court each other, then wouldn't she have picked him instead of Whit all those years ago?

Thoughts of his brother reminded Alec that he still hadn't told Isobel that his family was arriving in three days. He'd told himself they'd both been too busy this past week for him to share the news with her. But he recognized it as the thin excuse it was. Truthfully, he feared that telling her would mean an abrupt end to their courtship agreement. And he wasn't sure he wanted that now.

The song came to an end, and he thanked Mrs. Stone for the dance. Alec led the older woman to a chair then looked around for Isobel. He wanted another dance with her. On the other side of the room, he caught sight of her, talking with her last partner as well as with Stella and Franklin.

Alec moved through the crowd toward the small group. As he drew closer, he heard Isobel laugh again. His jaw tensed. It was his job to make Isobel laugh.

The ridiculousness of that notion had him shaking his head. If he didn't know better, he'd have said he was acting like more than a jealous suitor. He was acting like a man in… Alec didn't let himself finish that thought. As much as he cared for Isobel, as much as he didn't want to walk away from her when things between them ended, he wouldn't settle for anything less than a real match of mutual affection—one in which both of them saw the other for themselves.

Approaching the quartet, he smiled directly at Isobel. Her return smile scattered his logical arguments, rendering them unimportant. "Miss Glasen, may I have this—"

"Franklin," Stella interrupted, touching her beau on the sleeve. "Why don't you dance with Isobel this time? And I'll dance with Doctor Russell."

Alec caught sight of Isobel's confused expression, which surely matched his own, before Stella practically dragged him away. Bewildered, he began to move with the girl around the dance floor. Surely Stella hadn't set her cap at him. He dipped his chin to look at her. Her eyes were narrow as she regarded him in return, her expression firm with resolve.

No, she definitely hadn't switched her affections from Franklin to him. But then why had she insisted they dance?

"You look enchanting this evening, Stella," he said, anxious for something to say to end the tense silence between them. "Did you make your dress?"

Her face softened slightly. "I did, thank you. Franklin seems to like it, too." She glanced to where her suitor and Isobel were dancing and smiled. "Isobel looks so lovely in yellow, doesn't she?"

"Yes, she does." Alec didn't like the sudden calculation in the girl's smile. What was Stella up to? "I think she looks lovely in most colors."

The girl nodded thoughtfully. "It's true. Isobel is lovely in every way."

This time Alec offered a wordless nod in agreement.

"What are your intentions regarding her?"

The question took him by surprise, and he stumbled through the next dance step. Stella didn't comment, though she did look amused. In their few interactions, he'd never found her to be so frank. Bubbly and full of energy, yes, but not blunt.

"I'm not sure I understand," he hedged.

Stella lifted her eyebrows in a pointed look. "Isobel isn't just my employer, Doctor Russell. She is like a sister to me." She cast another glance at the other couple. "I want to know she won't be left heartbroken and without help when I leave."

"You're leaving?" This was the first Alec had heard such news.

She nodded, a genuine smile gracing her mouth this time. "Franklin asked me to marry him and I agreed. The wedding will be in two weeks, and after that, I won't be working at the dress shop anymore."

Alec cut a look toward Isobel. Though she appeared relaxed in this moment, he couldn't help wondering how the news of Stella's leaving had affected her. Would it also greatly affect her plans for continuing to design dresses or expand her shop? He very much hoped it wouldn't.

"Now do you understand?" Stella asked. Leaning in, she added in a half whisper, "Isobel told me you were only courting temporarily."

He nodded. "Then you know what my intentions are."

"As blind as bats, both of you," he thought he heard her mutter.

"I'm sorry?"

The girl expelled an impatient sigh. "She loves you, Alec."

"What?" Had Isobel actually confessed such a thing to her assistant? His gaze flew to Isobel's. She caught him watching and offered him a smile. One that went straight into his heart. "Did she actually say that?"

"She didn't need to. It was evident in everything she didn't say and everything she tried to deny."

Was Stella correct? A measure of hope shot through him, and Alec found it impossible to squash.

"Do you love her in return?"

Everything in him wanted to shout *yes*. But as he hesitated in answering, his old doubts reappeared, chipping away at his eagerness. "It isn't that simple, Stella."

"Isobel said the same," the girl replied, her attitude dismissive. "It doesn't have to be complicated, though."

He led Stella through a turn, grateful for a pause in this unforeseen, startling conversation. It was requiring far more concentration than Alec would have imagined to dance and talk with Isobel's assistant.

"Isobel was once engaged to my brother."

If he'd hoped to shock or deter Stella with that statement, he failed miserably. Instead, the girl nodded enthusiastically. "I know. She told me all about your brother."

"Then you can understand why…" Alec cleared his throat, hoping Isobel hadn't been extoling his brother's virtues. "It might be awkward for us."

Again his words had no effect on Stella's enthusiastic tenacity. "I don't see why. Isobel told me that she realized long ago she and your brother wouldn't have suited each other. He was a little too driven for her tastes." She wrinkled her nose, as if agreeing, then smiled. "She also had some rather favorable things to say about you, doctor."

"What did she say?" The question fled his mouth before he could stop it. Not that he didn't want to know the answer. But the entire exchange with Stella had him feeling as baffled and embarrassed as it did hopeful. "I'm sorry, Stella. Maybe you shouldn't—"

"Try to help you two?" Her smile increased. "Nothing would give me greater pleasure than helping my dearest friend."

He couldn't say that he didn't admire her fortitude or her desire to help Isobel. The latter was something he could readily identify with. However, what if Stella was wrong? Alec glanced at the girl's face. Nothing in her expression hinted at deceitfulness. If anything, she looked earnest and wise beyond her years.

"All right." Alec threw another look in Isobel's direction. Would he regret hearing what Isobel had said or be grateful he'd asked? "What did she say…about me?"

Stella lowered her voice, though he could still hear her well enough. "She talked about how she's never felt overpowered by your confidence as she sometimes did with your brother. You also have an optimism and humor she likes."

Nothing could have prevented him from glancing at Isobel once again. She caught his stare and raised her eyebrows in a silent question. Did his expression convey any of the surprise, confusion or elation coursing through him?

"But she didn't choose me back then."

Once again he spoke his thoughts without meaning to. Who would have thought Stella would turn out to be such a persuasive matchmaker or compassionate listener? This time, though, his admission about the past brought a familiar ache to Alec's chest.

The music ended at that moment. Alec lowered his arms, as did Stella. "If she had, would you still have come here and opened your clinic?" Her smile held no hint of smugness, only insightful patience and kindness. "For that matter, would she have opened her dress shop?"

Alec didn't need to consider the answer; he knew it at once. "No, probably not. For either of us."

"Then I, for one, am grateful she didn't choose you back then, Alec." The girl fell back a step and tilted her head, indicating the approach of Franklin and Isobel. "It doesn't mean anything if she's ready to make that choice now."

"Thank you, Stella." He hoped she knew how much he meant it.

"You're welcome." She spun around, tossing her next words back over her shoulder, "Now I'm going to claim back my fiancé."

Alec chuckled. Her parents didn't need to fear for her anymore, and not because Stella was getting married. The girl had clearly grown into the mature young woman they'd been hoping she would.

His mind still reeling from their conversation, he hesitated too long in moving toward Isobel. Someone else claimed her for the next dance before Alec could. Though disappointed, he also felt relieved to have some time to consider the information Stella had shared before he faced Isobel again. He selected a cookie from the refreshment table, then stepped aside to eat it. Not surprisingly, his gaze followed Isobel.

Was she ready to choose him now, as Stella believed? The girl's argument about the unlikelihood of either of them establishing their businesses returned to Alec's mind. Could that be one of the reasons his and Isobel's relationship hadn't progressed in the past?

He recalled Sunday's sermon about the trials of Joseph in Egypt. The pastor had talked about courage, but he'd also mentioned something about growth and timing in relation to the biblical story. But Alec had been paying a bit more attention to holding Isobel's hand than listening. Thankfully it didn't take him more than a moment or two to recall what Pastor Jonas had said.

The man had said that it might seem unloving of God to allow Joseph, His righteous, faithful servant, to spend a two-year stint in prison. However, Pastor Jonas had added, there must have been things Joseph needed to learn before becoming a great ruler in Egypt. And when the timing was right for God's purposes, when Joseph was ready, the Lord had provided a way for his release.

In terms of timing and growth, maybe things weren't so different for Alec and Isobel. The possibility brought a lightening to Alec's shoulders and heart, as if a heavy weight had tumbled off him. What if having several young ladies, including Isobel, choose someone else, instead of him, hadn't been for naught, even if those rejections had been difficult to weather? What if the Lord in His infinite wisdom knew where and what Alec needed to be, and Isobel, too?

Alec couldn't deny having found real fulfillment in his work at the clinic. In many ways, he felt greater contentment and passion practicing veterinary medicine here in Wyoming than he had working all those years at the dude ranch, fun as they'd been. Then to discover, so soon after arriving in Sheridan, that Isobel was living and working right next door? It was too unexpected to be coincidence.

Could that mean they were meant to be together now?

The hopeful thought brought a smile to his face as Alec watched Isobel moving on the opposite side of the crowded dance floor. If she could see him for himself, as Stella had indicated, did it really matter that she hadn't fully been able to in the past?

No, he told himself. *It didn't.*

Especially when he could now see Isobel more fully in return. And he loved her more deeply than he ever had in the past because of it. His smile increased, along with the hammering of his heart. He loved Isobel, and he didn't want their courtship agreement to end. Alec wanted their arrangement to continue, but only as a stepping stone to marriage, if Isobel would have him. It was time to risk his heart a second time, where Isobel was concerned.

Grabbing a glass of punch, Alec downed it in two gulps. The present song had ended, which meant it was time to claim a dance with the woman he was courting. And whom he hoped to keep courting—only for real this time.

To Isobel, the evening had been marvelous and fun from beginning to end. Almost like living inside an exquisite dream. Even the soft glow of the moonlight as Alec escorted her home felt dreamlike. Her only wish was that they could have danced every song together. Except, given the tender way Alec had regarded her as they'd danced to the final song, she might have been forced to sit down for most of the ball if he'd watched her that way the whole night.

Isobel glanced at his shadowed face, wishing she could better see his expression. He'd been unusually quiet since they'd left the dance. Perhaps he was just tired. Isobel, on the other hand, couldn't recall ever feeling so full of energy and optimism. She'd conquered her fear about the ball and it had turned out to be a great experience.

Some of the vibrancy coursing through her might have less to do with her courage, though, and more to do with the man walking by her side. "Did you enjoy the ball?" she asked. They were nearly to their street, but she didn't want the evening to end yet.

Turning to look at her, Alec smiled. "I did. You?"

"It was wonderful." She tucked her arm more snugly into his. "Thank you for letting me decide for myself whether to go through with it or not."

He glanced forward again. "You're welcome. I had no doubt you could manage the ball beautifully, but it needed to be your decision."

His confidence had her smiling until silence settled over them once more. Something must be on his mind. But what was it? Isobel recalled the strange look she'd seen on his face when he'd been dancing with Stella.

"What were you and Stella talking about while you were dancing?"

Isobel felt him flinch, though he tried to hide it behind a chuckle. "Ah, you know Stella. She was very animated."

"About?"

Surely Alec didn't care romantically for the girl. Stella was engaged, after all, and it hadn't been adoration in his expression as the two of them had danced. Isobel would have called it consternation or surprise, not affection.

"She talked about you, actually."

It was Isobel's turn for surprise. "What did she say?"

"How much she cares about you." She caught his sideways glance. "Stella also told me she was leaving after she and Franklin are married."

Isobel nodded. Was that what was troubling Alec? That she hadn't told him about Stella? "I'm sorry I didn't tell you about that myself. Preparing for the ball tonight has taken up so much of my thought and time lately."

"You don't need to apologize, Isobel." He placed his free hand over hers, bringing instant relief to her worry. "What will you do once Stella is gone?"

They'd reached Isobel's staircase, but she wasn't ready to go inside. Motioning for Alec to sit, she took a seat on one of the steps and arranged her skirt around her ankles. He sat beside her.

"I'll need to hire another assistant seamstress, which is going to take time."

Alec leaned forward. His casual demeanor, combined with his evening clothes, accentuated his good looks. "What about your plans for expanding or for designing more dresses?"

"I don't really know," she admitted with a shrug.

"Which is something new for me." Isobel gave a soft chuckle, which Alec repeated. "I'm trying to trust that God will let me know what I need to do, when I need to do it."

He turned his head to peer at her. "That's very wise of you."

"I appreciate that." She peeled off her gloves and set them in her lap. "But after a wonderful evening like tonight, I'd rather think of something else than the future of my shop."

For several heartbeats, her words floated unacknowledged in the quiet between them. Isobel shifted with embarrassment on the hard step. It wasn't that she didn't want to discuss her plans with Alec; she just wanted the loveliness of the ball to linger a little longer.

Then Alec twisted to face her. "I know of something else…you can think about."

His gaze lowered to her lips, causing Isobel's pulse to sprint in response. The moon illuminated the handsome features of his face.

"What is it?" she half-whispered, though she didn't need to ask the question. She knew the answer as clearly as if Alec had spoken it aloud. He intended to kiss her, and this time she couldn't think of anything she longed for more.

Alec kept his gaze locked on hers. Isobel's eyes resembled two golden pools of light and emotion. Did she understand that he wanted to kiss her? He wasn't sure until she leaned slightly toward him. One corner of his mouth lifted. Not only did she understand his honorable intention to kiss her but she welcomed it. His heart pounded in his chest as he matched her stance.

He'd wanted to kiss her ever since they danced together in the McCall's yard. Since then, that desire had only increased, especially now that he'd figured out how he really felt about her, about them.

Alec slowly brought his lips near hers, then he pressed a tender kiss to them. Though brief, the connection he felt in that single kiss made him want to sing loudly enough for all of Sheridan to hear. He'd kissed Isobel Glasen, the woman he loved with all of his heart. Reaching out, he cupped the side of her face with his hand and kissed her again, longer this time. How had he ever imagined finding and courting anyone else?

"I want to court you for real, Issy," he said when he released her.

"Y-you do? Why?"

"Because I care about you." He lowered his hand to hers, then held it against his chest. Could she feel his heart thudding rapidly with equal parts hope and uncertainty at what her response might be? "I want to court you as a means to marrying you. If you'll have me."

"You want to marry me?"

Laughing lightly, Alec nodded. "It shouldn't be much of a surprise. I already told you how smitten I was with you years ago." He gave her hand a gentle squeeze. "That feeling has only grown stronger since we started courting for convenience."

"I don't know what to say." She lowered her gaze to her lap.

Did she feel differently than he did? "I'm sorry if I spoke too soon about marriage. I only know I don't want our relationship to end, Isobel. Not now, maybe not ever."

"I don't want it to end, either," she said, lifting her chin. "I care for you, too, Alec."

The quiet admission still had the power to peal through him with the volume and strength of a chorus of bells. "Will you consider courting for real, then?"

"May I have some time to think it over?"

While he'd hope for a resounding *yes*, he could honor her desire for more time. "Of course. Take as many days as you need."

"Thank you, Alec." She bent forward and pressed a kiss to his cheek, then she stood. "I'll see you at church."

He rose to his feet, as well. "I'll be the besotted suitor sitting in the second row."

"Good to know," she said with a laugh. "See you tomorrow."

Alec waited until she went inside before he headed next door to his apartment, loosening his necktie as he went. Even without a firm answer from Isobel, he couldn't help singing to himself as he took the steps two at a time to his door.

He'd put his heart on the line by sharing his feelings with Isobel. But tonight had been different than the other times he'd risked it in the past. This time he would hold fast to the hope that Isobel would finally claim his heart as hers.

Chapter Eighteen

As she had during and after the ball, Isobel floated through the next few days, hardly daring to believe her new reality. Alec cared deeply for her and wanted to court her for real. That refrain hummed constantly through her thoughts—as she attended church with him, as she and Stella worked on the newest orders for dresses and as she considered Alec's courtship proposal.

Of course, there were still moments of self-doubt. Moments when she wasn't sure she could accept, knowing she could never give him children of their own. Then her mind would swing back to the euphoria of their first kiss and she would find herself clinging to hope all over again. Maybe Alec would be like her uncle, accepting of her condition and content to make a full life as a family of two.

She spent longer than usual on her knees the next three nights, praying to know what she should do. In her heart, Isobel knew what she wanted. She loved Alec and wanted to court him for real. But was that what God wanted?

By Wednesday morning, Isobel still didn't have a definitive answer. She couldn't deny the rightness she felt, though, each time she thought about Alec or becoming his sweetheart for real.

Perhaps that is my answer.

The idea descended like soft rain into her heart, and she couldn't wait to tell Alec. Before she agreed, however, she needed to tell him that she would always remain childless. Then he could decide if he still wanted to go through with their new courtship plan.

Excitement and apprehension turned her stomach into a mass of flutters, and each time she thought about speaking with Alec her pulse thumped erratically. She could hardly concentrate on sewing. Stella kept asking if something was wrong. Finally, by early afternoon, Isobel could stand the waiting no longer. She would go next door and see if Alec had a few minutes to talk now.

"I'll be back in a bit," she told Stella.

"Where are you going?"

Isobel didn't want to reveal too much just yet—not until she'd talked with Alec. "There's something I need to discuss with Alec. I'm going to see if he has a few minutes to spare."

"Take as long as you need," Stella said in a cheery tone, her eyes lighting with obvious delight. "I can manage the shop the rest of the afternoon."

She considered asking the source of Stella's enthusiasm, but Isobel didn't want to delay a minute longer or she might lose her courage. "I shouldn't be long."

Slipping out the door, Isobel closed it behind her. She greeted several people moving along the street, then turned toward the clinic. Movement at the edge of the sidewalk caught her attention. Two boys sat directly in front of her shop. The younger one was crying, while the older one held him stoically around the shoulders. Isobel glanced around. There were no adults conversing nearby, and neither boy looked quite old enough to attend school.

As she deliberated whether to see if they needed assistance, the older boy turned slightly, allowing Isobel to see his profile. The child looked as distressed as his companion, though he was apparently trying hard not to show it. His worry made her decision easy.

"Hello," she said kindly as she crouched beside the two boys. "My name is Miss Glasen. Can I help you, gentlemen, with something?"

The older boy glanced at her, relief mingling with the anxiety on his face. "I got us lost. And now I can't remember which store our mama and papa went into."

"I see." Isobel looked down the street in the direction of the mercantile. Could the brothers have wandered away from there? "Do you remember what your parents needed to buy?"

"They didn't need anything," the boy said. "They were just talkin'. So Ernie and me decided to explore."

If the family wasn't in town to purchase something, what other shops would they have gone into? "Can you remember what they were talking about?"

"Doggies," Ernie said. "I want a doggy, too, Harry."

"They were talking about dogs?"

Harry nodded. "And horses."

Understanding made Isobel smile. "I think I know

where they might be. And I just happen to be going there myself. Will you come with me?" She stood and offered her hand to Ernie.

"Where are they?" Harry asked as he climbed to his feet.

His brother stood, as well. After wiping his sleeve beneath his nose, he took hold of Isobel's hand.

"I believe they're right next door in the veterinary clinic."

"That's it, Ernie. The veter…" He glanced up at Isobel in consternation.

"It's an animal clinic," she supplied as she led the two boys next door.

Harry nodded. "The animal clinic."

Isobel held the door open for them, then followed the pair inside. A small crowd of people filled the waiting room. The sight brought a pang of disappointment to her. Alec wasn't likely to be able to get away to talk. "Do you see your—"

"Boys! There you are." A pretty blonde woman, holding a sleeping baby in her arms, rushed toward them. She looked vaguely familiar, though Isobel wasn't sure why. Ernie let go of Isobel's hand and clung to his mother's skirt. "Where did you two go?"

"I'm sorry, Mama." Harry hung his head. "We wandered off and I couldn't remember where you were. But this nice lady helped us." He lifted his chin and smiled at Isobel.

She smiled back. "Actually they didn't get far. They were right outside my dress shop, which is next door."

"Thank you for helping them find their way back

here." The other woman's expression reflected genuine warmth and gratitude. "I'm afraid we've been talking much too long for their tastes."

At that moment, a male voice called out Isobel's name. Only it wasn't Alec. Confused she turned toward the source and felt the color drain from her face. Whitman Russell approached her, smiling.

"Isobel Glasen. What are you doing here?"

The boys' mother turned toward Alec's brother. "Do you know this woman, Whit? She was kind enough to help our boys after they wandered off."

No wonder the woman looked familiar. This was Jocelyn, Whit's wife, and the boys Isobel had helped were Alec's nephews. "I...uh...live here, in Sheridan," she said, answering Whit's question. "I have for...years."

"What a coincidence you and Alec both ended up here." Whit shook his head, his arm encircling his wife's waist. "It's a great town, far more modern than I had expected. All of us decided to come visit Alec, even my parents. We're staying at..."

Isobel didn't hear the rest of what he was saying. Instead, she stared in shock at the other side of the room, where Mr. and Mrs. Russell were, indeed, conversing with their younger son. The entire family had surprised him with a visit. Only when Alec's gaze met hers, it wasn't surprise she saw reflected there. It was regret.

She didn't need more than a moment to ascertain the truth. Alec had known his family was coming—and he hadn't bothered to tell her.

Swallowing hard, Isobel turned to face his brother

and sister-in-law again. "I'm afraid I need to return to my shop. I'm glad the boys were able to find you."

"Thank you again for your help," Jocelyn said.

Isobel bolted for the door, but not before she heard someone call her name again. This time it was Alec. Ignoring him, she hurried outside. If she could make it into the dress shop before he caught up with her, she could hide in the back room. At least until she felt ready to face him and the confusing hurt mounting inside her.

But she wasn't so fortunate. Alec snagged her arm in a gentle grip outside the dress shop. "Isobel, wait. I can explain."

"Explain what?" she countered as she whirled on him. "Why I'm the last to know that your entire family have come to see you?" Her chest rose and fell with frustrated breaths, but she tried to calm them and her tone as she continued. "Even if you and I aren't courting for real, I had a right to know they were coming, Alec, after everything that's happened in the past. Why didn't you say something?"

He released her, but he remained close, as if afraid she'd disappear. "You did have the right to know. And I'm sorry I didn't say something. I wanted to. I planned to. But then I got caught up in us and in cleaning the clinic from top to bottom and putting in the wood paneling." Alec ran an agitated hand through his hair, causing it to stick up. "I needed everything to be perfect before they came, and then I forgot to say something about their visit. It's still no excuse, though."

"No, it isn't." She folded her arms, her anger tempering slightly. "They didn't know I live here, did they?"

He shook his head. "Not until now."

"Were you embarrassed to tell them?"

"Of course not." He tugged one of her hands free and held it in his own. "I've never been embarrassed by you."

The adamancy in his response filled her with some relief. There was still something about his manner, though, and his explanation that still didn't make sense. "Why did everything need to be perfect for your family's arrival?"

"I just wanted to make them proud." Alec shrugged, but he wouldn't look at her. "You know how it is? The younger brother always trying to get out from underneath the older one's shadow?"

Isobel frowned, her confusion escalating instead of decreasing. "You think you've been in Whit's shadow? For how long?"

"Most of my life," he admitted with a touch of frustration in his voice. "He's always been successful at everything. I never felt like I could compete, so I chose to do my own thing."

"Like your job at the dude ranch?"

Alec nodded and finally lifted his eyes to hers. "I was good at what I did there. Only it still wasn't good enough."

"What do you mean?"

His shoulders drooped as if he were suddenly exhausted. "My father was concerned about me not using my schooling to full advantage. So this spring, he challenged me to start my own clinic using half of my inheritance." Alec stared at something in the distance. "The other half would be given to me when I turned thirty in August, but only if my business was successful and I'd found a girl to settle down with and start a family."

His last words pierced her like shards of glass. "Is that why you courted me?" Had everything she'd felt between them been a ruse?

"No." He squeezed her hand. "We courted the first time because we both wanted the gossip to end. But my invitation on Saturday…" He tipped her chin up until her gaze met his. "That was real, Isobel. I want to court you because I love you."

She pressed her lips together to hide their trembling. He'd finally spoken of love, and yet it was too late. "Why didn't you tell me about your father's challenge before now?"

"I don't know." She heard the honesty behind the admission. "I guess I didn't think it really mattered."

But it did—far more than Alec realized. More than she had realized. "Your father isn't going to approve of you courting me, Alec."

"Why not?" He lowered his arm back to his side, though he still held her hand. "If this is about you being engaged to Whit in the past, it's all right. My family will understand when I tell them how I feel about you, and how I hope you feel about me." He lifted her hand to his mouth and placed a tender kiss against her knuckles.

Pain tightened her throat, and moisture stung her eyes. Once again, she'd come so close to finding a man who loved her in spite of her condition. Only this time it hurt far worse than it had the last two times. Because she loved Alec, more deeply than any other man from her past. And that made what Isobel had to do hurt more deeply, too.

"I can't marry you, Alec." She pulled her hand away from his, though everything in her cried out not to let go. "I hope we can still be friends, but I'm afraid that's all we can ever be."

His expression fell, splitting her heart in two. "Why? What about the other evening? You can't deny the feelings between us, Issy."

Ah, but she could. If that meant allowing this man she loved to fully embrace the life his family wanted for him. "I do care about you, but it isn't enough."

From the corner of her eye, Isobel saw several passersby watching them. That was good, she tried to reassure herself, though inside she ached with sorrow and humiliation.

She and Alec had initially discussed letting it be known around town that they no longer suited each other, and now would be as good a time as any. Then Alec would be free to court someone new, someone who could give him a family.

"Isobel—" He took a step toward her.

"It's over between us," she said, raising her voice so that passersby might hear. "Please don't try to see me anymore, Alec." She grabbed the handle of the dress shop door and wrenched it open.

Alec gripped the doorframe above her head. "Isobel, don't do this. I don't know what's happened, but I'm truly sorry for not telling you about my family or my father's challenge. I can understand why you'd be upset. It doesn't mean my feelings for you have changed, though."

"But other things have."

It was the closest thing she could come to telling him the truth. He didn't need to know about her inability to have children, not when he needed to settle down and have a family of his own.

"I have one last piece of business advice." She kept her words quiet so he alone would hear them. "The only one who's placed you in Whit's shadow is you, Alec. You don't have to stay there. You are successful and amazing in your own right. But others aren't going to see that until you do."

With that, she fled inside the shop, past a startled-looking Stella and into the back room. Inside, she twisted the lock on the door and slid down to the floor. Only then did she give in to the tears—as her heart broke for the third time.

Alec pushed his dinner around his plate, ignoring the hum of conversation at the table. Thankfully, there were enough people gathered in the dining room at the HC Bar that no one was likely to notice. If his family hadn't been visiting, he might have been eating with Isobel at their favorite restaurant at this very moment. Instead, his family was here and Isobel wanted nothing to do with him. And he couldn't reason out why.

Yes, he'd been a fool for not telling her sooner about his family's planned visit or what his father had insisted he do to receive the rest of his inheritance. But something told him there was more to Isobel's reaction than his blunder. Why else would she have looked down-right panicked when he'd told her about settling down and starting a family?

Did she not return his feelings? Alec couldn't believe that. Not after they'd danced at the ball and shared those two amazing kisses. Isobel had confessed to caring for him, too, and to not wanting their relationship to end. So what had happened this afternoon? Why had she ended things with him after all and asked him not to see her again?

At the conclusion of the meal, several of the women, including his mother and Jocelyn, volunteered to help Vienna clear the table and wash the dishes. Harry and Ernest joined the other children outside, while their father and the rest of the men remained seated.

Alec felt too restless and confused to contribute to any conversation, so he wandered out to the porch and sat on the step. He watched the children playing a game of *Blind Man's Bluff* in the yard. The very yard where he'd told Isobel how much he had adored her in the past and where he'd nearly kissed her.

Resting his elbows on his knees, he placed his head in his hands. He loved Isobel, and he'd felt fairly certain she loved him back—at least, until today. Everything in him had been hoping she would agree to let him court her for real, in preparation for marrying him. Instead, he'd been left hurting and alone all over again.

The front door creaked open behind him. Alec whipped his head up. To his surprise, Whit stepped out and dropped onto the step next to him.

"This is a first-rate dude ranch West and his wife

are operating here," his brother said, matching Alec's casual pose.

He couldn't recall ever seeing Whit so relaxed. "They've done a fine job, that's for sure."

"You have, too, little brother."

Alec cut him a glance. "Thanks." It came out more a question than a statement, which Whit must have recognized, given his chuckle.

"I mean it. You've done a fine job setting up that veterinary clinic of yours."

When was the last time his brother had complimented him? Probably not since Alec had graduated from veterinary school. "It's not like running a large corporation, by any means, but I enjoy it."

"It shows," Whit said, his gaze moving from Alec to the children running around the yard. "The few people who came in while we were there had only good things to say about you."

Alec didn't know how to respond. Isobel's earlier comment about his choosing to be in Whit's shadow nagged at his memory. "I hope Father sees it that way. I haven't had near the success the two of you have had, and chances are I never will." There, he'd finally admitted his biggest fear.

"There's more to life than success at business, Alec."

He turned to view Whit straight on. "Since when has that been your philosophy?"

"Since I met my wife." A contented smile softened his brother's expression. "I suppose that's not entirely true, though. It was when Harry was born. When I almost lost Jocelyn…"

"I'm sorry, Whit. I didn't know. That must have been terrifying."

With a nod, Whit glanced at his loosely clasped hands. "You were in North Dakota at the time, and when I finally wrote, she was out of danger. I realized something over those awful two days, though. All the successes I'd had in business didn't matter anymore. The only thing I wanted was more time with my wonderful, precious Jocelyn." His voice cracked with emotion. "When God granted me that, I vowed to work less and spend more time with my family. And that's what I've done."

Alec gaped in shock at his brother. Had he been so concerned over the years with proving his own worth that he'd failed to see such significant changes in Whit? "I'm sorry I wasn't around then."

"I don't fault you." Whit threw him a reassuring smile. "You were living your life and doing something you loved. In fact, I suppose I was a little jealous of you."

Alec's jaw went slack. "Why would you be jealous of me?"

"You were working on the ranch at a job you excelled at and liked." His brother blew out a sigh. "I guess as the oldest son I always felt obligated to follow in Father's footsteps. I've come to appreciate and enjoy my employment, but that was only after making the conscious decision that I'm where I would choose to be."

Running his hand through his hair, Alec could hardly believe what his brother had just shared. "I was always jealous of you. You succeeded at everything, Whit. In business, with the young ladies, with starting a family."

"What do you mean?" his brother good-naturedly shot back. "You were the fun-loving one who could get anyone to laugh or smile. That wasn't easy to compete with, little brother, especially when it came to the young ladies."

How misguided they'd both been in their opinions of each other. Regret coursed through Alec. "I guess neither of us chose to see things truthfully." He gave Whit a remorseful smile. "I apologize for my part in that."

He stuck his hand toward his brother. Without hesitation, Whit took hold of it and pulled Alec forward into an embrace. The brothers clapped each other heartily on the back as tears blurred Alec's vision. How wrong he'd been about his brother and about himself. It was little wonder that Isobel had told him what she had—that he wasn't in Whit's shadow, save for putting himself there—and she'd been right.

As if sensing what, or who, Alec was thinking about, Whit released him and said, "I still can't believe Isobel Glasen is living here."

"Yeah." Alec settled back onto the step. Memories of all that had transpired between them since his arrival in Sheridan flitted through his mind.

He sensed Whit watching him. "You followed her out of the clinic pretty fast when she left." Alec chose not to reply. "I know you cared for her in the past."

"You did?" Would this conversation never cease to shock him? He'd been certain neither his brother nor Isobel had known the extent of his feelings for her back then.

Whit nodded. "I wasn't entirely sure, though I suspected as much. The look on your face when Father announced our engagement was all the confirmation I needed."

"Why didn't you say something?"

His brother shrugged again. "Despite what you may think, Alec, I also cared deeply for Isobel back then. And I figured if she shared your feelings, then she wouldn't have agreed to marry me."

"What happened?" The question tumbled from his mouth. "Why did you end things with her?"

Lowering his chin, Whit returned to studying his hands. "It wasn't an easy decision, and believe it or not, it pained me to break our engagement. But in the end, I decided having a family was important to me."

"What does that mean?" Alec shook his head in confusion. "Didn't Isobel want a family?"

Whit frowned. "You don't know?"

Something akin to chilling dread made him shiver, despite the temperate evening. "What are you talking about, Whit?"

"Isobel can't have children."

Alec made no attempt to hide his shock this time. "H-how would you know that?"

"She told me, several weeks after we became engaged." His brother threw him a sad look. "It's something she's known for years. Apparently she's never had…" Whit's neck turned slightly red. "She's never had any monthly bleedings, so having children is out of the question for her."

Alec's breath whooshed out. He hadn't even realized he'd been holding it. Isobel's frightened expression when he'd mentioned his need to settle down and have a family made complete sense now. If he married Isobel, he would never be a father. The reality of his situation had him dropping his head into his hands a second time.

"I truly didn't mean to hurt her, Alec." His brother's pleading tone testified to his sincerity. "It's just that I wanted very much to be a father."

Nodding, Alec didn't lift his head. "Thanks for sharing what you did, Whit."

"You're welcome." His brother rose to his feet. "You still love her, don't you?"

"Yes," Alec said without hesitation. Although did it even matter? He was supposed to be settling down *and* starting a family.

Whit's hand settled reassuringly on his shoulder. "I've never known you to give up easily, little brother. Figure out what your heart is telling you and then follow it. Happiness for you is going to look differently than it does for me...or for Father."

Alec pressed his palms into his dry eyes as he listened to the sound of Whit greeting his sons in the yard. He'd thought his heart couldn't take any more bruising, but he'd been wrong. His conversation with his brother had healed some wounds and yet it had opened others. And even as doctor, he wasn't sure he knew how to fix an aching heart.

Chapter Nineteen

"I'm going for a walk, Aunt Jo."

Isobel picked up the Bible from her aunt's end table to take with her. She'd missed church services earlier today, in an effort to avoid Alec and any gossip about their courtship coming to an end. But the lovely sunshine outdoors couldn't be overlooked any longer, even if she still felt cloudy and gray inside.

After her disastrous conversation with Alec and a long cry in the back room, Isobel had made the decision to close the shop for a week. She needed time away from town and Stella needed time to prepare for her upcoming wedding.

Resolved, Isobel had packed Duchess and a small travel bag, rented a buggy from the livery and driven out to her aunt and uncle's home. She'd been there since Wednesday evening. Visiting with Joanna and Evan had done wonders for her weary heart. Isobel had finished some sewing projects and yesterday she'd started on a new gown for her aunt as well as Stella's wedding dress.

"Do you want some company?" Joanna asked, drying her hands on a towel as she moved from the kitchen into the parlor.

Isobel shook her head. "I could use some time alone, with my thoughts and the Bible." She hefted the book in her arms. "If that's all right."

"Of course."

Her aunt's warm smile inspired renewed tears, which she hurried to blink away. "You've been so good to me, Aunt Jo. Not judging me in the least, even though I didn't heed your advice about this courtship plan."

"Oh, Issy." Joanna wrapped her in a hug. "You can't predict who you fall in love with. And in spite of the concern I felt, I didn't factor in one important thing." She stepped back and brushed a strand of hair from Isobel's forehead.

"What's that?"

"That Alec Russell has fallen very much in love with you, too."

Isobel looked away. The hope in her aunt's eyes was too painful to see, especially when it matched the tiny seed inside her heart. One that refused to be uprooted no matter how hard she tried.

"Won't you at least talk to him?"

Isobel shook her head. "There's no point. He told me what his father is requiring him to do. Alec needs to have a family, and that isn't something I can give him. Plain and simple."

"There's nothing plain and simple about it," her aunt gently countered, "for either of you, I'm sure."

Isobel couldn't imagine Alec feeling as heartbroken as she did. Though the haunted look on his face right before she'd escaped into the dress shop would likely stay with her forever.

"I'm going to head out to the far pasture if you don't need me." She took a step toward the door.

Joanna waved her on. "Take as long as you like. Dinner will be ready when you return."

"Thank you," Isobel said, pausing with her hand on the doorknob. "I really mean it, Aunt Jo. You and Uncle Evan have been such a blessing in my life."

Her aunt directed another kind smile her way. "You are to our lives, too."

Opening the door, Isobel called for Duchess. The cat hopped down from the porch chair and came over to rub against Isobel's skirt.

"Issy?" Joanna called from behind her. Isobel turned back. "I know this is painful, even more so because it isn't the first time."

Isobel wordlessly lowered her gaze to the floorboards at her feet as the ache inside her yawned wider.

"Do you know who helped me through that first broken engagement of my own?"

She lifted her head to look expectantly at her aunt. "Who?"

"Your mother. Even though she was my younger sister, she let me cry, and then when I'd dried my tears, she took me by the shoulders. She told me, 'Joanna, listen to me. You are not the summation of your painful experiences or your seeming inadequacies. You are seen and known by God for the amazing woman that you are. And someday, if it's His will, you'll find a man who sees you as clearly and lovingly as God does.'"

Tears brimmed in Isobel's eyes again. Her mother

had passed away before Isobel became engaged to Whit, and yet she felt certain she would have received the same counsel as her aunt back then. And again after Beau…and now with Alec.

"That was when she shared with me her favorite scripture."

Isobel knew the reference by heart. "Colossians 3:15."

"Do you remember what it says?" her aunt asked.

Isobel gave a sheepish laugh as she shook her head. "It's been too long since I actually looked it up."

"Then maybe today is a good day to do so." Joanna pointed to the Bible in Isobel's hands. "I'll let you get on with your walk, my dear."

Isobel stepped down off the porch. Heading away from the house, she breathed in the loamy scent of sun-soaked grass and wind. Duchess followed along behind her, her ever faithful companion. Who would have known she'd come to love owning an animal? Certainly not her. Although, Alec may have suspected as much.

Thoughts of Alec renewed the pain in Isobel's throat and chest. She was grateful now that she hadn't revealed her inability to have children, or how she'd wanted to continue their courtship or how much she loved him. Even knowing she wasn't the right woman for him hadn't ended her feelings. If anything, those feelings had only deepened since she'd left him standing outside her shop. Try as she might, she couldn't bury her memories completely. Each day she recalled something else lovely that had transpired between herself and Alec.

Once she reached the far pasture, she dropped onto the grass beside one of the fence posts and positioned the Bible on her lap. Isobel didn't doubt that God knew of her most recent heartache or that He felt the regret and grief right along with her. And yet the loss of Alec from her life and the reminder of why no man would likely ever agree to marry her still overwhelmed her in quiet moments like these.

Isobel flipped the Bible open, yearning for relief from the constant hurt inside. Almost of their own accord, her fingers kept turning pages until she reached the third chapter of Colossians. Isobel bent over the book and read the beginning of the fifteenth verse aloud, "And let the peace of God rule in your hearts."

Why had this been her mother's favorite scripture? It had been many years since Isobel had heard her mother's explanation for loving this particular verse. She searched her memory for a clue. Something about peace and pain…

That was it! No matter how painful an experience might be, her mother had told her, there was always peace to be found if she remembered God's unchanging love and saw herself as He did.

Isobel placed the Bible on the ground beside her and drew her dress-clad knees to her chest. *How does God see me?* she wondered as she watched Duchess creeping through the grass toward an unsuspecting insect.

Surely God didn't see her as the world or her past suitors did. To Him, Isobel wasn't flawed or less than other women because she couldn't have children. She wasn't an old maid in His eyes, either. Then again, she also wasn't more important or better than those who could have children simply because she wore and designed beautiful clothes or owned a successful dress shop. Just as Aunt Jo had said to her, Isobel was much more than the summation of what she'd done or couldn't do.

A wave of peace rippled outward from her heart, encompassing her from head to toe. It wasn't the first time she'd felt such peace amidst great pain. This same feeling of peace had come over her after the death of each of her parents and after both her broken engagements.

God did see and know her. And when all was said and done, if she lost the things she currently treasured in her life—her family and friends, her cat, her shop, her talents, even Alec—Isobel would still be enough to God by being herself.

She brushed away the tears that had spilled onto her cheeks. The grief she felt at letting Alec go hadn't disappeared, but alongside it, she still felt peace. Best of all, she didn't need to do anything differently going forward with her life except be herself. And she could think of nothing else she wanted to be more than simply being...Isobel.

Hearing a knock at his apartment door, Alec stood up from the table and crossed the room. Could it be Isobel? He opened the door, hope throbbing hard inside him. But it wasn't the woman he loved on his doorstep. It was his father.

He did his best to hide his sharp disappointment behind a causal smile. "Afternoon, Father. What brings you back into town?"

The whole family had driven into Sheridan to attend Sunday services with Alec. He'd hoped Isobel would be there, too, but she hadn't been. Not that he would have known exactly what to say to her if she had come to church. Alec only knew he wanted—no, needed—to talk to her. To tell her that he still loved her.

He'd gone over to her apartment the other night, after his surprising conversation with Whit, but Isobel hadn't answered her door. The next day Alec had discovered the sign she'd hung on the door of the shop, announcing its closure for a week. He guessed she must be staying with her aunt and uncle.

"Are you going to let me in?" his father asked, raising his eyebrows in amusement.

Alec nodded. "Yes, of course. Come in."

He half-expected his father to sit on the couch in the parlor, but instead Howard Russell sat in one of the empty chairs at the kitchen table. "Still not eating much, I see." His father waved a hand at the half-empty plate of lunch.

"Still?" Alec returned to his own chair.

"You haven't eaten much at any meal you've taken with us."

He shrugged, unsure what to say. "Is there something I can help you with?" Surely his father hadn't ridden here to discuss his eating habits or the lack thereof.

"Your mother is worried about you." Howard set his clasped hands on the table top. "Frankly, so am I."

Irritation darted through Alec. He had done what he'd been asked to do, at least when it came to the clinic. The rest of it? Fresh grief swallowed his annoyance as his thoughts turned, yet again, to Isobel. He'd finally found the girl who saw him as himself, only she didn't want him anymore.

"I'm fine." As far as his business went.

Howard leaned forward, his gaze firm but loving. "How about you drop the act and be honest with me, Alec?"

"Be honest?" he repeated, his tone sharpening with frustration. Though it was mostly directed at himself. He blew out a calming breath, but it didn't prevent a mound of words and emotion from filling his throat, all begging for release. "All right. I've honestly thought for years that I was less than Whit. That he was and always would be more successful at everything."

He pushed his plate aside and rested his elbows on the table. "Nothing I did could compete. Especially when it came to the young ladies. So, in large part, I stopped trying. I figured I'd just be myself. But deep down, that was really only an excuse to keep from risking my heart again."

"And now?" His father's gentle tone surprised Alec. Maybe Whit wasn't the only one who'd relaxed since coming to Wyoming.

Alec ran his hand through his hair. He'd been doing that more and more the last few days, which meant the dark blond strands were beginning to stick straight up on their own. "Now I've learned that Whit was actually jealous of me all those years."

"Your brother told me about your conversation the other night."

Lowering his arm, Alec looked directly at his father. "Did he tell you we talked about Isobel Glasen?"

"He did," Howard confirmed, though his expression offered no hint as to what he thought of that news.

Alec sat back in his chair as a wave of weariness came over him. "I accepted your challenge, Father, for a number of reasons. One of them being to prove that I could be as successful as Whit at something." He rubbed his finger over a rut in the table top. "But what I've realized this last week is that I don't want to be like Whit. I want to be me, and I want to keep practicing medicine in my small clinic, even if that means I'm never as successful in making money as you and Whit have been."

"Is that what success is to you? Making money?"

"Maybe it used to be." Alec met his father's gaze straight on. "Not anymore, though. Success is doing something I love."

It's being with the woman I love.

His feelings for Isobel hadn't changed, not even after learning she couldn't have children. He'd let himself mourn that fact, but it hadn't taken him long to realize he wanted Isobel in his life more than he wanted a family of his own. Would his parents support his decision, though? He still wanted them to be proud of him. But after what Isobel had said to him the other day, Alec now knew the real person who needed to feel proud of his actions and choices was himself.

Letting her go wouldn't make him feel proud, and it would be throwing away his second chance with her. A second chance he now felt certain God had given them.

Alec squared his shoulders with resolve. "I've done what you asked me to do in getting the clinic up and running, and I'm grateful to you for giving me half of my inheritance to do that."

Howard gave a wordless nod, seeming to sense there was more Alec wished to say. And there was. He just wasn't sure his father would like it. But now that he was being honest—with Whit, with his father, and especially with himself—he knew what he needed to do and what he needed to say.

"I've also found a woman I love and want to marry, as you asked me to do."

"Isobel Glasen?"

Nodding, Alec bent forward, matching his father's stance. "I imagine you know of her background. She is unable to have children." He glanced down at his hands. "She also doesn't want anything to do with me right now. But suffice it to say, even if she won't have me, I'm not ready to court someone else for a while. Maybe not ever. Which means, I won't have fulfilled all of your tasks by the time it's my birthday."

"Are you saying you don't think you should be granted the rest of your inheritance?"

Alec lifted his head and peered directly at his father. "Yes, sir. That's what I'm saying."

"Then, fortunately, I'm going to have to change our agreement."

"I don't understand."

His confusion only grew when his father's mouth twitched with a smile. "Alec, my boy, you've done all that I have asked and more."

Howard held up a hand when Alec started to protest. "Not only did you set up a successful clinic, but you learned some important things about yourself in the process. And that is far more valuable than any inheritance."

"So you don't think I've failed?" This feeling of confusion was fast becoming a regular occurrence the more Alec talked with his family.

Howard gave a light laugh. "On the contrary, your mother and I both believe you have succeeded marvelously. Which means you will still receive the rest of your inheritance."

"Then why the worry?"

His father's demeanor softened in a way Alec hadn't seen in years. "Because we can all see how much you love Isobel, and yet you aren't doing anything about it."

"Wait." Alec rubbed his hand over his jaw, trying to keep up with yet another new surprise. "You don't mind that she can't have children?"

"Do you mind?"

He shook his head. "Not if it means losing her."

"Then what are you waiting for?" Howard motioned toward the door.

Alec frowned. "She told me not to try to see her again."

"Yes, and that sounds like a woman who is hurting and afraid."

Sudden understanding had him scrambling to his feet. "She's afraid that I don't still love her, that I'd rather have a family than be with her."

"Now you're getting it." His father wagged a knowing finger at him.

For the first time in days, a full smile lifted Alec's mouth. "Can I borrow your horse, Father, so I can go find Isobel?"

The grin his father offered him was nearly as validating as his next words. "Nothing would make me prouder, son."

Chapter Twenty

Removing his hat, Alec knocked on the Clawsons' front door. His heart hadn't stopped pounding since the ranch came into view and he'd dismounted in the yard. Isobel had to be here—he only hoped he would be allowed to speak with her.

"Good afternoon, Doctor Russell," Mrs. Clawson said as she opened the door.

Alec noted she didn't ask why he was standing there. Probably because the wise woman already knew. "I'd like to talk to Isobel, ma'am."

"She isn't here."

His shoulders fell as disappointment pummeled his gut. If Isobel wasn't here, where had she gone? "Do you know where I can find her?"

"Would you be good enough to tell me why?" The woman folded her arms over her apron. It was clear whose side she stood on. And yet her eyes shone with curiosity and kindness, not contempt.

Alec cleared his throat. If he had any hope of seeing

Isobel, he knew he needed to be open and honest with her aunt first. No matter how uncomfortable he might feel professing his love for someone who wasn't actually standing there.

"The reason, ma'am, is that I love your niece." He maintained a level gaze and felt a fraction of relief when Mrs. Clawson appeared pleased with his answer. "You see, I've loved her for years and that affection has only grown stronger and deeper since I came to Sheridan."

Isobel's aunt nodded in obvious approval, though she still guarded the door like a sentry. "Are you aware of why her engagement with your brother ended?"

"I am." Alec didn't lower his gaze or flinch at the woman's frankness. He wanted her, and Isobel, to know he wasn't going anywhere. "Even though she can't have children, I would still like to marry her."

He was surprised to see the woman brush a tear from her cheek. "I thought as much."

Stepping beside him on the porch, Mrs. Clawson pointed north. "She went for a walk and hasn't come back yet. So my guess is you'll find her out by the far pasture."

"Thank you." Alec grinned as he grasped her hand and pumped it up and down. "I'll treat her right, ma'am. I promise."

She smiled in return. "I know you will."

It was probably time to return to the house. Isobel stood and stretched her back, which had grown sore after sitting so long. "Duchess?" she called. "Here kitty, kitty." The gray cat bounded toward her through the grass.

Smiling, she reached down to pick up her Bible but movement in the corner of her eye captured her attention. Someone was coming her way. She straightened to better identify the visitor, and a startled gasp slipped from her lips. Her gaze collided with Alec's, and he stopped.

"Hello, Isobel." He held his hat in his hands, his expression penitent.

She swallowed hard. Hope and uncertainty fluttered as wildly as her pulse. "W-what are you doing here, Alec?"

"I know you asked me not to try to see you. And if you want me to go, I will." He fell back a step as if to prove his point. "But if you'll give me five minutes, I'll say my piece and then leave."

Did she want to hear what he had to say? She wet her lips in indecision, then dipped her head in a quick nod. "All right."

"Thank you." His entire demeanor radiated relief and gratitude. He narrowed the space between them to several feet. "I talked with Whit the other night. He told me about your engagement."

Isobel shut her eyes, bracing herself for the pain. But today she didn't feel any of the hurt, only acceptance. She opened her eyes and leveled a look at this man she still loved. "Then you know why we can't court for real or get married. I can't ever give you the family you want, Alec." She glanced away. "Or the family your parents expect."

"How long have you known?"

His question caught her by surprise, and she swung her gaze to meet his again. "About not being able to have children?" When he nodded, she answered, "Since long before I met you and Whit. We already knew Aunt Jo suffered from the condition. And given she was the eldest daughter and I was an only child, there was a great deal of worry throughout most of my growing-up years about me having it, as well."

"Is that what you meant when you said you'd learned the importance of caution?" He took another step toward her.

Isobel folded her arms and gave him a nod. "The doctor and my parents felt confident that if I was careful, then the monthly bleedings would eventually start." She stared down at the grass, feeling vulnerable and exposed at sharing something so private. "But they never did. By the time I was seventeen, we knew for certain. I would never be able to have children, just as Aunt Jo hasn't."

"Does your uncle love your aunt any less because of that?"

Was it her imagination or was Alec standing closer than before? "No." Isobel adamantly shook her head. "But Uncle Evan isn't like most men. He knew when he married Aunt Jo that they would be a family in their own right."

"What if I told you I felt the same way about you, Issy, as your uncle does about your aunt?"

Isobel's breath caught in her throat. Did he mean it? "What about your father? You're supposed to find a woman to settle down with."

"And I have."

Now he stood directly in front of her, his warmth enfolding her as pleasantly as the sun had earlier. After setting his hat on the ground, Alec reached up and cupped her face between both his hands.

"I love you, Isobel Glasen." His thumbs stroked away the tears slipping down her face. "I have from the first moment I met you, and I promise to love you every moment going forward."

Happiness flooded her senses. "You still want to court me?"

"Court you?" Alec repeated with a laugh as he lowered his hands to her waist. "I've already done that. I want to marry you, Isobel. If you'll agree to be my wife."

His words seemed nearly too wonderful to be true. "What about the other half of your inheritance? And disappointing your parents?"

"My father is the one who loaned me a horse to ride out here."

She widened her eyes in surprise. "He did?"

"Yes, and what's more, he agreed to still give me the rest of my inheritance on my birthday."

Shaking her head, she smiled at him. "Alec, that's incredible. But I'm not sure I understand."

"A very wise and beautiful woman reminded me that I need to stop placing myself in my brother's shadow. I need to be proud of me." He pressed a lingering kiss to her forehead that set her pulse thrumming rapidly. "Turns out, those lessons are of more value to my father, and to me, than just completing his tasks."

Alec placed another kiss against her right temple and then one against the left. "I also figured out what I want to use the other half of my inheritance on."

"What?" she asked, her voice breathless.

"I'd like to expand your shop, Isobel, to include your apartment."

Lifting her arms, she wound them around his neck. "Where will I live then?"

"As Mrs. Alec Russell you'll have free rein in my humble abode above the clinic."

Isobel pretended to think this over. "Isobel Russell, designer? It does have a nice ring to it."

"Are you still going to design dresses?"

She hadn't been sure until this moment, but now she could see the future—hers and theirs—with clarity. "Yes, but I'd also like to offer my clients gowns patterned after those in the magazines, though with slight variations in cut and style to fit them."

"I think that's a fantastic idea."

As he leaned toward her, Isobel fully anticipated his kiss. Alec paused an inch from her mouth. "I don't think you actually agreed to marry me yet."

"A terrible oversight on my part."

His deep laugh rumbled through the air. "Will you marry me, Issy?"

"Nothing would give me greater pleasure, Alec Russell." He bent toward her again, but a sudden thought had her frowning. "However…"

Alec's brow furrowed in consternation. "Did you change your mind already?"

"Never," she said, laughing. "It's just that everyone in town is going to think we're getting married because you won that race."

His slow smile renewed Isobel's erratic heartbeat.

"That's because I did win a race." Alec brushed a light kiss against her lips. "I won the race for your heart."

In that, he certainly had.

"Still, some credit needs to go to Stella and that horse of hers," Isobel murmured as she gazed into his blue-gray eyes.

Alec nodded slowly. "And to all the rumormongers, for making us want to court in the first place."

"I'm afraid we may have to invite the entire town to our wedding, then." She affected a deep sigh.

He winked at her. "It could be fun."

"If you're by my side, then it will be."

This time Isobel didn't wait for him to do the kissing. Tugging him forward, she pressed her lips to his in a long, glorious kiss. One that spoke of hope and love and a future as expansive and bright as the blue Wyoming sky above them.

* * * * *

Don't miss these other Western adventures from Stacy Henrie:

Lady Outlaw
The Express Rider's Lady
The Outlaw's Secret
The Renegade's Redemption
The Rancher's Temporary Engagement
A Cowboy of Convenience

Find other great reads at www.LoveInspired.com.

Dear Reader,

Giving Isobel and Alec a chance at love in their own story has been a real pleasure. It was also fun to have some beloved characters from my other two Sheridan-set stories appear in this one. I hope readers will take away from this story a renewed desire to simply be themselves—to remember we are enough just as we are.

A race for a bride event actually did take place during a rodeo in Sheridan in 1909. After reading this fun detail, I wanted to include a similar race in my story.

Horse colic was known to have been treated in the past using chloride of lime or spirits of turpentine. Likewise, veterinarians or "horse doctors" were once seen as being duplicitous and of low reputation. Farmers often believed they knew as much as the veterinarian and would use their own cures for their animals.

The School of Veterinary Medicine at the University of Pennsylvania was established in 1883. While not the first veterinary school established in the United States, it has the distinction of being the oldest accredited veterinary school still in operation.

I love hearing from readers. You can contact me through my website at www.stacyhenrie.com.

All the best,
Stacy Henrie